THE CREEK KILLER

A Harriet Harper Thriller

DOMINIKA BEST

THE CREEK KILLER
Harriet Harper Thriller series - Book 1

Copyright © 2020 by Dominika Best

ISBN: 978-1-949674-03-3

www.dominikabest.com
First Edition

For Dave
without you, none of this would be possible

Also by Dominika Best

Prologue
EL SEGUNDO, CALIFORNIA - SUNDAY, MAY 24, 1992

I woke up from a gentle shake. My sister's face hovered a few inches above mine, her eyes glistening wet. A grinding sound came from her jaw as it moved back and forth.

I shivered.

Natalie put her finger against my lips. "SSSH. Nod if you understand," she whispered.

I nodded.

My room was freezing from the cold wind blowing in through my open window.

"The monsters are coming for us. Be very quiet. We're escaping," she whispered.

I nodded again, biting my lip hard to not cry.

Was there a monster in my closet?

Behind my closed bedroom door?

My heart thrashed against my ribs like a bird trying to escape its cage. Why were the monsters after us?

I sat up.

Natalie slid away from me and pulled something closer to the bed. I peeked over and saw my favorite pink suitcase open.

I swallowed. My heart fluttered up, trying to find another way to escape my chest.

She'd packed for me a strange assortment of clothes and underwear and socks and shoes along with her t-shirts and underwear. She turned back to me and put one finger up.

"We have room for one toy. Pick your favorite fast," she whispered again.

A creak from somewhere behind my door startled Natalie. She froze in the middle of the room, her eyes blinking fast. I'd never seen Natalie like this before. I squirmed back into my pillows.

I wanted Natalie to stop scaring me. I wanted to go back to sleep. I wanted my mommy. Tears rolled down my cheeks.

But my mommy couldn't come. She went to heaven. I only had Natalie.

I opened my mouth to ask about Dad and Danny and Reece. Natalie vigorously shook her head.

"No time for questions. Toy. Now."

The urgency in her voice forced me out of bed. I looked around my childhood bedroom at my kindergarten art on the wall and my sticker collection books and my favorite headphones and all of my stuffed animals and dollies.

I didn't have a favorite toy. A small whimper escaped from my mouth.

I picked up a baby doll and a bottle closest to my pink-socked feet.

"Too big. Take Barbie. We have to go," she said, pushing on the suitcase flap for it to get close enough to zip.

I grabbed a naked barbie with long blond hair. I searched around for her clothes, but my room was too dark. I whimpered again and pressed my lips tighter together.

Natalie barely noticed as she snatched the naked doll from me and shoved it into the edge of the suitcase. She zipped the suitcase closed and picked it up. Natalie grabbed my hand and pulled me to the window.

"Have to leave through the window," she whispered. "We can't go back there."

"I don't have shoes," I said.

What I really wanted to say was I don't want to go. Tears streamed down my face and I couldn't stop my crying. The My-Little-Pony long pajamas clung to my body and goosebumps spread across my skin. I didn't want to let go of Natalie's hand.

Natalie didn't answer. Instead, she yanked the screen off the window frame. She lifted me up and pushed me through it into my mom's bougainvillea bush.

She came out right after me, holding a slightly larger suitcase. My mom's suitcase.

Natalie squeezed my hand. I held my suitcase to me as we walked across the perfectly trimmed lawn of my childhood home.

The night was dark. No moon appeared in the sky and the air smelled of garbage like it did sometimes. We stepped onto the sidewalk and Natalie started to jog.

My wet socks clopped against the pavement as I tried to keep up with her. My teeth chattered badly, and I couldn't catch my breath.

"Natalie, stop. I can't run this fast." I gasped.

Natalie looked behind us and her mouth opened and closed like the fish my dad once caught on the pier. Her chest rose and fell to the beat of my chattering teeth.

I looked where she was looking and saw the silhouette of a man.

"No," she squeaked.

She picked me up with her right arm and ran as fast as she could toward the intersection. My suitcase banged against her back. Sobs shook my sister's body.

I buried my head into her neck and squeezed my eyes closed. My sister's ragged breathing and the jerky motion forward filled my world. What was happening?

Ting. Ting. Ting.

I knew that sound. I peeked out and saw a car with no headlights waiting for us at the intersection, its door open. A woman I didn't recognize sat in the driver's seat. Natalie waved at her and shoved both of us into the backseat.

Natalie's harsh breathing turned into sobs again as the woman turned on her headlights and pulled away from the curb.

"Thank you, oh god, thank you," she gasped in between sobs.

"SSSH, child. You're almost safe. Conserve your energy now," the woman said, her voice gentle and kind.

I peered through the window as she drove through our sleepy neighborhood and onto the 405 freeway. I turned back to my sister.

"Where are we going?" I asked Natalie.

"Someplace safe, honey. Someplace where we will be safe." Natalie pulled me to her and hugged me tightly.

"Why are we running?" I asked in a small voice.

"I couldn't leave you behind." Her voice came out strangled against my hair. "I couldn't leave you."

We stayed that way the entire car ride. Only when the lady pulled to the curb of a well-lit building did Natalie let me go.

"Where are we?" My stomach sent growls through the rest of my body. My teeth chattered again.

"The bus station. We're going far, far away from here. I'm going to keep you safe. I promise you."

Jane Smith

My Monday night Krav Maga women's defense class had been full. Twelve women followed my every move in conference room A of the West Hollywood Recreational Center for a good hour.

The room smelled of sweat and ladies' deodorant. Some of my students had been coming for months, and one was new, her bruises fresh. I wiped my face with a towel and noticed the new young woman hovering nearby. The other women had left already.

"You did really well today, Katie," I said.

She peeled off the wall, her skinny arms dangling at her side, wrist bruises covered by long black sleeves. I'd used her as my partner in one of my demonstrations and saw the telltale signs of abuse around her wrists.

"Thank you, Jane. I...I wanted to ask how to maneuver away from someone who has you pressed against the wall?"

"There are a couple of moves I can show you, next class. Are you coming next week?" I asked.

She'd only taken one class and cowered when anyone placed their hands on her.

"I'm going to try. Can you show me now?"

I noted the urgency in her voice. She wanted to know how to keep safe.

Leave him, I thought.

I knew she wouldn't. Instead, I decided to convince her to come back next week.

I lunged at her.

She cried out and cowered against the wall, her hands outstretched in a defensive pose. I drew myself back. She wasn't ready for any of this.

I kneeled before her but made sure not to touch her. The girl was suffering from serious post-traumatic stress disorder. Many of my students came to me with similar symptoms.

"Ssssh, I'm not going to hurt you. You need to come back next week, though."

"You lunged at me," she choked out.

"I wanted to show you why you need to come back next week."

I was close enough to her to see tears dangling, clinging on her eyelashes. Fiercely hot liquid shot through my veins and waves of pinpricks flowed up my arms and down my torso.

Another girl damaged by another asshole.

"Why?" Her voice came out so soft I leaned in to hear her.

"I know you're used to getting hit. Your body needs to relearn how to move before it gets hit. That takes time. Our bodies freeze and we go into fight or flight like you just did. I can show you the moves, but you need to fight your body to move on command. That's why you have to come back."

"How long have you been doing this?" she asked.

I looked down at my muscled body clad in head-to-toe black yoga wear. My arms had been skinny like hers. I'd cowered in corners, too.

Until my sister, Natalie forced me into self-defense classes. Her insistence to be prepared for when THEY came.

"All my life. Since I was nine."

Fear flickered in her eyes.

"I don't have that long."

"You don't have to be as good as me to survive. But your mind-body connection needs training. Give yourself a month."

Leave him, I thought.

I'd been doing these classes for years in different cities and knew that no woman was ready to leave until she was. I kept my thoughts to myself.

"Thank you, Jane. See you next week," Katie said.

I smiled and rose to my feet.

"I'll be here."

I watched her walk out of the room wondering if I really would see her again.

I started folding over the IKEA gym mats and moving them against the wall in preparation for the next meeting. I'd been lucky to rent out the space on the cheap and was grateful to help women protect themselves from the monsters in their lives.

I could have gone to a gym, but that was too conspicuous. I could never advertise. My monsters were still out there.

My classes filled up through word-of-mouth and only women were allowed in. It was a way to give back and be part of a community. Be part of something. Otherwise, I kept strictly to myself.

I finished stacking the mats in a corner and grabbed my gym bag. I left the room and made my way to the unisex bathroom, two doors down. I slipped inside and opened the bag. I chose the dark-haired wig with a bob.

My naturally blond hair was cut in a short pixie style and currently was sticking out on the ends. I smoothed it down in the mirror and noticed the dark circles under my strangely colored eyes. I'd worn contacts for a while to obscure the unique color, pale almost-white-blue with a brilliant blue edge.

But I hated the feel of the contacts in my eyes and had ditched them some years back.

I placed the wig on my head and fitted it into place. I rounded my shoulders down to take on a stooped posture. I looked like a different person already. Amazing what posture and some fake hair could do.

I finished the transformation off with a ratty cardigan I'd bought at a thrift store down the road. I was ready to face the world.

I left the bathroom and my good mood dribbled out of me the further I walked. By the time I was out on Santa Monica Blvd, blinking against the harsh light of the afternoon, I had become a tightly wound woman filled with equal parts fear and anger, despite my best efforts at keeping the fear locked away.

Then I saw it.

My hands fluttered to my mouth as bile filled the back of my throat.

The time had come.

I scanned the surrounding road, having difficulty focusing on any one thing. Was I going to look? Information is power, Natalie's voice whispered in my ear.

I forced my legs to move to the front of the outdoor newsstand.

"LA Times," I croaked out.

I handed the man several dollar bills, my hands shaking. He handed me the paper and I read my old name on the front page. Under the headline, "Horror at Ballona Creek", the photos of five girls took up most of the page. One of the photos was of me at age eight.

The police had found my body buried at Ballona Creek.

LA Hall of Records

L APD Detective Harriet Harper flipped through the yellowed death certificates searching for Matthew Dunn, a husband she was pretty certain killed his wife and daughter in 1974. The smell of old paper and dust filled her nose as the pages turned. Harri frowned as she came to the end of the D's. No Matthew Dunn.

Even though the Los Angeles County Hall of Records Archive was in the middle of downtown Los Angeles, the archive was dusty, quiet, and empty, the smell of paper overpowering all other scents.

The archive was her first stop when searching for persons involved in the cases she was working on. As a detective in the Cold Case Homicide Special Section (CCSS) of the Robbery-Homicide division of the Los Angeles Police Department, the Hall of Records Archive was her second home.

"Are you going to be needing anything else?" Marg's voice penetrated through Harri's intense concentration. She was on a first-name basis with all the clerks and Marg was her favorite.

"I think this is the year I need. Thank you, Marg," Harri said without looking up.

Her cell phone buzzed in her pocket. She pulled it out and saw it was her Lieutenant, Violet Sanford. Violet rarely called her when she was out of the office.

Cold cases weren't go-go-go like other homicide cases. They involved DNA matches, paper trails, and searching through dusty records for long lost people.

"Hi Violet, what's up?"

"Where are you, Harri?"

"The archive. Why?"

"I need you back in the office. The task force is meeting in ten minutes."

"What task force?" She tried to keep the excitement out of her voice.

"The one I just fought to put you on," Violet said.

A fight meant Richard Byrne and the task force was for a homicide.

"Byrne, again?" Harri asked.

Lieutenant Richard Byrne was head of the Homicide Special Section (HSS) in the Robbery-Homicide Division (RHD). He was the reason Harri wasn't in Homicide yet.

"What do you think?"

"Violet, you are the best, you know that?"

"You must have done a real number on that guy."

"He did it to himself."

"Yes, he did."

"I'm walking as fast as I can."

"Run, Harri. The task force has been going since yesterday. You'll need to catch up."

"Running," Harri said as she packed up her files.

She clicked off her phone and dropped it in her computer bag. Lieutenant Violet Sanford was one of her fiercest supporters and Harri thanked her lucky stars each time she went to bat for her. Violet had confided that she'd come up against detectives like Richard Byrne herself and understood.

Lieutenant Richard Byrne wasn't dirty per se. But he was arrogant and would never cop to a mistake he'd made. His record was flawless as far as he was concerned. The higher-ups believed in his stellar close rate and promoted him to head of Robbery-Homicide Division.

Unfortunately for Harri, one of her previous cases hinged on a big mistake Richard made on closing one of his cases. Internal Affairs was called in. Harri struggled at the LAPD since. Until Violet stepped in.

"Thank you, Violet," Harri said under her breath.

She'd heard through the grapevine about the find down in Playa del Rey. A multiple gravesite uncovered yesterday. Everyone down at the PAB (Police Administration Building) was talking about it.

The task force was pulling in the best detectives and not keeping it strictly RHD which was odd. Richard didn't usually work that way. She'd overheard detectives angling to be assigned to the task force.

Harri hadn't bothered because overcoming Richard's dislike would be impossible for her even if she did have one of the best closing records in the Cold Case Unit. But somehow, Violet had managed it. Excitement fluttered in her stomach like a hundred butterflies taking to the skies. Soft and gentle at first but overwhelming in its intensity a moment later.

She'd been waiting for an opportunity like this for the last two years.

"I can't put these back, Marg," Harri said.

"Got a new case?"

"Yes."

"Good luck. I'll put them back. Don't worry about them," Marg said and waved her off.

Harri rushed out of the quiet room and down the corridor. She broke into a run, her computer bag thumping against her back. No way she wasn't going to be late.

She exploded through the double doors into the blinding afternoon sun. The PAB was three blocks away down a tree-lined street. If she ran, she'd get there in five minutes, ten minutes late for the meeting. She'd be sweaty and gross, but she wouldn't be horribly late. She could slip in and stand in the back with the uniforms. It was the best she could do.

She gulped down the smoggy, hot air and sprinted, dodging people and cars. Her heart hammered in her chest with anticipation.

DETECTIVE ROB LAKIN, one of her team members in Cold Case, met her the moment she got off the elevator on the eighth floor.

Rob was legendary in the department for being both a walking crime encyclopedia and a friend to anyone he met, often using his Brooklyn accent to disarm even the crankiest of witnesses. At a slim six-foot-five, Rob towered over most of the other detectives in RHD and had gotten the nickname of Ichabod. He found the moniker endlessly amusing.

"You're late. And sweaty? Did you run here?" Rob asked, grinning at her.

"What do you think?" Harri asked, panting. She swallowed the air-conditioned air a couple of times and bent over to regulate her breathing.

"I was at Records when Violet called."

"I know. She told me to wait for you."

"She did, did she?"

"Yes."

"Thank you," Harri said.

Rob slapped her playfully on the back.

"You're a lot more out of shape than you look."

"Ha-ha," Harri said. She was thankful for the reprieve he'd given her before going into the meeting.

"You're on this too?" Harri asked, although unsurprised. He was one of the best detectives she'd ever worked with.

"Wouldn't want to miss this one, would I? David Swisher is head of this task force."

"Not Richard?" This surprised Harri.

"Came from above. Complicated case."

"Richard must be pissed."

"He is."

"Gilead is running the show?"

"Yeah. Gilead wanted two detectives each from HSS, CCSS, and SAS. We have Jackie Render and Jorge Hernandez from Special Assault, Tom Bards and David Swisher from Homicide, and us."

She'd worked with Jackie and Jorge back in Hollywood Division and knew them to be good detectives. They were part of the SAS (Special Assault Section) dealing with crimes with a sexual component.

Neither was much interested in politics and the truth of each case came first with both of them. She'd heard something similar about Tom Bards. They'd never crossed paths, though.

"Strange that Richard isn't heading up the task force, though," Harri said.

"It's odd. I'm sure he's wheeling and dealing in the background."

"Watch my back you mean?"

"Something like that."

Richard's animosity toward Harri was well known throughout the division. Rob led Harri down the gray corridor to wooden double doors labeled Conference Room #5.

"Ready?" Rob asked.

Harri rubbed the drying sweat off her face with her sleeve and noticed the trembling in her hands. She coughed, trying to diffuse her uneasiness. Harri grimaced and forced a now-or-never-let's-do-this smile. This is what she wanted. A chance to prove herself.

Rob opened the double doors.

3

Police Administration Building
(PAB) - Los Angeles, CA
DAY 1

H arri Harper and Rob Lakin arrived last for the meeting. The rest of the task force team members filled the room, sitting at makeshift workstations.

Detective Jorge Hernandez tacked up the last of the crime scene photos of mummified remains on the cork-board wall at the back. A portable whiteboard stood to his right.

Harri had seen Jorge around the halls as Robbery was on the same floor as Cold Case. He reminded her of an over-excited puppy each time she saw him. He had dark, floppy bangs that he constantly shook out of his long face, lanky limbs, and a goofy toothy smile he gave everyone.

Jorge was the youngest on the team by a good number of years. She'd heard he had a good head on his shoulders and was solid.

It made sense he'd been chosen by Richard Byrne. Richard loved mentoring young male detectives. He believed it was the best way to keep the LAPD the way he liked it.

Jackie Render, red lipstick, and nails perfectly manicured, no hair out of place and pulled back in a tight bun, handed a white binder to both Harri and Rob. Harri knew Jackie had two small girls at home and she marveled at how put-together Jackie was at all times.

Harri glanced down at her black slacks and white button-down shirt and noticed two small soup stains peeking out from behind her suit-jacket. She didn't understand where Jackie pulled extra time from. Jackie cleared her throat.

"Copies of the murder-book as it stands right now," Jackie said.

Harri grinned. "Thank you, Jackie." Her nerves settled somewhat on seeing her friend.

"Excited to work with you again, Harri," Jackie said.

She turned to Rob. "We haven't met."

"Rob Lakin. Good job on the Giovanna case last month," Rob said. He pumped Jackie's hand up and down.

His exuberance widened Jackie's smile. Jackie nodded. "I was happy to close that one. Court date is set for next month."

"I'm sure it'll stick."

"It will. We built a solid case against him," Jackie said.

Harri had heard about Saul Giovanna, a serial rapist, from some weeks back. He'd raped seven women before the eighth finally reported the crime on the urging of her mother. He targeted the immigrant community knowing full well they'd be too terrified to come forward.

"Sorry we're late," Rob said and looked around. "Where is everyone?"

"This is the core team. Once we have our tasks, we can grab support staff as needed to help," Jackie said.

Harri couldn't take her eyes off the crime scene photos. "We still need to go to the burial site," Harri said.

"That won't be necessary. Your time can be better spent elsewhere," a man's voice interrupted.

Harri followed the voice to Detective David Swisher, the only one wearing a suit and tie.

With black hair slicked up as if he was still a frat boy in college, he stepped up to the small group.

She put on the most neutral expression she could muster. Out of the corner of her eye, Harri noticed Jorge had stopped going through his binder to watch the interaction. Everyone already knew about the politics, apparently.

"Welcome to the task force. We've not met." He extended his arm.

Harri took it first. David's grasp was limp and sweaty. He turned to Rob and Harri fought the urge to wipe her hand on her pants.

"Detective Robert Lakin," Rob said and gripped the other man's hand in his so hard, David winced.

David pulled his hand away, face reddening.

"Why is it not necessary for us to go to the crime scene?" Rob asked.

"The crimes were committed elsewhere and since the burial itself is over twenty-years-old, not much exists of the original site. Your time will be spent better going through all the paperwork," David said and stalked to the whiteboard across the room.

Rob flashed Harri a side-grin. He'd thrown him off his game on purpose. It was good to have allies.

"We should begin," David said.

Harri and Rob sat in the nearest chairs to their left. Jackie wended her way through the cast-off chairs to the front of the room and joined Jorge at a small table.

The conference room opened and Detective Tom Bards, the legendary DNA expert, and creator of the Cold Case Special Section almost twenty years ago walked in. His gray hair was swept back. He wore a suit like David, but his was well-worn and comfortable. He had a prominent long nose and a mouth set in a thin line. Harri heard his tongue was sharp and his wit was dry. He was a man not to be messed with.

"Looks like you started without me," Tom quipped, his eyes boring into David's. "Again."

"I...I... thought you weren't coming today," David said.

"What made you think such a thing?"

The question hung in the silence of the room.

Tom walked toward David and took a seat directly in front of him.

"Don't let me interrupt you," he said.

David blinked rapidly and drops of sweat appeared at his hairline. He cleared his throat. Once, twice, and inhaled deeply. He plunged in.

"I'm sure most of you know each other, so no need for introductions. As to be expected, the media knows of the discovery of the gravesite and the find is front-page news."

"That was less than twenty-four hours? Do we have a leak?" Tom asked.

"We are investigating that. The task force is under a media blackout at this time. The PR team led by Seth Gibbs will handle all media inquiries and statements. CO Parker assigned us ten uniforms to help with the hotline and doing the door-to-doors."

"That's not going to be enough," Jackie said. "I'm going through missing person's files and I need at least three more detectives to help me."

"Why do we need to do door-to-door interviews if the crime-scene is so old?" Harri asked. The uniforms could be used elsewhere like David had mentioned to them.

David reddened at her question.

"I'll have the detectives assigned to you. What's your update on that?" David asked.

He motioned for Jackie to join him at the whiteboard. When she did, he left her up there and slid into his seat.

His body became less rigid, Harri noticed. David Swisher's demeanor surprised Harri. He was less sure of himself now that Tom was in the room. She filed that knowledge for later use.

David Swisher's foot tapped against his chair leg making a clicking sound. Jackie shot him a look. His leg stopped.

Jackie began.

"I'm compiling a list of missing girls between the ages of 12-17 who disappeared between 1991-1996. The forensic pathologist provided me with the ballpark timeframe. I started with Southern California. In Los Angeles County, that's around 140,000 girls in that age range. That includes runaways, abductions, and disappearances. It would be helpful to narrow down the timeframe, even with three extra detectives," Jackie said.

David Swisher stood back up and faced the room.

"I was going to get to that. The forensic pathologist, Leonard Richards of OCME (Office of the Chief Medical Examiner) has given us a preliminary dating on one of the two mummies they've gotten to the lab as 1991-1993. That shaves off a year at least."

"What about the scrap of paper found at the bottom of the bin?" Harri asked. She'd started to skim the evidence they'd gathered in the murder-book. "It has a date."

"That's right. Dr. Richards did find a scrap of the front page of the LA Times paper from July 1992. Apparently, it was in excellent condition. I'm surprised it's in the book already," David said.

"I called Dr. Richards this morning and he sent that extra info over. I wanted to make sure everyone on the task force was up-to-speed on all the developments. I will focus on 1992, which leaves me with about 50,200 girls to go through. I will need those detectives," Jackie said, smoothing her hair down.

Harri knew Jackie's nervous tell and that was it. What had Jackie nervous?

Having explained her piece, Jackie sat down.

The debrief felt so disjointed to Harri. Strong undercurrents shifted the tone of the meeting each time a member talked. It was weird.

David stood alone in front of the empty whiteboard. He pointed to the photos Jorge pinned up.

"As you can see from the photos, the mummified remains were enclosed in plastic storage bins. Dr. Richards and his team have managed to get two of the bins out and to their lab. The other three are forthcoming. I spoke to Dr. Richards this morning. He'll be doing dental x-rays first thing for ID as soon as they process the inside of the plastic bins. He'll send the x-rays over to the NCIC (National Crime Information Center) and we'll see if they get any hits. Most likely tomorrow."

Jorge raised his hand. David nodded at him.

"I can handle the gravesite. I'm familiar with Ballona Creek. I mean, I know its history. It used to be the site of the Sanford Hughes Hangar." He looked at each of them for some sort of recognition. "The movie director. The one that flew airplanes."

Harri vaguely remembered that name.

"Oh yeah, the one that Leonardo DiCaprio played in that movie," Jackie cut in.

"Yes, that one," Jorge grinned.

"We need to find access and ownership to the site for that time period. Let's stick to 1991-1993 for now. Who laid down that foundation? What company was there at that time? There is some confusion as to when the Sanford Hughes Airport closed and who took over the site after that," David said.

Jorge scribbled notes inside his case file, nodding his head. David stopped and waited to see if anyone had any questions. When the team stayed silent, he went on.

"Going back to that scrap of paper," David said.

"Seems like that was left deliberately. Could be a false lead," Detective Tom Bards' gravelly voice cut in.

"That's what you and I will be working on. There was a spate of abductions in 1992 in the South Bay, centered around El Segundo," David said.

Could David be angling to work with Tom Bards then? Was that part of the unspoken dialogue going on? Harri wasn't sure how advantageous politically that would be to David. He was running the task force after all. But having Tom Bards as a friend could help with promotion if the task force succeeded.

A cold shower of pinpricks marched down Harri's back. She didn't do well in political intrigue and had gotten burned each time she'd been caught up in it. Rotating her shoulders to get rid of the feeling, Harri focused back on the case. She grew up in El Segundo and remembered the cases well.

Two sisters and three high school girls all disappeared that summer. Her parents barely allowed her and her sister, who went to high school with the missing girls, to leave the house. Harri was about to go to ninth grade when that happened so didn't know any of the girls personally, but she remembered her sister Lauren crying in her room over Maggie Johnson's disappearance.

"Ballona Creek is nearby El Segundo. It would have been a perfect dumpsite back then. The place was wild and over-grown," Harri offered.

David Swisher didn't acknowledge her or her comment. He kept his focus on Tom.

"I've pulled the five case files from El Segundo PD for us to start working on."

"Wouldn't that be better for us to dive into?" Rob inter-jected. "We're cold case and are used to looking through files that old."

David deigned to look at Rob at least.

"You'll be looking through old case files too, while we wait for Dr. Richards to do his thing. I want you to go through old cases looking for similar homicides where the body was mummified, stuck in a plastic bin, or had eyes carved into their chest."

The detail of the carving of the eyes was not in the murder-book.

"I don't see that detail in the notes, nor the crime scene photos," Tom remarked.

"Dr. Richards called me before this meeting. He found the carvings on both girls. He should be emailing the photos to the team."

David met Harri's eyes. "Oh, and Officer Harper, you will be managing the hotline. Due to the intense media interest, the phones are already ringing off the hook with tips."

Her heart catapulted to her throat.

"It's Detective, Detective Swisher," Harri managed to get out over the lump in her throat. Her cheeks burned.

David didn't bother correcting himself.

"This is going to be a hard case everyone, so slow and steady is the pace. Overtime has been approved. Use it."

David's grin told Harri he was happy to have the upper hand again.

"Any questions?"

When no one spoke, he adjourned the meeting and the team disbanded. Rob and Harri fell in behind everyone else.

"You all right?" Rob asked.

"Swell," Harri said, but couldn't hide her grimace. Manning the tip hotline was a job for a rookie uniform, not a Detective Level 1 like she was. The demotion and lack of respect was expected from Richard Byrne's lackey. It still burned her, though.

"I'm going to speak with Violet about running it up the chain of command to get me some uniforms to help with the calls. I won't be able to do this alone."

She'd been in uniform when a severed head had been found in Griffith Park years ago. The detectives set up a tip line for the case and the phone didn't stop ringing for a week. If she remembered correctly, there'd been at least three officers manning the phones initially. That's what she'd ask Violet for. At least, for this first week.

"Don't let him get to you. Take the opportunities as they come," Rob said as they entered the CCSS bullpen.

"Thanks, Rob." She gave him her best I-am-thankful-for-you smile. "Let me know if you need any help to read through the files," Harri said.

He nodded and disappeared into his cubicle.

Harri headed to Violet's office to get the room, phone bank, and staff issues resolved.

4

Silver Lake, California
TUESDAY, AUGUST 7, 2018 - DAY 2

H arri Harper pulled into the drive of her home at 2 AM that morning. Strands of hair escaped from her and her ears rang from the noise of the ever-buzzing phone lines. She'd spent the whole day wrangling the setup of the tip line.

The evening news broadcast the story and the phone number for any information. The moment the segment ended the phones began to ring and hadn't ceased since. When Harri spoke to Violet earlier about getting uniforms to help her man the lines, Violet had suggested five uniformed officers instead of three. CO Gilead Parker had ok'd the shifting of manpower to the tip line and, when the phones started ringing, they could have easily used three more bodies.

Harri assigned the five officers, including herself, to one of two twelve-hour shifts to spread out the load. Three officers worked on each shift and the tip line was getting over a hundred phone calls an hour.

The story of five mummified girls in Ballona Creek played to a national news audience and the tips were coming in from as far away as Alaska and Maine.

She took the six steps leading to her front door, her tension slowly dissipating with each riser. Her three-story modern home sat perched on a ridge along the side of the hill.

Her family's tragedy had paid for the million-dollar home as she'd never be able to afford it on her detective's salary. She'd used most of the estate that had been left over to pay for it, leaving just enough to take care of her dementia-riddled father in a private clinic out in Ojai. She had no other family.

Two years after her sister Lauren disappeared in the Willamette National Forest up in Oregon, on a sunny day, Harri found her mother on her parents' bed, unresponsive. At the autopsy, Harri found out her mother swallowed as many pills as she could find and died. Apparently, the loss of her eldest daughter was too much for her to overcome.

Her father, a successful contract attorney working with the film studios, hadn't fared much better in the years after the disappearance. After leading searches into and around the vicinity of the Tamolitch Pool trailhead for months, her father turned to alcohol to ease the pain.

Early-onset dementia took whatever bits of mind he had left. She kept him in a home in Ojai for memory-care patients. Her parents had set up trusts for both of their daughters and since Harri was the last living relative, it all went to her. She'd rather have her family a hundred times over than the money. Instead, all she had was a beautiful, empty home.

Harri opened the door and tossed her keys into the glass dish on the small entry-way table. She smelled the flowers from the kitchen and couldn't help but smile. Freesia. They were Lauren's favorite and she got them every year from the Trader Joe's on Hyperion. Her life was filled with the ghosts of her long-gone family. The boxes of all the evidence she'd gathered on her yearly trips to the Willamette Forest to find her sister's body filled up her second bedroom.

She took the stairs to the third level of her home, where the master bedroom and bathroom were located. Dierdre, her interior designer, called the look inside Boho chic decor. All the furniture was Birchwood, leather, cream, or dark metal with splashes of colorful textiles, green plants, and art decorating the walls. The feel was eclectic, colorful, and stylish. All it needed now was a family.

Her home was what she aspired to have her life resemble. At present, the two were diametric opposites. Harri entertained the CCSS crew every year at Christmas time, but the rest of the year she wandered the rooms, soothing her grief with the spectacular views of the opposite hillside and Silver Lake Reservoir.

Harri reached her bedroom and undressed, thinking maybe she'd finally get that older dog she'd been considering for the last ten years. Someone to keep her company, but who wouldn't mind sleeping the whole day during her shifts.

Smiling at that, she stepped into the shower and let the water wash away the aggression and anger she'd been holding onto toward Richard Byrne and David Swisher.

By the time the hot water ran out, she was too tired to feel much of anything. Harri pulled on a white fluffy robe and brushed her teeth. When done, she walked out of the bathroom and flicked off the light in the bedroom.

The lights of Silver Lake twinkled back at her. She flopped down on her bed, her mind wandering back to the summer of 1992.

"MOM, I WANT TO GO SURFING," Lauren *whined as she grabbed a jug of orange juice from the fridge. Harri and her mother sat at the kitchen table eating some Eggo waffles. Her mother had talked to the neighbor, a busybody named Mrs. Landry, and found out that another girl had never come home. It was the third disappearance in the last month.*

"*You know kids run away all the time,*" Lauren reminded her mother as she poured herself a glass of orange juice.

"*But so many in the same summer? From the same town?*" her mother asked, her brow furrowed.

"*I was watching America's Most Wanted,*" Harri began.

Her mother put her hand up to stop her. "*I don't want to hear anything about that,*" her mother said, biting her lip.

"*Are you going to let me go then?*" Lauren asked.

"*Absolutely not. I don't want you leaving this house without me or your father.*" She turned to Harri. "*That's you, too,*" she said.

"*Mom, it's summer. You can't keep us home forever,*" Lauren whined.

Harri knew her sister was learning to surf on a shortboard and hoping to compete in her age division come this fall. If their parents didn't let them out of the house, no way would she be ready for that.

"*The competition in Huntington is only three months away. Who is going to snatch me out of the water, Mom? And I promise you, I'm not planning to run away.*"

"*It's too dangerous out there, Lauren. You're not going anywhere today. I have to go to work today. So, both of you, stay inside. Why don't you go and watch movies with your sister in the den,*" her mother said and by the look on her face, it was final.

Lauren rolled her eyes and stomped out of the kitchen, orange juice in hand.

"*Eat some breakfast,*" her mother called out after her.

Harri grabbed another Eggo waffle off the plate. "*I'll eat hers, Mom.*"

Her mother tweaked her nose and smiled.

HARRI PUT her hand over her chest like her old therapist said to do when the pain became unbearable. The memories kept tumbling in.

Lauren and Harri watched loads of MTV and reruns that summer. Their mother would chaperone them to go to the local library for books, but other than that even the beach was a no-no without her mother or father present.

The sisters took to watching old reruns of Monty Python's Flying Circus and all the available Monty Python movies late into the night to laugh. As the town became more and more terrified, and Lauren's friend Maggie disappeared, they clung to the hilarity of the movies.

The two of them stayed in that whole summer.

The disappearances mysteriously ended when school started again. All the students spoke about the missing girls at first. Then other concerns crowded out the conversations like college applications, SATs, and Friday night's football game. The overall consensus of both teachers and students alike became the missing girls ran away from home.

Harri relished that summer and how close she became with Lauren. Most seventeen-year-olds didn't hang out with their fourteen-year-old little sisters, but that summer the sisters had been inseparable. She had another two years with her sister before the disappearance that changed everything.

Lauren went off to the University of Oregon in the fall of 1994. Within a week of getting there, Lauren inundated Harri and her parents with stories of her hikes and mountain biking in the Willamette Forest.

She'd fallen in love with the wildness and ruggedness of the surrounding countryside and spent most weekends outdoors. Lauren and her two new friends set off on the popular McKenzie River Trail on Saturday the 24th of September 1994.

As the story went, the girls didn't bring enough water and before they went too far, Lauren volunteered to go back to the car to get more. She was never seen again.

Harri and her parents joined the search for Lauren that Sunday. After a week, the search was called off and the rangers didn't believe she'd be found alive at that late date. Her family and about five volunteers, including her two friends, searched for another week.

Lauren vanished without a trace.

She'd never gotten to the car and the searchers found no trace of her walking back on the path.

Her family fell apart that weekend.

Harri curled up into her down comforter, her terrycloth robe wrapped around her, and closed her eyes, the opening theme of Monty Python's Flying circus playing in her memory.

5

Jane Smith

DAY 2

O ur old names were Natalie and Lindsey Peters. Every news outlet was running the story on the discovery of my sister and me along with three other girls' bodies excavated down at Ballona Creek in Playa del Rey.

But we had run and survived.

We had gotten new names. Natalie's had been Rebecca; my name was Mary.

I hated the name Mary. It was so plain.

But, Jennifer, the woman who'd taken us in, said it was a good, safe generic name. She'd told me another little dead girl gifted me her name and I should be grateful.

Jennifer was good like that. She always told us the truth. We lived in fear of whatever was after us for six years. And then Jennifer came home with the news.

My brothers and my father had died in a car accident in the Philippines in 1996. We were finally safe. Or so we thought.

I was fourteen and my sister still hadn't told me who the monsters were. I'd always assumed it was one of them. Perhaps Danny.

He was the oldest and seventeen when we ran. I'd heard Reece crying in his bedroom the night we left through the open window. Monsters didn't cry, did they?

I WALKED into the kitchen as Jennifer and Rebecca, my sister loved her new name unlike me and wanted me to call her that solely, argued about it.

"I don't believe it. This must be some sort of scam they are pulling," Rebecca said in a strangled voice.

"Honey, we could also see this as the best of luck. You and your sister are free now," Jennifer said, taking Rebecca's hand in hers.

"Why? Why are we free now?" I asked, pulling out a chair and sitting next to them.

"Your father and brothers died in a car crash in the Philippines. Several months ago now. They just sent back the remains to be buried. Looks like some lawyer is handling the arrangements," Jennifer said.

Rebecca flashed her an angry look. Rebecca never wanted me to know anything.

"I'm old enough to know what we've been running from," I said, getting angry at Rebecca all over again. This had been a point of contention with us for the last two years. She refused to tell me why she'd upended my life.

"What did they do?" I asked her for the millionth time.

"I will not destroy you like they destroyed me," she said, her face pale.

"Rebecca, you've been surviving and doing a damn good job of that. Now, you can flourish," Jennifer said, her voice soft and soothing.

Rebecca pulled her hand away from her. Her eyes were big and glistening with unshed tears. "I can't. I won't believe it. I don't feel safe," she whispered.

I couldn't imagine what my family had done to her to make her so terrified.

"Safety will come. Time sands down the sharp edges of fear. I've seen it in my clients," Jennifer said.

Rebecca trembled and pulled her legs into her chest.

"You didn't know them. They are devious. Tricky…evil," Rebecca muttered.

"Let me make you some lemon pancakes. Today is the first day of your new life. Your future is bright and shiny. C'mon girl," Jennifer said and jumped up.

She pulled Rebecca into a big hug and motioned me to join them. I did.

"Those bastards are gone. Think of the future," Jennifer whispered fiercely.

I still wanted to ask what they did to her, but now wasn't the time.

MY MOMENT NEVER CAME, and I never did find out what happened. We tried to do as Jennifer suggested.

Rebecca thought of college and what she might like to study. It had been out of the question before the news, but as the days passed by, she became more excited about what options were open to her now.

She'd always wanted to live in San Francisco and decided to go to San Francisco State. Jennifer beamed with pride when she told her she wanted to do pre-law and eventually go to law school.

It had been a hopeful year and Rebecca opened up. Her face brightened and she smiled more. But Rebecca never stopped going to her self-defense classes.

When I asked her about it, her answer was always the same. Never hurts to be prepared, she'd remind me.

What we didn't realize was the darkness still searched for us.

We thought we were safe.

We were wrong.

So. Very. Wrong.

. . .

I LAY BACK in my bed, my laptop next to me. I'd read all I could about the crime scene and the five mummified remains. I wondered who the girls were who took our place. My heart pattered at a steady feverish pace.

It was time for me to decide. A decision I'd avoided making since Jennifer and Natalie's murders.

My stomach grumbled.

I hadn't eaten since yesterday. Since I saw the paper and managed to get home.

I'd vomited the moment I stepped into the safety of my apartment and stayed in bed all day with muscle aches and feverish skin, knowing the time had come.

Wasn't this the reason I came back to LA? Once and for all to face the monsters?

This discovery had forced my hand.

I sat up, hand in mouth, biting the skin off the side of my thumb. I had preached to my students to welcome the fear.

Understand it and use it.

Embrace it, even.

Thank it for keeping them safe.

I'd trained all my life for this moment.

Was I ready to come out of the shadows and face my pursuers?

My monsters?

6

PAB - Los Angeles, CA
DAY 2

Harri Harper punched in the code for the conference room that she'd found in her email. David Swisher decreed each detective had their own code to get into the room so he could track the comings and goings of the detectives on the task force.

The email claimed it was to control the dissemination of information. Good luck with that.

Harri was sure it was Richard Byrne who fed the best information to his secret mistress, a reporter at the LA Times named Lucinda West.

The two top lead sheets she carried slipped out of her grasp and fluttered to the floor.

"Crap," she muttered and stooped down to scoop up the sheets. Her hands betrayed a minor shake. As if on cue, her heart dropped into her stomach and then pounded away against its captivity.

Get a grip, a small voice sounded in her head. She couldn't keep up with the anxiety over these meetings. David Swisher was a cop, the same as she was. What was he going to do to her besides shaming her in front of her peers and playing his petty games? She'd survived worse.

Harri pulled her shoulders back and jutted out her chest in a power stance. She lifted her chin and opened the door.

The meeting had already started. Despite Harri's best efforts, her cheeks flared red. David Swisher had given her the wrong time.

Keeping her chin and posture the same, she walked to the nearest chair.

Rob nodded as Jackie swiveled back to see what the commotion was. Tom Bards didn't bother to turn around and David stood in front of the still-empty chalkboard, triumph dancing in his eyes and a I-gotcha-Cheshire-cat smile on his face.

He licked his lips.

Harri met his eyes and gave him a wide grin. His smile faltered.

"Hi everybody. Sorry, I'm late. I was waiting on these new lead sheets," Harri said, waving the sheets in front of her.

"The phones must be ringing off the hook," Jackie offered.

"They are. Please continue, I didn't mean to disrupt the flow," Harri said.

Detective Jorge Hernandez, in the middle of taking bites of a bagel, gave her a thumbs up.

"All right," Jorge said, his mouth full of bagel. He took a swig of coffee and managed to get whatever was in his mouth down his throat. "As I was saying, the dumpster sat next to what used to be the Ash Ghost hangar. For all of you not up on your LA history, that would be where Sanford Hughes built his massive wooden airplane during World War Two."

"Fun fact, the Ash Ghost flew for two minutes before crashing into the Santa Monica Bay," Rob said.

"I saw that. Crazy," Jorge said and flopped his bangs out of his eyes with his hand. He shuffled his notes.

"The site became a Hollywood soundstage in 1995, but before that, it was the Sanford Hughes Airport, with several landing strips for smaller aircraft. The airport closed down in 1985 and the site sold to the McDougall Company to build components for helicopters."

"That's not going to be easy to get information from them," Tom Bards turned in his seat to face the rest of the detectives. "They have government contracts. Military."

"I've already hit that wall, Tom. Anyway, per our new time-line of the body dump occurring sometime at the end of 1992, the foundation was poured under McDougall's watch," Jorge continued.

"Wait, so do we have definitive confirmation that the bodies are of the missing girls from El Segundo in 1992?" Harri interrupted.

"I'm going to get to that once Jorge is done," David Swisher said without taking his eyes off of Jorge.

Harri raised an eyebrow at Rob. He shook his head. Harri took that as a let-it-go suggestion. She'd been thinking the same thing.

Jorge finished off his bagel and crumpled the white paper into a ball.

"As Tom said, the McDougall Company deals with big government contracts. I have calls out to two managers, Daniel Novten and Lawrence Sherman, for lists of workers on-site in the summer and fall of 1992. It took me hours to even get those two names. I'm tracking down other ways to interview the two men," Jorge finished.

"Thank you, Jorge. As Jorge mentioned, NCIC (National Crime Information Center) came back with preliminary matches to Maggie Johnson and Jennifer Lynch from the dental records available in their missing person files," David said.

"That was fast," Rob remarked.

Typically, bureaucracy moved slowly and bodies in that state would take weeks to get identified.

"I pulled some strings with the necessary people," Tom said before David could answer.

With that one statement, Harri knew who held the power in the room. David did, too.

The color had left his face and he pursed his lips hard enough to make them match his pale, sweaty skin. The tip of his tongue slipped out past the colorless flabs of flesh.

Harri couldn't tell if he was at the height of fury or panic.

David turned to the pictures of the victims behind him, hiding his face from the team.

"Dr. Richards contacted a well-known forensic odontologist to come and fully x-ray, measure, and compare the mummified remains with the files they have for the missing girls from 1992 on NamUs (U.S. Department of Justice's National Missing and Unidentified Persons System)." His voice sounded distant.

"We have the prelim results, not the definitive results that will hold up in court-of-law," Tom said.

"We should have definitive results for full identification in several days. In the meantime, we move forward under the assumption these are the five girls that disappeared in the summer of 1992 from El Segundo," David said.

He turned back to face them. He'd used that time to get himself under control.

The tension dribbled out of Harri. David had his own worries to deal with. She could handle him.

"I checked in with NamUs this morning and they only have files on Maggie Johnson, Jennifer Lynch, and Lisa McNeill, three of the missing girls from 1992. The other two girls, Lindsey and Natalie Peters aren't in either of the databases," Tom said.

"Meaning we have no biological records to match to the

Peters' sisters?" Rob asked, jotting down the information into his notebook.

"So far we haven't found any. They have no remaining relatives. The father and brothers died in a car accident in the '90s," Tom said.

He didn't have to get up to the front of the room to be heard. Harri noticed the team all leaned in when he spoke.

David noticed it too, apparently as he spoke in a louder voice to pull the attention back on him.

"I've been in contact with El Segundo detective Peter McDonald. The original files from the cases that he'd sent up didn't have any leads. The girls all disappeared around two weeks apart through June and July. They all disappeared on their way home. No witnesses came forward regarding any abduction attempts."

"Seriously? Someone must have seen these girls walking?" Jackie cut in.

"You would think so, but they interviewed over 100 people and not one of them saw the girls after they set off from each destination."

"We are going to have to re-interview all those witnesses," Jackie said.

"I agree," Harri said. "People give up more secrets after this much time."

"We need more men," Rob said.

"I'll take care of that," Tom said. "I'm also making copies of the case files for all of you. I agree on the re-interviewing. It will be a team effort."

David didn't like the sound of that. His lips had disappeared again.

Tom's demeanor stayed the same. His body was relaxed and his eyes watchful.

David continued. "As I was saying, Detective McDonald called me with new information not included in the case files of the missing girls. The original detectives, both deceased, were zeroing in on a suspect around the year 1995. His name was Christian LeGuerre, and he'd come on their radar when he was under suspicion for strangling his next-door neighbor Lorraine Benjamin, who was seventeen-years-old at the time."

"Do we have that file?" Rob asked.

"Was he prosecuted?" Jackie asked.

"No. The district attorney refused to prosecute because of a lack of evidence linking him to her death."

"How did the detectives connect him with the disappearances then? We're going to need the original murder-book," Tom said.

Many detectives wrote ideas and thoughts and inconsistencies in the margins of the original murder-books. A detective having access to the murder-book knew the full history of the case.

"He would have been eighteen in 1992 and at El Segundo High School with the missing girls. Both of the deceased detectives believed that the sophisticated nature of the Lorraine Benjamin killing showed a mature killer. One that had killed before," David said.

"You need to call Detective McDonald for that murder-book," Tom said.

"It's already done. I put Sergeant Thomas in charge of receiving it and making copies for all of you," David said.

"All right then," Tom said.

David frowned. Their roles had changed again.

"Is Christian LeGuerre still alive?" Harri asked.

"He is and living in El Segundo with his parents," David said.

The relief on the change of topic was evident and he even managed a small smile for Harri. Harri almost felt bad for him.

Almost.

"Sounds like a real winner," Jackie commented with a grin.

"Jackie, what have you found?" David asked.

He'd gotten control back of the room and his friendly smile had disappeared. The repugnant bro dude was back.

"My team is narrowing down the pool of missing girls. We are still slogging through close to 30,000 names. I've been going through various databases to see how many returned home or if their remains were found."

"That's a shocking number of missing girls," Rob said.

"We've got it down from 50,000 girls," Jackie's voice softened. "It is a disturbing amount of girls for one year."

Harri knew that Jackie had two small girls at home. Digging through so many missing girl files had to be getting to her.

"Gilead assigned Harri some extra officers. Harri, could you lend some hands to Jackie?"

"We are barely keeping up with the calls as it is. We have five uniforms answering the hotline in shifts. We have a leak somewhere. The tip line went bonkers last night after the evening news. They all led with the dental records and the connection with the '92 disappearances. Who else besides us knew about that?"

"All the crazies must have come out," Jackie asked.

"Hundreds of them. We're barely keeping up with the lead sheets. They've not stopped or slowed for that matter," Harri said. "When things slow down, perhaps we can help you with the calls, Jackie."

"I'm going to need more bodies. Looks like Harri can't spare any," Jackie said.

The cardigan she wore shifted and Harri noticed the white shirt underneath was stained with coffee. Harri had been with her when she'd spilled that coffee on herself.

Yesterday.

Jackie hadn't been home yet.

"I'll look into that," Tom said.

"Thank you, Tom," Jackie said and scrubbed her face with her hands.

"Are we certain yet on the two identifications?" Rob asked.

David nodded and wrote Maggie's and Jennifer's names on the whiteboard.

"Maggie and Jennifer are two of the mummies. We can start on pinning down each girls' timeline."

"Am I still working on the missing girls' list?" Jackie asked.

"For now, yes. When we get definitive confirmation on the identity of the other three bodies, we can drop that line of inquiry to focus on the timeline."

"All right," Jackie said, biting her lip. She didn't look thrilled by his answer.

"Rob, have you found any cold cases that have similarities to the girls?"

Rob shuffled some papers and nodded as Gilead Parker walked into the room.

"Gilead, I wasn't expecting you," David said. His gaze pierced each one of them, in turn, to see who'd called him in.

Rob raised his hand.

"I asked Gilead to call in a profiler to help us with my line of inquiry. I found a match in MO to Jeremy Evans."

"The plastic bin killer?" Jorge asked.

"That same one. He killed six women in the Central Valley, burying them in plastic bins. He's been in prison since 2000."

Today wasn't David's day. He dropped into a chair, face red.

"Hello team," Gilead said. "I wanted to touch base and first thank you all for the hard work you're doing to help these girls. I've been in touch with Quantico and Melissa Jeffries is on her way to LA. She'll be arriving later this afternoon. Let's all play nice, all right?"

His smile was all white teeth and warmth, but his eyes stayed cold and calculating as they swept over the team.

Harri felt the undercurrent again. Gears moving behind the scenes in inextricable ways. Harri felt bad for David Swisher. He was caught in a rip current that took him further out to sea and he didn't yet realize it.

FBI involvement typically meant more political minefields, as well. Harri was happy, though. She knew Mitzi Jeffries.

Melissa "Mitzi" Jeffries, Harri's instructor in a Quantico profiling course last year, had been a Miami homicide detective, then a small-town sheriff before taking her training at the FBI. Mitzi, now a criminal psychologist at the BSU, Behavioral Science Unit, traveled to different jurisdictions both to give talks on profiling techniques and to assist police departments in particularly difficult cases. She was a vivacious blonde woman with a big voice and Harri had liked her instantly. She couldn't wait to see her again.

"Keep me appraised of all the developments," Gilead said and took all the oxygen in the room with him.

For once, David Swisher stayed seated as he pulled his thoughts together.

Harri and David's eyes met.

He'd seen her smile.

She knew David would get his small petty revenge now. Tiny ants crawled up Harri's spine and goose-pimples sprouted on her skin. Harri feared the fury she saw in his eyes.

"Detective Harper, why don't you go pick up the profiler this afternoon? Show her the burial site and provide her with all necessary case files. It sounds like the five uniforms have the tip line under control," David ordered.

Harri gulped down her laugh. That was the best he could do? She hiccuped a sort of snort.

Her reaction confused David.

Harri beamed at him.

He frowned.

"Sure, I'd love to pick Mitzi up," she said.

His eyebrow raised at Harri's use of the profiler's nickname. He didn't understand why but knew she'd bested him.

The meeting broke up soon after. When Harri returned to her desk, she scrolled through multiple emails from IT support of the digitized 1992 El Segundo files.

"Does that task force seem odd to you?" Rob appeared at her elbow.

"Very. I almost feel bad for Swisher," Harri said.

"Don't. And don't underestimate him."

"I won't. Although, I wonder why Tom Bards isn't heading the team."

"The way things are playing out he soon will be. Trust me. I've got some years on you. Something's up between those two."

"No joke. We should be working toward bringing those girls home to their families and finding the bastard who did it, not playing interdepartmental politics."

"Shit flows down from the top," Rob said.

"Yeah, it does. Can I see that Jeremy Evans' file? It's on the server, right?"

"Let me show you where it lives," he said and motioned her to move over.

He knelt beside her and took control of the mouse. He clicked through the folder structure until he found the right one and double-clicked on the folder icon. Ten numbered documents lived in the folder.

"This is the complete file. He didn't do the carving of the eyes nor the mummification. But, disposal in plastic bins is rarer than I thought," Rob said.

Harri took over the control of the mouse.

"Gonna interrogate Mitzi on that drive, aren't you?" Rob asked.

"I want to prepare, that's all."

"You were one of those extra-credit students, weren't you?" Rob pushed himself off the ground with some effort.

"How did you guess?" She winked at him and clicked open the first file.

"Happy reading, nerd," he said as he held his back and pretended to hobble over to his desk.

"I'm getting old," he called out, but Harri waved him off.

She had two hours before she had to get on the road, and she'd be damned if she didn't have the entire file read by then.

7

Jane Smith

DAY 2

I placed the frozen pizza into my shopping cart, my eyes scanning my surroundings. My paranoia was off the charts since the article. This was the first time I'd left the house, forced out by my hunger.

This particular Trader Joe's supermarket, located on La Brea Avenue, was busy all day long. Crowds typically made me feel safer. Everyone was too busy getting through their grocery list to pay me any mind. That's what I wanted. But not today. Today was different.

I itched my hairline. The mouse-brown wig I'd chosen wasn't made out of real hair and itched like crazy. I slumped my shoulders even more than usual. My contortions hurt since I had perfect posture, but I wanted to look like a wallflower. Nothing to see here folks, I hoped my entire being shouted.

My cart, loaded with the essentials for the week: eggs, coffee, bread, frozen meals, crashed into a grocery cart coming around the corner from the fruit aisle.

"Hey," I said in a loud voice to the pony-tailed mean girl wearing huge sunglasses and maneuvering the offending cart into my aisle.

"Watch where YOU'RE going," she stated loudly as she pushed past me.

"Brave of you," I said.

She didn't respond.

The knuckles on both hands whitened as I gripped the bar harder and maneuvered my basket toward the cashier.

My eyes blinked fast. A cold sweat broke out on my back. A bead formed near my neck and traveled down my spine. The skin prickles made both my hands numb. Not the best place for a panic attack, I thought.

Even with all my training and vigilance, I'd tweak, and the panic attacks would roll. I feared taking medication because I needed to be aware. At ALL times. If my students could see me now. Hypocrite, the nasty voice whispered. I ignored it.

It was time to make my exit.

"YOU ARE FINE, YOU ARE FINE," I repeated my mantra under my breath.

My eyes darted to the customers in front of me as I searched for the shortest line.

A strangled cry escaped my lips.

My brain registered what I saw before I could make sense of it. My heart thrashed against my ribcage and wilted the next moment. My hand pressed down on my chest hoping to calm the beat. I blinked, not believing who stood several lines away from me. The only other person I'd ever known to have my exact eye color.

Reece Peters, my brother.

My supposedly dead brother.

The last time I'd seen Reece, he was twelve. The older version of the boy I remembered stood two aisles away from me. His resemblance to my brother was beyond uncanny, all the way down to his electric blue eyes.

So, they didn't burn in a fiery car crash in the Philippines after all.

We had known it, Natalie and me.

Jennifer tried to convince Natalie otherwise, but in her heart, she knew. She grasped at the hope, ignoring the instinct that had helped her survive.

And the hope had killed her. Ran her down. It killed Jennifer, too.

I was the only one left standing. The only survivor.

I STARED down at my cart, trying to make sense of my thoughts. My rational thoughts. It was an argument I had with myself every day. Either my brothers were alive and hunted us down or I'd been wrong about Natalie's monsters and I was running from an unknown.

But this man standing less than thirty feet away from me proved my gut right.

My rational brain took over. You haven't seen him in over twenty-five years. It could be a doppelgänger? I saw the teenager he'd become from the pictures announcing their deaths in the car crash. I hadn't kept any of the newspapers. They would be online, though. I could check.

I snuck a peek back at him.

Our eyes met.

His eyes were my eyes.

I left the cart in line and hurried toward the exit, trying not to hyperventilate. I ducked my head down and didn't breathe again until I hit the parking lot.

I ran to my BMW and jumped inside. Only then did I survey the lot to see if he'd come out after me. The parking lot was busy, but I didn't see the man from inside the store.

With trembling fingers, I started the car. After the deaths of my sister and Jennifer, I kept tabs on all the news articles about

Daniel and Reece Peters. Their names never surfaced again after their joint funeral.

I gulped for breath, my heart still thrashing to escape my chest. I fought to stabilize my breath. Getting out of this parking lot now was my only objective.

I pulled out of my parking spot.

A horn shrieked in protest.

My foot slammed the brake.

A car sped by me, coming out of nowhere, horn blaring.

My ears rang from the sound as I took a right and drove down La Brea. I lived in West Hollywood, but I never drove straight home.

I took countermeasures anytime I left my house. I had learned how to avoid people following me from Jennifer's old neighbor, Marcus during my high school years.

Both Rebecca and I had learned at Jennifer's insistence. She'd gotten him involved when a boy kept showing up at our front door, asking for Rebecca.

A boy she wasn't interested in.

Jennifer, worried about a stalker situation, corralled Marcus into teaching us. He never did say how he knew what he knew. But he had some great tips.

I used every single maneuver he taught us now. I took rights and lefts, and pulled sharply into traffic, always keeping my eyes scanning all the surrounding cars. I didn't see any that were familiar.

After driving around the city for close to an hour, I headed home, eyes peeled for any familiar cars.

IN MY NOW MORE LUCID state, I doubted he'd recognized me. His face didn't spark any familiarity for me. But those eyes? Could another man have those same eyes and not be my brother? It could be a possibility, I supposed.

And why would he come back to Los Angeles? With that unique feature, he almost dared people to recognize him for who he really was. And after a successful faked death? It didn't make sense.

Then again, that's exactly what my sister and I did in a way. We had been declared missing and Jennifer had bought us new identities. Yet, here I was in my hometown, as well.

I could have gone anywhere in the world too, but I didn't. After all of my running, I'd come home. I wondered if the discovery of the mummified girls made him come back, too. Maybe he didn't live here, but the girls brought him home.

I pulled into the underground parking of the apartment building and turned off the car. I waited for any suspicious sounds.

When none came, I stepped out of the car, my keys sticking out from in between my fisted fingers. I walked to the front of the building and pretended to dig around in my purse while I observed my surroundings. Seeing nothing out of the ordinary, I took the steps two at a time and opened my door, fingers still shaking from the lingering adrenaline.

Dropping my purse to the ground, I rushed into the kitchen and opened the fridge. I needed water. I gulped down the water, closed the fridge, and flopped down on my couch.

The rush of anxiety chemicals through my body made me woozy, my surroundings seemed unreal.

I pulled off the itchy wig and ruffled my hair with my fingers. I stretched out my back and heard a crack. I groaned. I stretched down to touch my toes and felt my muscles release.

I hoped my transformation was enough to put him off track. I'd have to change my look more frequently. I'd gotten lazy and rotated between the mousy wallflower, the bobbed yoga girl, and the pony-tailed girl next door.

I righted myself and pulled my knees to my chest.

I closed my eyes.

I pictured the man in the check-out line. Maybe, it wasn't my brother and just my crazy mind playing tricks on me.

But someone had been after us all those years ago. And they got Natalie and Jennifer and almost got me. I snapped my mind shut before the memories of that ghastly night could deluge me.

Hannah, my last Skype therapist, would be proud of me. It was part of my training in my battle with PTSD and survivor's guilt. My fear had made me housebound for several years. Thank god for Skype and tech-savvy therapists. And the Krav Maga. The need to help other women finally pulled me out of the house.

The questions rattled in my brain.

Could I believe what I saw?

Should I act on it?

I stared into the tree right outside my window, taking peace from the green all around me. I needed to tell someone about who I was. The police failed me before, though. Why would this time be different?

Because I was a different person now, and not a lost teenager, I reasoned. They would have to listen to me. I was a citizen who paid her taxes on time.

My name was fake, though. The police would interrogate me like before. They'd have to corroborate my story and would look into what happened that night when Jennifer plunged from the third-story window. They would see I was the main suspect and had disappeared before being questioned.

I shifted my gaze to my built-in bookcase of books, filled to the brim, their riotous colors making my eyes blink faster. The bookcase reminded me of Jennifer and our home in Seattle.

It reminded me that not one of the cops believed me about the intruder in Jennifer's house back then.

What would change now?

And I had run.

I changed my name again and escaped over the border into Canada, like my sister and I had always talked about if anything went wrong.

And everything had.

The police had bodies though, two of which were supposedly my sister and me.

I squeezed my eyes shut and let the tears flow down my cheeks. I wished my sister and Jennifer were here. They would tell me what to do.

Jennifer would swear at how corrupt the cops were, she'd been a defense lawyer, and Natalie would goad her into an even greater torrent of cuss words at the justice system. I didn't think they'd want me to go and talk to the police.

Natalie would tell me to run.

But I'd been running and I was tired. I didn't want to run anymore. Like my therapist said, the only way to heal is to embrace the demon inside you.

Face it.

Let it in.

If I told my truth, I'd be able to step into the light. Out of the shadows for once and for all. Maybe, in my own way, I could help find justice for those girls.

I was sure I was supposed to be one of them. The police should know someone had taken my place.

8

LAX - Los Angeles, CA
DAY 2

C onstruction at LAX jammed cars into all surrounding lanes making the crawl toward the arrivals terminal painful. Harri Harper white-knuckled it into the furthermost right lane amid a cacophony of car horns and swears coming from the other drivers.

"Damn, that was ugly," she said under her breath and drove up to the arrivals terminal of American Airlines. She pulled on the parking brake and turned on the flashers. Melissa "Mitzi" Jeffries, her Farrah Fawcett hair as audacious as Harri remembered it, strolled out of baggage claim, a small suitcase rolling behind her. Harri beeped and Mitzi waved in her direction.

Harri exited the car and hugged Mitzi.

"It's great to see you, Mitzi," Harri said.

"You too, honey. Thank you for the ride."

"David Swisher instructed me to take you to the body dump. Are you up for going now?"

"I don't really need to see the burial site. It's technically not the crime scene. Plus, these girls were placed there over twenty years ago and, from what I've found on the internet, a lot has changed since then."

"All right, I'll take you straight to the PAB then," Harri said.

"I'm surprised you have time to wrestle with LAX traffic on such a big case?" Mitzi asked.

Harri had no way to answer that without going into the politics.

"I have the perfect opportunity to pump you for information." Harri flashed a grin.

"At least you're honest," Mitzi chortled.

"I try." Harri hefted the suitcase into the back seat.

"How's the new unit?" Mitzi asked.

"How did that news travel all the way to Quantico?"

"I get around."

"You know everything," Harri quipped.

"And don't you forget it," Mitzi said and hopped in the car.

"How did you know?"

Harri slid into the driver's seat. A car honked for the spot and Harri waved at the pissed off driver.

"Violet Sanford asked me for a recommendation. Seems like she went above and beyond," Mitzi said.

Harri hadn't known that.

"Oh, my goodness. Thank you, Mitzi!"

"I like your brain. It was easy."

"How are you liking the unit?"

"The cases are interesting, and we've closed a bunch of them. Feels great. I've been angling for Homicide."

"Want to run with the big boys, eh?"

"Something like that."

"What's the problem? You have a unique gift to make connections that others don't see. Homicide would be lucky to have you."

Harri's heart skipped several beats. She pressed her arm into her chest willing her heart to calm down.

"Richard Byrne doesn't think so."

"Who's he?"

"The reason Violet needed to contact you for a recommendation."

"I see. One of those. Every department seems to have one," Mitzi said.

"Yes, they do seem to proliferate," Harri said.

Mitzi watched Harri closely. "You all right?"

"Yes. Tell me about Jeremy Evans."

A horn blared again.

"All right, all right." Harri waved to the irate driver and pulled back into traffic.

"Jeremy Evans killed in the Central Valley throughout the early 90s to the early 2000s. We caught him in 2002."

"How did you catch him?"

"He made a mistake. They all do, eventually. His last victim was seen getting into his beat-up truck by a worker walking home from the fields. The worker was brave enough to come forward with the license plate. The case broke open after that. The police put him on surveillance and gathered enough evidence to convict him. He'd killed twelve women before that."

"You profiled him?"

"I did."

"I didn't see the profile in the case file?"

"I'm not sure why it wouldn't be. He fit the profile about eighty percent, not my best work. But after we had a name I was able to help with the prosecutor's case."

"Are there similarities you're seeing between the two cases?" Harri asked.

"Strangulation. They both used plastic bins for body disposal. The Central Valley victims weren't mummified

57

though, nor did their bodies show as much damage as the mummified girls."

"The forensic pathologist has noted the hyoid bone had been broken, along with broken fingers, lacerations to their abdomens, and bite marks," Harri said of the Ballona Creek girls.

"Jeremy Evans didn't bite. He'd left scratches on two of his victim's breasts, but no other visible marks. He was more into strangulation to the brink of death and then bringing his victims back. He'd torture them for several days before finally killing them. The victims had multiple bruises on their necks from the multiple strangulation attempts. He preferred nylon rope."

"Is he good for the Ballona girls?"

"I don't think so. The main fantasy doesn't match."

Harri thought of the course Mitzi taught at Quantico and learning that each multiple killer functioned inside their own specific fantasy.

"It's the aspect of the mummification, isn't it?" Harri asked.

She maneuvered their car through traffic onto the 110 North headed toward Downtown.

"Yes, mummification is specific and vital to this killer's fantasy. Jeremy Evans was your typical sexual sadist," Mitzi explained.

"The strangulation over days?"

"Yes. It's watching the person die over and over." Mitzi said.

Harri gripped the wheel harder.

"Mummification is different."

"Tell me," Harri said.

"That detail speaks to a different personality type. Why mummify a body?"

"To preserve it? Like the Egyptians," Harri said.

"Right. Keep the body in a very specific state. Unlike the victims of Jeremy Evans. He wasn't interested in the bodies after death."

"Mummification takes time."

"Exactly. The body is treated with the utmost care. Jeremy Evans didn't care about the bodies in that way. He couldn't figure out where to store them so they wouldn't be found. That's why he chose the storage locker."

"We can never fully understand the perverse fantasies these killers have. The forensic pathologist's report on the bodies makes me think sexual sadist, but the mummification speaks more to a pathology of necrophile. Those two personality types are opposite to each other."

"Split personality?" Harri quipped.

"Something like that."

They fell silent. Harri focused on the traffic crawling toward downtown as Mitzi stared out the window.

"Why do you think they asked me to come here?" Mitzi asked.

It was a direct question and surprising coming from an FBI agent. Harri knew Mitzi spoke what was on her mind and didn't enjoy playing politics.

"Honestly, I don't know. I joined the task force yesterday and have been dealing with the tip line since. I am not part of the team that's actively investigating the case."

"But isn't Rob Lakin with the cold case unit?" Mitzi asked.

"He is. The detective running this task force is part of the HSS (Homicide Special Section). Rob is going through the cold cases, I'm on tip-line. I'm following instructions," Harri said.

She didn't really know of any other way to put that without getting into politics and talking crap about other officers. She tried to keep her nose clean.

"I'm hearing what you're saying. This is a high-profile case.

I thought LAPD would want first crack at it. BSU profilers don't usually get on a case this early," Mitzi said.

"Rob was the one who asked for you. He'd be better to ask about that," Harri said.

It was an odd question with tension behind it. Harri didn't want to get into the politics during what could be her only opportunity to speak with Mitzi.

"Are you going to interview Jeremy Evans?" Harri asked, switching tactics.

"Most likely. I was the profiler who was on the team when they caught him, so I know his tics and how to get information out of him. IF there's any information to get. I've interviewed him two or three times over the years. He knows me. We have history."

"That's a horrifying thought," Harri said.

"Part of the job. I've worked on equally gruesome cases in the years since then. It's amazing how creative these guys are in destroying other humans. I guess, in the end, it's in the spectrum of human behavior."

"What do you mean? You think that certain parts of the population are always going to be like this?"

"I do. And there's very good evidence that serial killers have existed throughout the history of human civilization. I mean, haven't you heard that even dolphins murder without cause these days," Mitzi said.

As the skyline of downtown Los Angeles loomed before them, Harri mentally went through everything Mitzi had told her. If she had any more questions, now was the time to ask.

She had a pretty good idea that she'd be in the conference room helping on the tip-line and being kept out of the action the moment she dropped Mitzi off.

But her mind was blank. Mitzi, as always, explained her thinking thoroughly. Harri didn't have anything else to add or ask about.

They drove into the parking lot and Harri helped Mitzi get her luggage out of the car. They walked along Main street, passing several homeless people camping out in front of the transportation building.

"That's pretty astonishing to see how many homeless encampments have sprouted up," Mitzi said.

"There are 68,000 more homeless people on the streets this year," Harri said.

Mitzi shook her head and a look that Harri couldn't identify crossed her face.

"Washington like this?"

"It's not this bad," she said as they went into the front doors of the PAB.

Harri helped get Mitzi to the checkpoint and brought her to the task force conference room. Mitzi said hello to Rob and then Gilead turned up and took her to his office for a private conversation.

As Harri had expected she was put back on tip-line duty.

9

Jane Smith
DAY 2

Natalie's voice followed me all the way to Police Headquarters downtown.

Keep your eyes forward.

Make eye contact and then look away. Don't challenge people but make them aware you are aware.

Wear headphones, but never have anything playing.

Walk with keys in between fingers, ready to gouge if need be.

Take a circuitous route to wherever you are going, in case of a tail.

Take public transport.

Yell "fire" if ever grabbed.

HER WARNINGS PLAYED in my head as I took the metro to Union station. I wore my girl-next-door getup. A blonde wig with bangs pulled back in a ponytail and a headband for good measure. I wore navy pants and a white shirt, all baggy. I hoped I looked like a typical boring girl as I could.

Her voice stayed with me as I waited in the large lobby of

the Police Administration Building for detectives working on the Ballona Creek Girls case. They made me wait fifteen minutes before arriving to take me up to an interrogation room.

A tall, fit woman stepped off the elevator. Her brown hair was pulled hard into a ponytail and her hazel eyes were bloodshot with dark circles underneath. But her gaze was sharp, calculating, searching. She reminded me of one of those odd-looking supermodels. All high-cheek bones and legs. She didn't look like a cop.

"I'm Detective Harper. This is Detective Lakin," she said.

A man turned up behind her. He looked like a family man, well-rested, and taken care of although extremely tall and gangly. The two made quite the pair.

"What is this about?" the woman asked in a clipped tone.

"I need privacy. I don't want to talk about it here in a lobby. It's about the Ballona Creek bodies."

I looked around. The lobby was empty, but for us and the intake officer.

"Please follow us," Detective Lakin said.

I followed them to the elevator. The building did not look like a police headquarters, but more like a fancy office building. One that held finance guys, or bankers.

The elevator ride was silent. They led me to a small interrogation room as I'd assumed they would.

I felt naked and defenseless.

The room was small and dark with a buzzing fluorescent lamp above my head. It had four chairs and a single table, and it was hot and stuffy. A sudden surge of vertigo made me grasp the back of the chair. I lowered myself into the chair and crossed my arms at my chest.

I took a deep breath.

I needed to convince them that I really was Lindsey Peters without any real proof.

"Water? Coffee?" Detective Harper asked.

"No, thank you." I slid my scarf off my neck and placed it in my lap. I could hide my nervous hands in it.

"You left your name with the intake officer. Are you really Jane Smith?" asked Detective Lakin. He opened his notebook and wrote.

"It's the name that I use now. I've had a long list of aliases since I escaped with my sister."

"Escaped?" Detective Harper said. "Who are you purporting to be?" she asked coolly.

Her eyes met mine. In other circumstances, I'd like this woman. Her hazel eyes told me she'd seen things. There was sadness behind them and she understood the darkness.

"The newspapers said they found my body down at Ballona Creek. My name was Lindsey Peters when I was eight years old."

Detective Harper sat back in her seat as Detective Lakin wrote in his notebook.

She scrutinized me.

I sat still, keeping my eyes on her.

She leaned in.

I leaned in as well.

"Lindsey Peters disappeared back in May 1992," Detective Harper stated.

"Yes, the night of May 24th. It was a Sunday night."

I recounted our midnight escape and how we met the mysterious woman at the end of the street who drove us to the train station. Our trip to Seattle, Washington and meeting Jennifer Stevens. All the fake paperwork and the new names.

"Did your sister take your birth certificates? Passports?" Detective Harper asked.

"No. I don't know. I never thought to ask," I replied.

"You don't have any kind of documentation then?"

I shook my head. I knew this would happen, but I couldn't

keep the disappointment from flowing into my stomach, causing acid to swirl around it.

"You never contacted your family again?" Detective Lakin asked. His voice sounded bored.

"No."

"How did you get to Washington?" Detective Harper asked.

I closed my eyes, remembering the days after the escape.

"We went to Oakland first, by train. I remember it was Oakland because we met another woman who gave us a car to drive up to Seattle and she said we were in Oakland."

"Who were these women?" Detective Harper asked crisply.

"I asked Jennifer about that. She was part of a sort of underground railroad for abused women. The woman in Oakland was in the same group."

"What about the woman who picked you up in El Segundo?"

"That was Natalie's teacher, I think. They knew each other."

"Where did you get these fake identities?" Detective Lakin asked.

"Jennifer. That was her job in the network. She was a defense attorney."

Detective Harper and Detective Lakin exchanged a glance.

"Why should we believe you? Are you here to waste our time? Get on the front page of the LA Times."

"God, no," I exploded.

Detective Harper pursed her lips. The lines on her forehead scrunched up.

That wasn't the right reaction to give them. I pulled myself together. I needed to get some control back.

"You can't tell anyone I've been here. Please. I wanted to help with the investigation, tell you we lived. But they can't know I'm alive and in Los Angeles."

My gut churned, waiting for them to say something.

"Who was your sister running from?" Detective Harper asked, her tone friendlier now.

"She never said. Wait, she called them monsters. That's how she always talked about who she ran from. Who she protected me from."

"Monsters?" Detective Harper leaned back in her chair, her lips pursed again, her eyes sharp on me.

"That's right. I was only eight at the time," I retorted.

"What happened to make your sister run that night?" Detective Harper asked.

"She refused to speak about that night."

"Can your sister corroborate any of this? Where is she now?" Her questions were coming faster now.

"My sister died in a hit-and-run in 1999."

"I'm sorry to hear that. Can we speak to Jennifer Stevens?" she asked.

"She was killed the night of Natalie's funeral."

The look between the two detectives was easily readable. Disbelief.

"Killed? How?"

I gulped. The truth would win out. I had to believe that.

"Home invasion."

"Where were you?" Detective Lakin asked.

"I was at Jennifer's side. She saved my life by standing between me and the intruder."

The detectives fell silent.

I was too afraid to say the wrong thing. We sat like that for the eternity of five minutes.

"Do you have any other family that could support the fact that you are Lindsey Peters?" Detective Lakin asked, his gaze boring into mine.

Could I trust them with the suspicion that my brothers

were still alive? That I'd seen one at the supermarket? They would think I was a total loon if they didn't already.

"My brothers and father died in a car crash in the Philippines in 1996. We didn't have any other living family that I knew of. It was just my father, my two brothers, my sister, and me. My mother died in childbirth when I was five, along with my little sister. As far as I knew my parents were only children and the grandparents were long dead."

"How are we supposed to believe you without any proof?" Detective Harper asked.

"I don't know. I can give you DNA and fingerprints, but I doubt I'm in the system. I don't remember being fingerprinted back then."

"Did they find who killed Jennifer Stevens?"

I shifted in my seat and cursed myself for giving them a tell. They could find out for themselves I was the prime suspect.

"I don't believe so. I left the country that night. I went up to Vancouver to another of Jennifer's crew. We had planned it that way if something went wrong. If they found us."

"You keep saying they?" Detective Harper asked.

"My sister always said they."

"Did Jennifer tell you who you were running from after your sister's death?"

"She didn't get a chance. She went down to San Francisco to meet with police and identify the body. She was down there dealing with paperwork and then back to Seattle to do the funeral. We barely spoke in those six days. I barely remember them myself."

"And why do you live under an alias now?" Detective Lakin asked me.

Our eyes met over the table. I refused to look away.

"Because I don't know who's after me. All the people who were close to me are dead and I'm the only one still alive. I think the only reason why is because I've been underground all this time," I said.

"Why have you come forward now?" Detective Harper asked. "I can't imagine it's just civic duty. Especially if you've been running all these years?"

My cheeks burned. I wanted to tell them about my brothers. Fear kept my mouth closed.

"I am, was Lindsey Peters. My sister Natalie Peters and I escaped from 1011 Lomita Street, El Segundo. We are not the girls in that grave. Which means you still have to identify two girls whose parents are looking for them."

"And you have no idea who the monsters were?" Detective Lakin asked again.

"I always assumed it was one of my brothers. But she refused to say. When we discovered that my brothers and father had been killed in a car crash in the Philippines, my sister started to relax, live life a bit more. Not be so scared all the damn time. But then she was killed a few years later, so there is that. I guess we were wrong."

At last, I laid out my suspicion.

I was still frustrated with myself over not pushing my sister harder on what had been really going on. Each time I asked, she instead sparred with me, making sure my fighting techniques were up to par.

She drilled safety into me.

How to protect myself when I was alone.

To always lock the door when I was home.

She forced me to do women's protection classes and martial arts. But never told me who.

Who was coming?

"She taught me to protect myself. She never wanted to talk about the past after we got to Seattle. But it was something that haunted her because she screamed pretty much every night that I lived under the same roof as her."

"Let's go back to the home invasion. Walk us through it," Detective Lakin said.

He stared at my face intently. Was he trying to see the eight-year-old girl from the LA Times in my face?

"We cleaned up after the wake at our house. We hosted some friends of ours from high school. We had finished up the dishes and started to prepare for bed. Jennifer heard the noise first. She ran into my room and told me we had to get out of the house. When I came back out, the man was in the hallway. She told me to run and I did."

I wished I had asked for that glass of water. My throat was parched. My shoulders slumped remembering that horrible night.

"I ran away. She put herself in between me and the man who'd come to kill me. I ran down the stairs and out the door. She hit the pavement almost in front of me. I sprinted up the street and never went back. I called 911. Then I disappeared."

I didn't mention that I'd been wanted for questioning in her death for years after. Probably even now.

I took a deep breath and finished the story.

"Jennifer had made a plan for me if anything went wrong. She had a contact in Vancouver, British Columbia that I was supposed to go find if something happened. I'd always carried a key to a storage facility on the other side of the border. It was on a chain that I wore around my neck. She'd squirreled away new papers, clothes, and money for me there. I went to live with her friend until I was of age."

"What was the contact's name and phone number in Vancouver?" Detective Harper asked.

I bit my lip. I couldn't expose the woman who'd kept me safe for all those years.

"I can't give you that information."

"Why not?" Detective Lakin asked.

"I don't want to expose her like that. She's still active in the group."

"The underground network for abused women?" Detective Harper asked.

She didn't sound like she totally believed it.

The two detectives glanced at each other. After a few more seconds of silence, Detective Lakin closed his notebook.

"Proving your identity is near impossible without the proper paperwork," Detective Harper said. "And the lack of corroborating witnesses to your story."

I pulled out a small manila folder from my backpack. "These are my current dental records. I don't know if they'll help since I was eight at the time. I have no idea if my dentist in El Segundo still has them on file. But it's the only proof I can give you." I slid the manila folder to them.

Detective Harper took the manila folder and peeked inside.

"We will run these down," Detective Lakin said.

I stood up to shake his hand.

"I hope some of this helped," I said.

He grasped my hand in a strong grip. Detective Harper followed suit.

"Please leave your address and telephone number so we can keep in touch. If this checks out, your story I mean, then we are going to need to speak to you again," Detective Harper said.

"I can't give you my address. How about just my phone number?" I asked.

"We need both your address and your phone number. You came here in good faith and we want to believe you. So, in good faith leave us a way that we can find you."

I hadn't thought they'd need my address. My survival instinct kicked in. No way I was going to give them where I live.

"I took a huge risk coming here today and you don't believe me. I can see it on both of your faces."

They didn't correct me.

"I won't give you my address since it will go into your computer system and then it's out there, easy to crack and get." I sounded paranoid, but I didn't care.

"We will protect the address. This is the LAPD. We don't get hacked," Detective Harper said in a disbelieving voice.

"I'm a developer. I work in internet security. Anyone can get hacked." I wrote down my cell phone number on the notepad that Detective Lakin put in front of me.

"My phone number is all I can give you. Can I go now?" I asked.

Detective Harper held up her hand and took out her cellphone. She punched the number into her keypad.

My cellphone buzzed in my backpack.

Satisfied, she nodded at Detective Lakin. He shook his head and pointed at the pad.

"We need an address."

I sighed and wrote an address down. He didn't specify what address. They weren't going to like it when they discovered the yogurt stand off Santa Monica Blvd.

Detective Harper opened the door. "I'll lead you out," she said.

We didn't speak as she led me to the elevator and back to the lobby.

"Thank you for coming in," she said.

"Please believe me. I want my identity back and justice for those girls," I said. "We escaped and they took our place."

Something in her eyes flickered. Was that pity or compassion? I hoped it was the latter. I needed all the compassion she could muster. I needed her to help me find the monsters.

I choked back tears as a wave of sadness crashed over me

and turned away from her. The door swooshed closed behind me.

I scanned the street and slumped my shoulders. I needed these detectives to help me find my brothers' new identities. Slowing my walk, I made sure to keep my eyes down, face pointed to the ground. I'd clocked at least three cameras on the entrance. I'd taken a huge risk coming here.

First step was to prove I was Lindsey. I needed to find a witness to corroborate the night of the escape. The woman who drove us to the bus station. My sister called her Barbara. She'd been Natalie's teacher.

I would find her and bring her in with me to prove who I really was. Who Natalie had been. Maybe she could even tell me what really happened back then.

10

Cold Case Bull Pen - Los Angeles, CA
DAY 2

The Cold Case bullpen stood almost empty aside from Rob Lakin hunched over files at his cubicle across from her own. Detective Harri Harper, mind reeling from Jane Smith's crazy story, flopped into her chair and rolled it over to Rob.

"Whack job or a break in the case?" Harri asked.

"I know, right?" Rob asked, not looking up from the file.

Harri scootched in closer and peered over to the file.

"Better question. Do you think she was wearing a wig?"

"I'm a guy," Larkin shrugged. "How am I supposed to know about wigs?"

"You're also a detective."

"Ha. Ha. I didn't notice that, though. Her eyes were incredibly unique, however. Attractive girl. Terrified, but attractive."

"She changed her body posture, too. When I walked her out," Harri observed remembering how the woman's back rolled in when she walked outside.

"What do you mean?"

"What were your impressions of her when she was speaking to us? About her body language?" Harri asked.

"She had good posture. Even through her baggy shirt, I could tell how physically fit she was. She looked like a gym rat."

"That was my impression, too. But then when she walked away her posture changed. She rolled her shoulders in, stooped like an old man, and shuffled her feet. I wouldn't recognize the woman who walked out of here from the one we interviewed."

"Talented actress then? Do we believe her?" Rob asked.

Harri chewed on her lip. "I'm intrigued. She's not your run-of-the-mill fruitcake. What are you reading?"

"Natalie and Lindsey Peters' file."

"Anything?"

"Not much. The only thing that jumps out at me is that the father, one Christopher Peters, didn't report his daughters missing until two days later."

"That's weird."

"It is up to a point. He explained that he believed his eldest had run away with a younger daughter in tow and assumed they'd come back in a day or two. He wanted to give her time to cool off, he claimed."

"Does the file explain how the Peters girls were lumped in with the other disappearances?"

"Christopher Peters went to the media. He was adamant they be included in the main investigation," Rob said, rubbing his lips. "Wonder why?"

"To have more resources looking for his girls?"

"The girls he didn't report missing for two days?"

"Right?" Harri asked, sitting back in her chair.

"Are we believing her?"

"She's terrified of something. Did you see how her hands were shaking?"

"We need to corroborate the two deaths," he said,

gesturing at the file.

Harri leaned in.

"Let's say that we do find out that Jennifer and Rebecca Stevens died the way Jane Smith said they did. That still doesn't prove her identity as Lindsey Peters."

Rob rubbed his face.

"And, if we do prove she's Lindsey Peters, then what? The sisters ran away. They don't connect to our case."

"Natalie Peters was at the same school as the other girls," Harri said. "That's one connection."

"We have two girls who haven't been identified yet, we should be finding their names."

The truth of that statement smacked Harri silent. She pursed her lips, mind racing down different lanes of inquiry. What if the Peters' girls were connected? How would they fit into the investigation?

A woman waved, yanking Harri out of her thoughts. It was Mitzi.

"I happened to be passing by when I saw you go into the interrogation room with that woman. I hope you don't mind, but I watched your interview with her," she said, pulling an empty seat to their little group.

She sat down.

"What a story," Mitzi said.

"Did you believe her?" Harri asked.

Mitzi's vast years of experience interrogating suspects and taking witness statements could bolster her gut instinct that Jane Smith brought another dimension to their case.

"She looked haunted, like an abused spouse on the run from her husband," Mitzi said. "She reminds me of victims who have been in manipulative relationships where they are fearful of everything and everyone to a type of paranoia."

"You believe her then," Rob asked.

"She didn't show signs of lying. I believe that she believes everything she said," Mitzi said.

Harri noticed the undercurrent of excitement in her voice. She'd been pulled into the story.

"You mean tells. I didn't catch any, either," Rob said.

"Did you notice she kept her voice flat during most of the interview? She didn't look away when you asked her questions. Kept her emotions well hidden. Those are all signs of trauma."

"Is she Lindsey Peters?" Harri asked.

"She sure thinks she is. But if she's not, who told her she was Lindsey Peters and why?" Mitzi asked.

Harri had wondered something similar. The pull of the darkness beneath Jane Smith's story was tickling Harri's brain. As if an answer to a question they hadn't even considered had been given to them and they didn't know how to find the question. Yet.

"Or we have an abused woman coming in to get her fifteen minutes of attention," Rob added.

"Say she is telling the truth. About everything. Someone has left a trail of bodies searching for her," Harri said.

A shower of cold prickles cascaded down her face. She'd felt that sensation before. And it hadn't turned out well for the witness she'd been looking to re-interview.

"She's in danger."

"Jane Smith told us as much," Rob said.

"Well, what about this? She is telling the truth, but she's confessing to the killings of her sister and her adopted mother," Mitzi said.

Harri cocked her head at Mitzi in a do-you-really-think-that sort of way.

Mitzi held up her hand.

"Hear me out. Imagine this scenario. Natalie Peters is getting abused by a family member. She plans her escape but doesn't want to leave her sister behind in fear the abuse will continue with her sister as the new victim."

Mitzi paused.

Harri shifted in her seat and stretched her leg out.

"Girl, stop fidgeting. You're making me nervous," she teased and patted Harri on the knee.

"Ok. Natalie flees from her home with her sister to protect her and it's traumatizing for both girls. Natalie never tells her sister why they ran. That's okay for a while since Lindsey is still young, but when the teenage years hit that becomes a problem."

"Do trauma victims strikeout, though? I've always heard they tend to be more victimized?" Harri asked, doubtful of the direction the theory was going in.

"Devil's advocate. Lindsey doesn't understand why her sister is so vigilant and fearful. She resents her sister for all the fear. What if Lindsey's trauma over this clandestine life bubbles over? She runs her sister over. Jennifer Stevens finds out and tries to get her to get help, turn herself in and she pushes her out the window?"

"It doesn't feel right," Harri said. "Where's the proof?"

"The Seattle police might have it," Mitzi said.

Harri tapped her feet on the carpeted floor, expelling nervous energy.

"I don't buy it. Why would she come to us with this story? What's her impetus? She must know her story will be scrutinized," Harri said.

"We're talking years of hiding an identity, mix that in with teenage emotions and the trauma of that night? I mean, could the scenario be possible with that level of fear and paranoia running through the girls?" Mitzi asked, tossing her hair back. "Or she's being hunted by an individual who wiped out her entire family."

"When you say it like that," Rob said.

"It's a wild story is all I'm saying," Mitzi said. "Could go either way."

"Does she tie into our girls in Ballona Creek in any significant way? Because if she doesn't, we should push this to another jurisdiction," Rob added.

"Are you wanting to drop this into someone else's lap?" Harri asked. "They were from Los Angeles."

"Running away is not a crime. The deaths happened in two different jurisdictions. The precincts might want us to contact their cold case units," Rob said.

"Lindsey was only eight when her sister took her. Technically, that's kidnapping," Harri pointed out. "I'll give both jurisdictions a call when we come to that point. First, how do we determine she's connected to this case? Proving she's Lindsey Peters would be a start, but then if she's alive it's not part of our case," Harri said.

Both Mitzi and Rob nodded.

"Now who gets to tell David Swisher about Jane Smith? I don't think it should be me," Harri said.

"That guy turns his face away every time you talk. It's something else to behold," Rob said, a frown forming.

"That I can handle. It's not like it hasn't happened before. The active demoting me is driving me nuts, though," Harri said.

"I'll go tell him," Rob said.

"Thank you," Harri said.

She and Mitzi returned to their desks.

Harri took in the new stack of lead sheets waiting for her and sighed.

It was going to be a long day.

HARRI MANAGED to get through eight of the lead sheets when Rob reappeared at her elbow. His expression told her all she needed to know about his meeting with David Swisher.

"Looks like your conversation didn't go very well," Harri said.

"Swisher thought Jane Smith belongs in a looney bin with that story. He didn't care to hear any theories on the subject. We're moving forward as if Natalie and Lindsey Peters are the remaining two mummies. Before he dismissed me though, he assigned you to look into Jane Smith."

"I see. If I find that Lindsey Peters and Natalie Peters aren't part of our mummy case, then could Swisher find cause to put me on that new case and off the task force?"

"It's what he wants, I'm sure. His reasoning was that this falls under the anonymous tip category and since you're in charge of the tip-line, you are the person to chase it down."

"Isn't that what we have the uniformed officers for?" Harri asked.

Harri had spent many years chasing down anonymous tips while in uniform. She'd gotten some good leads a handful of times, but usually, they came to nothing.

"It's not what you wanted to hear, I know," Rob said.

"Her story deserves to be investigated. I'll follow the thread wherever it takes me," Harri said.

All victims mattered and deserved justice. She wasn't going to play politics to stay on the task force. She'd do her damnedest to corroborate Jane Smith's story.

"She still could be connected to our girls. There are too many coincidences for my liking."

"I agree. All right, I'll leave you to it," Rob said and went back to his desk.

Harri logged into the California database and searched for Rebecca Stevens. Her file came up as the fifth entry, but when she clicked on it, she found the file hadn't been uploaded to the database yet.

She picked up the receiver and dialed the number for the San Francisco precinct.

11

Jane Smith
DAY 2

I bounced back and forth from left foot to right foot, watching the six-foot-tall woman. I'd gone back to my old Krav Maga class in Pasadena. I needed to find my power again. My safety.

She made a move and lunged at my chest. I welcomed her and wrapped my arms around her. I twisted both of us to my left and used her momentum to slam her body to the ground. Once she was on her back, I pretend pounded her face and did one last stomp.

My instructor, Daniel, nodded and I held out my hand to help my opponent to her feet. She heaved herself up and bounced up and down. It was my turn to be the aggressor.

We switched positions and I lunged at her. Her technique was as good as mine. My body flopped to the ground within seconds and I groaned on impact. It had been months since I'd trained this hard. She mimed hitting me in the face and pretend-stomped me in the head. I waited for Daniel to nod before getting up.

On and on we trained hard for the next hour. This particular class also had us work on disarming aggressors of their knives and guns. By the end of the second hour, I was dripping with sweat and exhausted. And for the first time in days, I wasn't afraid of my own shadow.

I knew these moves. I'd trained enough to get in whatever position was necessary to disarm someone, or to slip out of their grasp, or to protect myself from an assault. I pictured my brother Reece's face on each one of my sparring partners. It was the only way to prepare my mind for what was to come. To practice getting over the shock of coming face to face with the monsters and surviving. Not freezing. I could never freeze.

Natalie drilled that into me.

"Good job, everyone!" Daniel called out.

Finally, the class was over.

Head down, I moved for my gym bag at the edge of the sparring room. It was more like a gigantic warehouse. Some of these guys enjoyed the grunge of a warehouse workout space. The location made the practice more real for them I always thought.

The gyms rarely had locker rooms to change in. I liked the idea of no locker rooms since no one could corner me to chit chat. The problem was I couldn't change into a disguise discreetly until I got to the car. It was enough of a hassle to make me move around gyms.

I never came to a Krav Maga class more than once or twice. That anonymity thing was crucial to me. The double doors slammed behind me as I blinked several times in the darkness. The small parking lot adjacent to the gym didn't have any streetlights. Weird seeing as many women were attacked in dark parking structures or lots. Was that an advertisement for how much women needed the lessons?

I rolled my eyes at the thought as I approached my small silver series 3 BMW. There were four cars exactly like it in the thirty-space parking lot. I hit the button to click the lights on. Best way to be anonymous in LA was to drive a silver BMW.

All the entertainment assistants in town trying to keep up appearances had one and silver was the color.

Throwing my gym bag into the passenger seat, I slid into the driver's seat and closed the door. I engaged the locks and pulled out my dark-haired bob wig. It was the easiest one to put on in the dark.

The double doors opened and more of the class started filtering out into the lot. I shoved the wig on my head and checked myself in the mirror. Good enough, I thought.

I pulled out of the small lot onto the residential street. I was sure no one noticed my transformation.

I breathed in.

The class had brought me back to center. I didn't feel as out of control as I had after the police interview. More like an interrogation, I thought. The cops didn't believe me of that I was sure. I drove toward the 210 West, the freeway I used to get back home.

My mind was clear.

I couldn't even feel the fear anymore. Well, maybe just a little. In the far outer edges of my consciousness, though and that was okay.

At least, I could think clearly and plan now.

I was calm.

I was peaceful and my body was relaxed. Now, what was my plan?

I followed the signs onto the freeway and merged into five lanes of red lights. Traffic at rush hour. Fully anonymous now, I allowed my mind to wander.

The first thing I needed to do was to get that female cop, Detective Harper, on my side. I felt her wanting to believe me.

The man was skeptical, but she'd watched me closely. She studied my body language to see if she could find my tells. I had them, but I'd been telling the truth. I think she knew that.

I needed more solid evidence of that escape. Someone to corroborate my story.

Since Jennifer and Natalie were dead, there was only one other person who had been there that night. The woman who'd given us the ride to the train station. Natalie had told me she'd been a teacher at El Segundo High School. I would start there.

I knew exactly how I'd do it. One of my students had been a substitute teacher in the LAUSD school district. Using my hacking skills, I would create the perfect cover as a substitute teacher for snooping at the high school tomorrow. I doubted the El Segundo database would be too difficult to get into.

I smiled. I was back in control. Slow and steady, I thought.

I inched forward toward home.

12

Police Administrative Building (PAB)

WEDNESDAY, AUGUST 8, 2018 - DAY 3

Detective Harri Harper ran a hand through her disheveled shoulder-length hair and rubbed her eyes. The coffee from the break room couldn't cut through her exhaustion after staying at her desk all night. The letters blurred on her computer screen.

She pulled off her reading glasses and closed her eyes.

Ugh, she thought. She needed more caffeine. The adrenaline of the search faded hours ago and Harri should have gone home to sleep.

She'd gone down the rabbit-hole of the Jennifer and Rebecca Stevens murders. After an unsuccessful attempt to get either of the files on the two deaths through the usual police database channels, she'd called both the San Francisco Police Department and the Seattle Police Department to access the files that way. For the rest of the night, she'd pulled up anything she could find on the three women, Jennifer, Rebecca, and Mary Stevens.

Her phone rang.

She grabbed at it, pushing the receiver off its holder and

into her lap. She scooped it up and put it to her ear, flustered she'd lose the call.

"Detective Harri Harper speaking," she said.

"Detective John Larrabee from the Seattle Police Department. I saw a message on my desk that you called about the Jennifer Stevens murder," he said.

"Good morning Detective Larrabee. Thank you for calling me back. I'm following up some leads on a current case that we have down here in Los Angeles and the Jennifer Stevens murder has come up," she said.

She didn't want to color their conversation in any way when it came to getting information on Mary Stevens AKA Jane Smith or Lindsey Peters.

"I was the lead investigator on that case, in fact. That's one of my go-back-to cases. It was a long time ago, but I can't let it go. I read over the murder-book every year to see if something jumps out at me. Make some calls, that kind of thing," he said.

"Mind if I ask what keeps bothering you about it?" Harri asked.

"The whole case never sat well with me. There wasn't any evidence of a break-in, although I had a feeling there should have been."

"Why did you think there should have been?"

"The crime scene didn't sit right with me," Detective Larrabee said.

"Why?"

"Seattle back then was a smaller city. Jennifer lived in a ritzy neighborhood where everyone knew each other."

"Are you saying that people kept their doors open?"

"Something like that. Not her, though. Jennifer Stevens installed a pretty hardcore security system. Her neighbors said that Stevens always kept her doors locked. Her security was impeccable."

"As if she was waiting for something bad to happen?"

"I looked to see if she'd been burgled before, but we had nothing on her at all," he said and sighed. "The gathering after the funeral of the oldest adopted daughter, Rebecca, gave someone a perfect moment to get into that house, wait for everyone to leave, and strike. I could never prove it, though."

"And the main suspect ended up being her other adopted daughter, seventeen-years-old at the time, named Mary Stevens?" Harri asked. "Do you think Mary Stevens did it?"

Many times, detectives had a strong suspicion of who the perp was but couldn't definitively prove it.

"Honestly, I can't answer your question. Mary Stevens disappeared that night. We declared her missing a week later, but she never resurfaced."

"Why didn't you think that whoever killed Jennifer Stevens also took Mary Stevens?"

"Again, no evidence of break-in or disturbance. And the deeper I delved into the family, the weirder the story became."

Harri leaned in, licking her dry lips. Her heart swooped toward her stomach. The path to breaking this case appeared in her mind's eye. Her research had led her to the same conclusion.

"Why weirder?" she asked.

"Let me get to that. First, the story that was circulated by the DA and my superiors ran like this - Mary Stevens, heart-broken over her sister's death, argued with Jennifer throughout the house and in the heat of the moment pushed her. Jennifer lost her balance and fell out of the second-floor window."

"I'm hearing hesitancy in your voice," Harri said.

"It didn't feel right. You know when you walk into a scene and everything looks like it's pointing in one direction, but you have this gut feeling that you're missing something?"

"Yes, definitely have encountered that feeling," she said.

"I had that feeling in spades. From speaking to all the

neighbors and the few friends the girls had, I heard about a loving, caring family that rarely fought with each other."

"You must have spoken to their school friends?"

"The friends said both the girls seemed… haunted."

"Is this why things got weirder?"

"Exactly." Detective Larrabee's voice faded out.

"Hello? Detective Larrabee?"

Loud sounds spewed out of the receiver and Harri pulled it away from her ear. The phone fell silent.

"Detective Larrabee?"

"I'm here, sorry about that. All right, where was I?"

"Investigation got weird?"

"Right, the school counselor. I spoke with her and she shared that Rebecca must have had a traumatic event in her past as she suffered from classic symptoms of PTSD."

"Did the younger sister exhibit the same symptoms?" Harri asked.

"No, as far as the counselor had seen Mary didn't have the same symptoms, but she kept to herself. Here's the thing," he said and exhaled into the phone.

Harri pulled the phone receiver away from her ear again.

"No family pictures hung on the walls or were kept in family albums from what I found inside the house. No photos to see what Mary Stevens even looked like. I searched through the girls' school yearbooks and came up short."

"The yearbooks?" Harri was surprised at the complete erasure of the girls.

"That surprised me, too. I asked the high school principal to pull up the girls' files and found notes from Jennifer Stevens every year excusing the girls on picture day. I saw the girls' school records myself. These girls did exist.

"But no photos of them."

"None. I assumed the girls were part of witness protection," he said. "I know that sounds nuts, but it was the best I could come up with."

"Any forensic evidence indicating an intruder?" Harri asked.

"They'd had tons of people over for the gathering after the funeral. Fingerprints everywhere. We managed to get most of them identified since half the high school turned up. We did find three prints that could not be identified, but no indication when they were left."

"Was the security alarm on when she fell?"

"Evidently," he said. "It was still armed when the unis first responded."

"Any evidence Jennifer Stevens committed suicide?" Harri asked.

"None. The coroner told me that the angle of fall was not consistent with a jump. She was too far away from the window. All evidence suggested a strong shove. Here's the other thing." He paused and sipped a liquid on the other end.

"Her hyoid bone was broken. I asked if it broke on impact. The coroner believed she was unconscious when she fell through because her arms weren't broken."

"Her arms weren't outstretched on impact?"

"You've seen that before then?" he asked.

Before Harri could respond, he continued.

"Her head hit the pavement first. And then the coroner found fingerprint bruises on her neck. She was strangled first, lost consciousness then pushed out the window."

"Hard for a young girl to strangle her mother."

"Strangling a human takes force and time. I couldn't wrap my head around a seventeen-year-old girl having enough power to fight off her mother while strangling her to the point of unconsciousness. I still don't buy it."

"I don't, either. All the newspapers that picked up the story went with Mary Stevens being guilty. Did that come from you?" Harri asked.

She hoped the question didn't come off too edgy. "I know sometimes leaks happen from higher-ups," she added.

"My lieutenant at the time went with that angle. He's no longer in the department. The problem was always the lack of evidence of an intruder. Besides the fingerprints on Jennifer Stevens' neck that is. It was easy to pin that on Mary Stevens since she disappeared before we could question her and get her story. She became the de facto killer," he said.

"But you didn't believe that back then?" she asked.

"The lack of photos gave me pause. They still do. After all these years, I believe Jennifer Stevens hid those girls from someone. That someone found them and got them all," he said.

"But no proof to corroborate that theory," Harri added. "And you still didn't think Mary Stevens had been kidnapped by the strangler?"

"That's right. Nothing in the murder-book to prove my theory. It's a damn shame. We all have those cases. I'm sure you have some of your own."

She did. A picture of her sister's smiling face floated through her mind.

"Who called the death in?"

"Anonymous 911 from a payphone. I always believed that was Mary Stevens. It was a young woman, crying, per the operator."

"I see."

Harri's mind churned that detail. It matched Jane's statement.

"All right, your turn. What do you have? Why call me now?" he asked.

"A woman came into our headquarters yesterday with information on a current case," Harri started.

"Is it the mummified bodies in the creek? The case all over the news?" he asked.

"I can't comment about that at this time. The woman's name was Jane Smith. She claims she used Mary Stevens as an alias for Lindsey Peters."

Silence. She imagined Detective Larrabee's face from the audible guffaw from the other end of the line.

"Well, I'll be damned," he exclaimed. "What's she like?"

"She's fierce. She's," Harri searched around for the right word to use, remembering the girl's demeanor. Her body language challenging the LAPD cops to believe her all the while her eyes shining strangely.

She'd seen that look in her mother's eyes when her sister disappeared.

Her father's eyes, too. She'd not fully understood what she was seeing at the time of the interview, but now she did.

"Fear. This woman was scared for her life," she said.

Her thinking on Jane Smith shifted. Initially, her night of research led her to believe the woman was more killer than victim. The recognition of the fear in Jane's eyes made Harri a lot more sympathetic to the woman's story.

"I'll be on the next flight out to Los Angeles," he said.

"Before you do that, I need help in finding any evidence connecting this woman with Mary Stevens. From everything you told me, there are no photos. Maybe the fingerprints on file? Something in Jennifer's estate?" she asked.

"I can send you the fingerprints we couldn't identify."

"Who handled Jennifer's estate?" Harri asked him.

"She designated her friend Philip Jerome as her executor. I'll call him and see if he kept any items. I checked into the case several months ago."

"What happened to the house?"

"The owners sold it a year later. It's changed hands four times now. Nothing there to see from the original crime. We have the evidence box, but you'll have to come up here to see that. What I can do is send you the list of items stored inside. It's mainly Jennifer's clothing and jewelry."

That evidence wouldn't help Harri uncover Jane's identity.

"If Mary Stevens is Lindsey Peters…" Detective Larrabee's voice faded.

Harri heard clicks through the phone.

"Then this IS the Ballona Creek case," Detective Larrabee said. He waited for her to answer.

The case was all over the internet. She didn't have a chance to keep that from him. And really why would she try? She wanted his help.

"You didn't hear it from me."

"Fair enough. I'll see what I can dig up on my end. Jane Smith is a pretty innocuous name. Do you have eyes on her?" he asked.

"Honestly, my LT thinks she's a crank and wouldn't put uniforms on her. I have her phone number and her address, but I bet you the address is fake. She was too concerned over her security to give us the real one."

Harri chewed on her lip. The fact she didn't know where Jane Smith concerned her. She worried the woman would disappear into thin air and take this case with her.

"I hear your concern. I would be, too."

"Thanks for that, Detective."

"You wouldn't be the first one she's disappeared on."

"She came to us, though. Still haven't figured out why."

Could Jane Smith's need to reclaim her identity be so strong as to keep her contacting the police? Harri sure hoped so.

"Thank you for the call, Detective, and I'll help any way I can. I want to know what happened back then. It would make an old detective happy," he said.

"We'll get to the bottom of this, Detective. I'll keep you in the loop."

They said their goodbyes and hung up. Harri leaned back in her seat, her heart thumping. This puzzle drew all her attention. This was no runaway case.

13

PAB - Los Angeles, CA
DAY 3

Detective Harri Harper entered the conference room and found herself there first. She took a seat and read through the new lead pages she'd gotten from the uniformed officer moments ago. Detective Jorge Hernandez came in soon after.

"Morning," she said.

"Hey," he mumbled back.

Jorge looked as exhausted as she felt. He clutched his coffee cup to his chest. He lowered himself into his chair and closed his eyes.

The rest of the task force filed in soon after. Jackie smiled her way and Rob gave her a thumbs-up as they passed her. David Swisher arrived last and headed straight to the whiteboard, standing in front of the pictures of Maggie Johnson, Jennifer Lynch, and Lisa McNeill.

Natalie and Lindsey Peters' photos had been clipped off to the side.

"Good morning everybody," David Swisher said. "Hope everybody got some sleep last night. I know this case is moving fast, which is good. But make sure you take some hours to take care of yourself. It's too early for burnout." He flashed a quick smile.

Harri sat up straighter and put her lead sheets down. From what she understood, everyone had so far come up empty.

"As you may have heard, three of the girls have now been positively identified with dental records. Their families have been contacted by myself and Detective Bards."

"We are tracking down all the original witnesses listed in the police report to recreate the timeline of the twenty-four hours leading up to each of the three girls' disappearances," Detective Tom Bards said.

David Swisher nodded and held up his hand to stop Tom Bards from speaking further.

"Let's hear from the rest of the team first," David said and turned to Jorge Hernandez, who was about to take a sip of his coffee. "Jorge, what have you found about our dumpsite?"

Jorge put his coffee down without taking the sip, a strained look on his face. David was making friends left and right, Harri thought.

"I finally got a list of employees that were working that summer at the McDougall Company. I've managed to track down two, a Robert Daniels and a Jackson Letts."

Jorge paused and read through his notes.

"No one knew of any concrete being poured in that general vicinity. It was pretty wild back then, they told me. And the wetlands in the creek surrounded the airport, which is what McDougall liked about that site in the first place."

He rubbed his eyes with the back of his hand. His exhaustion was evident.

"Jackson informed me that if somebody had poured concrete at the site one night, somewhere off in the distance, nobody would have noticed."

"Have you run background checks on the employees yet?" Tom asked.

"I have one word for you. Military."

"Hit a wall?"

"You can say that again. I managed a basic background check, but the walls came up fast. From what I could find, they were all vetted and records were clean. I extended the timeline out to January 1993 since making a mummy takes time."

Jorge turned to David.

"I spoke to the coroner about that. In arid conditions, it takes about two weeks. In an enclosed location, about two months. With the torture seen on the bodies, I'm assuming they weren't killed immediately."

"Good assumption," David offered.

Jorge shrugged and flipped his bangs back.

"I wanted to make sure I had enough of a timespan since I didn't think McDougall would cough up information twice. It's been like pulling teeth from them," he said. "I'm in the process of tracking the employees from that fall."

"Impressive to get as far as you have with a military contractor," Tom said.

"Thanks. It's been interesting. Today, I'll be finishing up the background checks. Talk to whatever employees I can find about anything suspicious that they might have seen," Jorge said.

"All right, great." David turned toward Jackie. "Jackie, what's your status?"

"Before I get into that," Jackie said. "Where are we with Natalie and Lindsey Peters?"

Harri nodded and was glad Jackie asked the question. The addition of the two sisters didn't sit well with her because of Lindsey's age. The girls didn't fit the victim pattern.

"What do you mean?" David asked.

"I spoke with the forensic pathologist and she said that none of the bodies was of an eight-year-old girl. If neither of the two bodies that are still unidentified is that young, then Lindsey Peters isn't one of our victims."

"They don't fit the victim profiles," Harri added. "At least, Natalie does. Lindsey is too young. And the killer took a big chance to grab both of them at the same time. How do you control both of them? On top of the fact they disappeared together at night."

Rob and Jackie nodded.

"I agree with Harri," Rob added.

"Me, too," Jackie said.

Jorge and Tom focused back on David. Tom sat back in his chair; his eyes partially shut. David shifted from one foot to the other, clearly thinking of how he should respond.

The room was silent.

"I'm the liaison for the forensic pathologist. The more time we take away from Dr. Richards with unnecessary questions…"

"The question is relevant," Tom cut in.

"Last I checked this was a team. I also couldn't find you last night," Jackie said to David.

David opened his mouth and closed it again. Harri looked away, not wanting to see his tongue flick around his pale wet lips. This guy was a terrible leader and Harri was surprised Richard Byrne chose him. The choice had to be political.

Jackie continued. "I narrowed down the age ranges of the girls to make my list more manageable and pertinent. Dr. Richards told me the last two bodies were both aged around fifteen-years-old. Her guesstimate came from the condition of their teeth and the length of their leg bones. My list sits at about 5000 girls missing during that month in the Los Angeles area in that age range."

David nodded as he picked up a dry-erase marker and wrote Jane Doe #4 - fifteen-years-old and Jane Doe #5 -

fifteen-years-old. He kept his back to the rest of the detectives. Harri wondered if he was trying to pull himself together again.

"I'm confirming the names on the list as still missing, or if they've been found dead or alive. Since Natalie and Lindsey Peters disappeared on the same night, are we assuming the sisters disappeared together?" Jackie asked.

"David?" Tom asked, watching David's back.

David still had not turned around. He didn't want to face the team.

David nodded. "The last mummy is not Natalie Peters then."

He faced Tom; his eyes boring into the older man's. Defying him to contradict him.

Tom smiled.

"I don't think we can rule that out yet. What if Lindsey and Natalie Peters were grabbed, but since Lindsey was so young, she didn't fit the killer's victim profile? She could have been dispatched fairly quickly and her body buried elsewhere," Tom surmised.

They were watching a slow-motion car crash. Harri wanted to look away, but her curiosity got the best of her.

"Fine," David snapped.

Harri cleared her throat.

"What?" David snapped at her now.

Harri lifted her chin. "A woman came in claiming she was Lindsey Peters."

"NO?" Jackie exclaimed, turning in her seat to look at Harri.

"Yes. Rob and I took her statement."

"Is she for real?" Tom asked.

"What's her story?" Jorge asked, pulling his chair closer to Harri's.

"That they ran away from their family in the middle of the

night. She was eight at the time. Her sister initiated it," Harri explained.

David pulled up a chair next to Jorge. Even Tom turned his chair around. The team now resembled an AA meeting, Harri thought wryly.

"Where is Natalie Peters?" Tom asked.

"The woman claimed her sister died in a hit-and-run in San Francisco in 1999."

"Can we corroborate that?" Jorge asked.

"She also claimed the woman who adopted them was killed on the night of Natalie's funeral. She gave me the names of the two victims, Jennifer and Rebecca Stevens, and those deaths do check out. There's a catch, though," Harri said.

"She's the prime suspect in the murder of the adoptive mother, Jennifer," Rob said.

"No way," Jorge interjected.

"She went under the name of Mary Stevens," Harri said. "Now, she calls herself Jane Smith. Has a license in that name."

"Did she provide proof of her identity as Lindsey Peters?" David asked. "She sounds like a crank."

"There is one last strange piece to this puzzle," Harri said.

"Beyond the unbelievable strangeness you've already told us?" Jackie asked.

"When I spoke to the lead detective on the Jennifer Stevens case, he found quite the puzzle himself. The family home contained no pictures of the girls. No photos of them in their school yearbooks, no team pictures, nothing. The girls were ghosts."

"Damn. So, no way to prove her story," Jackie said.

"Natalie was cremated, too. No DNA to match to. But I'm not sure what that would prove. We have no records to match to. Detective Larrabee is searching through Jennifer's estate for birth certificates or paperwork proving name changes or who the girls actually were."

"How can there be no photos of teenagers?" Jackie wondered.

"That's what bothered Detective Larrabee," Harri said.

"How did she try to prove she was Lindsey Peters?" Tom asked.

"She knew the address of the Peters family, everyone's name, ages at the time. All information she could find on the internet, though. The woman has been in hiding since 1999 because she never knew who was after her and her sister. Her sister told her the monsters were after them."

"You caught a live one," Jorge remarked.

"There's something there," Harri said. "I can't put my finger on it yet, but…"

She stopped herself short before she admitted to everyone that she believed Jane Smith. The woman was clearly haunted by something and the fear in her eyes was real.

But was she Lindsey Peters?

"You think this is a worthwhile lead?" Tom asked.

"I do," Harri said.

"Due to the age of Lindsey Peters and this new development, perhaps David was right," Tom amended and nodded to David.

"If we go with the assumption that the two remaining bodies aren't the Peters sisters, Jackie can keep trying to match the missing girls to our last two victims. Harri, you keep digging into Jane Smith, and her links to Lindsey Peters. If she does turn out to be Lindsey Peters, then we can fully rule them out as part of this investigation."

"So, the Peters sisters were lumped in with the other three girls because they disappeared at the same time," Rob said.

"Correct. No bodies were found back then so why not

lump the disappearances in? Makes for a bigger headline," Jackie said.

"The father went to the media to get his girls attached to the other missing girls," Harri said, keeping her face as neutral as she could.

The thump, thump, thump of Harri's heart drowned out her colleagues' discussion. She'd given him a reason to kick her off the task force. She hadn't foreseen this outcome. Acid sloshed in her stomach and crept up her esophagus. She put her hand over her chest, the heartburn excruciating.

"You all right?"

Someone touched Harri's arm. Harri couldn't distinguish the voice through the noise in her head.

Harri nodded.

"Heartburn. Too much coffee," she said to no one in particular.

The voices of her colleagues grew louder. Harri focused on Tom's deep voice and the conference came back into focus.

"We've spoken to the immediate families of Maggie Johnson and Jennifer Lynch. Calls are out to the family of Lisa McNeill. They moved out of state in the intervening years. We're slowly piecing together each of the timelines."

Cases were made and murderers were convicted on details put together on the victim timeline of the twenty-four hours leading up to the crime. During interrogations of suspects, those inconsistencies proved useful in cornering a suspect in his lies.

"David and I are re-interviewing the list of witnesses available from the original case file. We need help. Jorge, can you start doing background on both Maggie and Jennifer? Boyfriends, friends in common, enemies in common, that sort of thing."

"Great, I'll get on that Tom," Jorge said.

The door opened and Mitzi Jeffries walked in.

"Howdy, folks. Y'all look intimate. Am I interrupting something?" Mitzi quipped.

David jumped out of his chair as if he'd been caught cheating at something.

"Just wrapping up," David said.

"Perfect timing, Mitzi," Tom said.

"I've got a preliminary profile. Can I join your trust circle?" Mitzi asked with an arched eyebrow.

She sat in David's chair forcing David to drag another one over to squeeze between Jackie and Rob.

"This one has been a doozy for me. The treatment of bodies pre-mortem vs. post-mortem sure stumped me."

She took a deep breath, and her voice became clipped and clinical. All the cheer she'd just flung out into the room vanished.

"Pre-mortem, the killer tortured the victims. Fingers and toes were broken on all five of the bodies. Bite marks were found on their abdominal and breast regions. Because of the mummification of the bodies, the coroner and forensic pathologist couldn't determine if the victims were sexually assaulted, but I'd hazard a guess that they were."

Mitzi stopped and let that info sink in.

"The preliminary cause of death was manual strangulation. Each of the five victims had the hyoid bone broken, with darkening around their necks. Our killer used his hands. A sexual sadist has these kinds of fantasies and inflicts them on his victims."

The room was silent. Mitzi glanced down at her notes before continuing.

"Typically, sexual sadists are sociopaths who enjoy watching the pain of their victims. I would put the age of our man between twenty to thirty-five, Caucasian, and well-to-do to upper-middle-class. These girls were all very high-risk targets."

Harri hated the high-risk versus low-risk designation for victims. She understood that it was a form of shorthand, but the terms made certain victims more worthy, more special than the victims designated low risk. Kids living on the streets, prostitutes, and other low-risk victims were just as worthy of justice as the high-risk, high profile victims. At least, that's the way Harri policed.

"The girls came from middle-class to upper-middle-class homes in a small community. An outsider would be noticed by more than one person. This killer is part of that community and hid behind a mask. I'm talking about somebody like Ted Bundy here," Mitzi said.

"The mummification doesn't sound like a sexual sadist," Tom said.

"That's right. It doesn't fit with the usual fantasies of sadists. The mummification process wasn't accidental. It fits into the fantasy. Mummification in his fantasy suggests a very different pathology. As I said before, the sexual sadist wants the victim alive. That's part of the fantasy. The bodies after death aren't that important to these kinds of predators. However, mummification has been known to be a part of the ritual of a necrophile."

Mitzi leaned in and Harri followed suit.

She was glad they were sitting in a circle, able to see each other's faces and reactions. Harri drew comfort from the other detectives that wanted to nail this asshole as bad as she did in light of the horrors these young girls went through.

"Wait, like a guy who has sex with dead bodies?" Jackie asked, her face screwed up in disgust.

"Yes. Like Ed Gein. He was the guy used as a template for the guy in the movie Psycho and Silence of The Lambs. He dug up women's bodies to harvest their skin and then made lampshades and furniture out of it. The sex tends to be post-mortem with these guys."

"That doesn't fit the profile of the pre-mortem condition of the bodies," Harri said.

Mitzi turned to her.

"Exactly," she said, pointing to Harri. "The profile of the necrophile is opposite to that of a sexual sadist. The necrophile tends to be shy and very easily cowed over. Think of the sexual sadist as the bully, and the necrophile as a cowering victim. The necrophile is someone who would not want to be in the spotlight. He hides in plain sight. He'd be that weird guy."

"He'd stick out in a small community such as El Segundo," Harri said. "I lived there. Everyone knew everybody and gossiped. It really was a small town back then."

"Did you know any of these girls?" Tom asked.

Harri knew where he was going with that question.

"No. I was only ten at the time. Lindsey Peters must have been at my elementary school, but I don't remember her. My sister went to El Segundo High School."

"Did she know the girls?"

"I think she did. Not well, but I remember her saying one of them was in her English class." Harri flashed back to that summer. "My sister was big into surfing back then. Not that into school."

Lauren had been missing almost as long as these girls had been.

"That detail has to be part of the profile. These girls were taken in such a small tight-knit community. This man would still be twenty to thirty-years-old, white Caucasian, middle-class to upper-middle-class. But he'd be the odd man out. These guys don't really look people in the eye. They're afraid of people. It's why they feel so comfortable with the dead bodies. They can't talk back. Can't make fun of them," Mitzi said.

"We are searching for two killers then?" Tom asked.

Jackie groaned. Another complication in an already complicated case.

"That's where I was going with this. One killer enjoys the game in the pre-mortem stage. The second takes over after the first is done. These killers are very close. And by close, I mean a narcissist and his victim. Someone he could have complete control over. We know of killer teams from the past. They tended to have familial relationships like Buono and Bianchi."

Mitzi stopped, her hand floating inadvertently to her mouth. She took a nibble at one of her cuticles. Harri had seen her friend do that before. Something bothered her.

"What is it, Mitzi?" Harri asked.

"This profile is still incomplete. We are missing something vital. I scheduled a meeting with the forensic pathologist later today to help me narrow the profile down further," she said.

"And Jeremy Evans?" Rob asked.

"I'm meeting him tomorrow at Chico. I have to fly out the next day for Maine, another profile. But I'll be on call and will finish this profile as soon as the post-mortems are done."

"Thank you, Mitzi," Tom said.

Mitzi waved him off. "Don't thank me yet. The profile is still not very useful. We're missing something."

Harri had overheard Mitzi talking this morning to someone about another case up in Maine and couldn't imagine traveling from precinct to precinct with these kinds of horrors happening.

"Do you think that Jeremy Evans could be good for this?" David asked.

"No, I don't because of the treatment these victims endured. The fantasy doesn't match."

"All right, thank you." David turned to Rob. "Any other cold cases you could connect with ours?"

"I did find one other cold case. Her name was Charlaine Lewis and she was found in Hollywood in an alleyway, raped and strangled. The reason why she connects is she had eyes carved into her chest like our mummified girls."

"The eyes match the carvings from the Ballona Creek Girls?" Mitzi asked.

"Pretty exactly, in fact. From everything I could gather from the police reports, the killer had been interrupted by Charlaine's pimp."

"The victimology has changed, though," Mitzi said.

"And why not abduct her? You don't have much privacy in an alleyway."

"Didn't stop Jack though, did it?" Jorge asked.

Jackie groaned and covered her face with her hands.

"Really, Jorge?" Harri asked.

Jorge shrugged. "I'm not wrong."

"Anyway, the killer ran into the crowd and the pimp never saw his face. It's still an open case. The pimp became the main suspect, but there wasn't enough circumstantial evidence to get a conviction. I'm running down the pimp today to see if I can get him to give me any sort of description of the man."

"The carving of the eyes on Charlaine Lewis's chest is a detail more closely resembling the fantasy of our two killers than the plastic bins of Jeremy Evans," Mitzi said.

"When was this?" Tom asked.

"In 1998."

"They learned from their mistakes and began choosing low-risk victims?" Mitzi asked.

"Could be. Could be our last two unknown victims were low risk."

"I'm on that," Jackie said.

"I won't keep you all any longer. Thank you all for your good work," David said and stood up.

The other detectives followed suit, and everyone headed for the door. Everyone, except Harri. She glanced over at the victim wall and her chest constricted again.

For the time being, she wasn't connected to the task force and she wasn't sure how to feel about that. The task force had been a hot mess under the leadership of David Swisher, true. But it was a plum assignment. High-stakes and all that. At the same time, a mystery had been plopped in her lap and she wanted to see it through. The mummified girls needed justice, but so did Jennifer and Rebecca Stevens.

Harri took one last look around the room and stood up. Follow the case where it leads, she thought. And this case had dropped Jane Smith right into her lap.

14

Jane Smith

DAY 3

I walked through the doors of El Segundo High School as if I belonged there close to the end of the day. I'd easily hacked my way into their school database and entered my name as a substitute teacher in case anyone checked why I was there. I'd also prepared stories to give for certain questions I might encounter. I'd spent most of the night researching the teachers at the high school, but the computer records didn't go back to the early 90s. My next step was yearbooks. All I needed was a name.

I'd studied the building layout of the school and knew the library shared a wall with the principal's office. I wished it was on the other side of the building, but luck wasn't with me in this regard. The library housed all the old yearbooks and that's where I was headed.

Once I passed the principal's office, I gulped down air and willed my heart to stop pounding in my ears. I quickened my pace. Almost there, I thought.

I grabbed the handle of the double doors and pulled. Nothing happened.

What? My heart rocketed up to my throat.

The door was locked.

I pulled harder, but still nothing. I'd picked a day the library was closed? Unbelievable. Heat bloomed in my cheeks.

Calm down, Natalie's voice whispered in my ear. I breathed in again.

I stood at the door and looked left to right. No one was in the hall and I couldn't see any cameras. Didn't mean they weren't there, though. I checked the time on my watch. There was another period left before the end of the day. I had forty-five minutes to get this done.

My sister taught me to pick a lock years ago and I'd brought a kit, just in case. At least I was prepared. Somewhat.

The bell rang and kids streamed out of the classrooms. I used the diversion to pull out the lock pick. I was about to slip the key inside the keyhole when footsteps drew closer to me. I put my hand in my pocket and snuck a peek. A haggard-looking security guard headed toward me.

I joined a small group of students hurrying by me and slipped into the first empty classroom. I sat down at the desk and pretended to be working while glancing at the door every few seconds. The guard walked by the classroom without looking inside.

My shoulders relaxed. That was close. Time for another tactic, I thought.

Teachers could be chatty. Maybe I could find someone who worked back then. Satisfied with this new plan, I waited another five minutes before heading out to the teacher's lounge.

I opened the door and found one teacher inside. A lady in her fifties, wearing a frilly pink shirt, drank a cup of tea while reading a romance novel. I put on my best smile and sat down next to her.

"Hi there. My name is Jane Locarno. I'm substituting for Mrs. Baker. Could I ask you something?" I asked.

The woman looked up confused and saw me, looked down at her novel as if she really wanted to get back to it, but was too polite to say so. She closed the book and gave her full attention to me.

"What was your name again?" she asked.

"It's Jane. Call me Jane," I said.

"Could you repeat your question? I was really into my book and didn't hear you," she started to explain.

I waved her off.

"I totally understand. I love my shifters, too," I said, pointing to the book cover of a woman with werewolves snaking around her legs.

She gave a small laugh. She was warming up to me.

"I'm substituting for Mrs. Baker. I've been wanting to substitute here forever because I'm looking for a woman who worked here in 1992. I need to contact her, and I've been unable to locate her. Here's the really silly part," I paused, hoping she'd believe my story. "See, my mom was best friends with a woman named Barbara when I was a little kid. Barbara is the reason I became a teacher."

I smiled for effect. "Unfortunately, my mom died, and I never knew Barbara's last name. I know that she worked at El Segundo High in 1992. Do you know of any teachers that taught back then? I so would love to reconnect with her."

"You need to speak with Lucy Deacon. She was an old-timer that retired last year. She taught for over thirty-five years right here at El Segundo High," she said.

"Oh, my goodness, she sounds exactly like the right person to ask. Thank you so much. Does she still live in the area?" I asked.

"Yes, she does."

She surveyed me. The teacher trusted me enough because she gave me the address.

"Thank you. I so appreciate it. I'll let you go back to your book. Thank you again," I said and left the lounge.

I couldn't believe my luck. Lucy Deacon could tell me about my sister and what she was like that spring before we ran away and fill in some holes. She would have known my whole family.

My brothers.

The image of my brother at Trader Joe's supermarket rose into my consciousness, but I pushed it away. I wasn't ready to face that fear yet.

I went back to the empty classroom and searched around the drawers until I found something to keep me busy. I graded math sheets I'd found in the drawer while watching the door. The security guard sauntered by the classroom every fifteen minutes.

I was stuck.

The bell finally rang for the end of the day. Students jostled and hurried by the open classroom door, doing their best to get out of the school as fast as possible. Thirty-five graded math worksheets sat stacked to my left and I'd run out of time. I needed to act now.

Lock pick in hand, my bag slung around my shoulders, I trudged to the door.

The hallway was clear.

I ran-walked to the library doors. I pulled out my pick, my hands shaking visibly. Now or never.

I jammed the pick inside and almost cried in relief when I heard the click of the tumbler opening. I slipped inside without anyone noticing.

The familiar smell of the dark library calmed me. Books had become my refuge after my sister and Jennifer died. The calming effect of the books enabled me to focus on finding those old yearbooks.

The section holding the yearbooks lived on the last shelf of the last stack on the back wall. The layer of dust indicated the yearbooks hadn't been touched in years. I crouched down to see the years on the spines better. Damn.

The years between 1988-96 were missing and yet 1965-1987 were all accounted for. As were 1997-2018. Just not the years I needed. I flipped through 1986 but didn't find the mysterious Barbara. I pulled out the yearbook for 1997. I opened the book but then froze at the sound of a rattling. Was that a key in the lock? I licked my lips, as my heart rattled around in my ribcage.

Spooked, I shoved 1987 and 1997 in my backpack. I had to get out of there. Keeping low, I tiptoed to the edge of the stacks and peeked around the corner to the door. Seeing no one there, I strode through the reading tables and slipped out of the library. The doors clicked closed behind me. I was almost out.

My steps quickened. I wanted out of this school now. I opened the exit door and stepped outside. I gasped and braced for an attack at the flash of movement to my left.

Someone tapped me on the shoulder. I turned and found a woman right behind me with the security guard standing behind her.

"I'm Principal Martin. I don't think we've met before?" she asked me while holding out her hand. She stepped down to my level.

"I am the substitute teacher for Mrs. Baker. My name is Jane Locarno," I said.

"Bobby, the security guard has been curious about why you wanted to get into the library so badly," she said.

"I'm not sure what you mean?" I asked her.

Bobby the security guard stayed in the doorway.

My stomach turned over, sending bile into my throat.

"You've been lurking around the library all day long," he said.

"Could you please open your backpack?" asked the principal.

"What?" I demanded in an outraged tone. "I'm a substitute teacher. I made $50 today. Why are you hassling me?"

"Please open your bag, Ma'am," said the security guard.

I heaved the backpack to my front and opened it up. "See there's nothing in here," I said.

"Aren't those yearbooks?" the security guard asked, peering over my shoulder.

I pulled the yearbooks out and handed them over to him.

"I found these on Mrs. Baker's desk. I wanted to see what people looked like back then. I was six years old and thought it be fun to look at them," I said ad-libbing.

"You know that's school property," the principal said.

"I'm back tomorrow. I was going to bring them back then. But now that you have them, I should get going. I have another appointment," I said.

"You should come inside. I'd like to check your credentials," Principal Martin said.

I ignored the request and took the steps two at a time. Once I hit the flat pavement, I sprinted across the lawn and down the street. My heart tried to escape my ribcage, while I fought off the urge to throw-up. I checked behind me, but neither of them followed me. That didn't calm my heart nor my stomach. I picked up my pace.

I unlocked the rental car and got inside before I made a bigger scene of myself. At least, Ms. Lucy Deacon existed. I didn't need those yearbooks anyway, I told myself and hoped I was right.

. . .

I DROVE out of the neighborhood and parked at a gas station off Sepulveda Blvd. Only then did I pull off the wig and take off the fake glasses. Using facial wipes from my purse, I wiped the pale foundation off my face to get back my natural golden skin. I hoped seeing me might waken some old memories in Lucy Deacon because my dead sister and I looked alike.

15

San Francisco, CA
DAY 3

Detective Harri Harper pushed through the white double doors of the quaint red brick building that was the SFPD- Richmond police station. The lobby, however, resembled any other police station lobby. Flyers hung from cork boards and blue chairs hailing from the 1980s lined both the end walls. Seven people sat waiting for their turn as the intake officer flipped through a binder in front of him. At least there wasn't a line.

"I'm here to see Detective Peter Gallagher. He's expecting me," Harri said.

Detective Gallagher hadn't sounded too pleased to hear she was arriving today to look at the murder-book. She'd hoped there would be a willingness on the part of SFPD to cooperate with her, but after the phone call she'd had with him, all bets were off.

"Name and ID?" the intake officer asked.

"Detective Harriet Harper. LAPD," Harri said and showed him her ID.

He noted the badge number and name in his spreadsheet.

"Have a seat." He gestured to one of the uncomfortable blue chairs.

She wandered over to the nearest corkboard instead. She was still pissed over the phone call with Gallagher and wanted to expel some nervous energy. Harri would see the murder-book on the case and she didn't care how unfriendly he was.

On the flight over, Harri reviewed the case file she'd put together on Jane Smith's story. Proving definitely that Natalie Peters transformed herself into Rebecca Stevens was her main priority. She'd clipped the photo of Natalie Peters out of the LA Times and needed the crime scene photos to confirm the two teenagers were the same person.

HARRI PACED BACK and forth in the small lobby until she finally surrendered to sitting in the hard, blue plastic chairs. Harri checked her watch. It'd been 40 minutes since she'd first arrived and still no Detective Gallagher. Her irritation grew with every passing minute.

She had to see that murder-book.

Harri plastered a smile on her face and breathed deep. The door to the bullpen behind the station guard finally opened and a red-haired man sauntered out.

Of course, Harri thought, Gallagher was one of those.

Harri stood up and faced him straight on, flashing her warmest smile. He nodded to her and gave her a why-are-you-here-I-don't-have-time-for-this smile. Police departments didn't love sharing their information on big cases with other jurisdictions, but his level of irritation was unwarranted.

"Thank you for seeing me, Detective Gallagher. Detective Harriet Harper of the LAPD."

She stuck out her hand. He grasped hers. His palms were sweaty and warm. She fought the urge to pull her hand away and wipe it off.

"Do your murder-books generally not get digitized? Would have saved me a trip."

"Not ones that old."

"Gotcha," Harri said.

"What's your interest in Rebecca Stevens?"

"Tying up loose ends is all."

"Follow me back to the conference room. I'll show you what we have."

That didn't sound promising.

Harri followed him back through the door into the bullpen. All bullpens were cubicle-land now and had been for a decade. The interrogation rooms ran along the front wall with several larger conference rooms on the smaller right wall.

Detective Gallagher led her to one of the conference rooms. A thin folder lay on the table. That didn't bode well.

"That's the file?" she asked him.

"That's all there is," he said. His tone was almost apologetic. Almost.

"Were you the lead on this?" Harri asked.

"Yes. Sit down and I'll fill you in on all that I recollect."

"Where is the murder-book?" Harri asked, still standing.

"Gone," he shrugged his shoulders. "I located this file with the case number. There was a complete murder-book, but files were misplaced when the department shifted storage sites a few years ago."

"Why would this thin file be in its place? Wouldn't it have gone missing, too?" Harri asked.

"I don't know how to answer that, Detective," Gallagher said. "I can tell you about the case from what I can remember," he offered.

Harri hadn't expected this.

She pulled out a notebook and pen from her satchel and sat down. "Go ahead," she said.

"The victim, a college student attending San Francisco

University, crossed the street on her way to class. A car careened into her at high speed."

"Any footage?"

"The city didn't have cameras on that particular street. Due to the early hour, around 6:30 in the morning, we found one witness. He couldn't give us a license plate or ID of the driver. Just said it was a male, driving a dark, four-door sedan. No skid marks."

"Did she die at the scene?" Harri asked, not looking up. She noted down the information in her notebook.

"No. She never regained consciousness and died later that day at the hospital. The car traveled at a high speed and her body had been flung into the air. She hit her head on the pavement, hard," he said.

Harri looked up. "High speed?"

"The traffic investigator saw that from how far the body traveled after impact," Gallagher said.

"Name of the investigator?"

"I don't remember."

Harri cocked her head at him. She wasn't sure why that sounded like a lie to her, but it did.

"Did you do a sweep of body shops?"

"Yes, but came up empty," he said. "The case went cold, fast. It's still an open unsolved."

"Who identified the body?" Harri asked.

"Her mother came down to identify her. A Jennifer Stevens. That's in the file," he said and pointed to the sliver of a folder.

"Don't you find it strange that the murder-book is gone, and this is left in its place?" Harri asked.

"I don't know," he shrugged. "It's unfortunate. These things happen."

"Do they though? I've never had a murder-book go missing," Harri said, irritation creeping into her voice.

"I'm not sure what you're getting at. It was a hit and run that went cold almost twenty years ago. I'm surprised I remember as much of it as I do. I haven't seen the murder-book in years. I filed it correctly. After your call, I went down to records to get it. This is all I found."

Harri opened the file and found a form with the basics of the crime and its case number. It resembled a placeholder file. There were no personal notes, no photos, no canvassing notes. The entire investigation was gone.

"You were in charge of this file, right?" she asked him.

Gallagher's hackles went up. Wrong question to ask.

"Are you accusing me of something?"

"No, I'm not accusing you. Who else had access to this file? Cold Case Unit? Traffic Division? Anyone else I can track down?" Harri asked.

"Why are you so into this case?" he demanded. "Want to share with me why an LAPD cop is up here on a twenty-year-old hit and run?"

"I'm trying to identify the victim," Harri said.

"Rebecca Stevens?"

"Yes. Did you know her mother was killed a week later? On the night of the funeral?" she asked.

"Didn't her little sister do that? I remember reading that in the paper. Bad luck for the family," he said.

He didn't sound very sorry.

"I don't understand the need for identification," he said.

She sat back and regarded him. He stared back at her.

"Right now, neither do I. Bosses sent me up here. Looks open and shut though," she lied. Something smelled fishy and she didn't want to give out any more information. She figured the SFPD had similar protocols on taking out old case files as the LAPD. There had to be a log somewhere of every officer who looked at the file.

"Did you check the sign-out log?" Harri asked.

"Of course. Besides me, only two other officers checked it out. The cold case detective in 2002, Lewis Hill, and my Lieutenant, Gary Lane, that same year. They both signed the file back in."

"You never went back to it?" she asked him.

"No. I'm not good with cold cases. We have an untold number of hit-and-runs here, and many go unsolved."

"Don't you find it odd that there's no digital file online and the murder-book has gone missing, with this in its place?"

He guffawed at that.

"Honestly, I've seen so many things disappear in the past twenty years I'm not surprised at all. Anything from so long ago that is not in the computer and digitized is nonexistent as far as I'm concerned."

Detective Gallagher's blue eyes regarded her. He was waiting for her to say something.

"Right."

That didn't sit well with him.

"We have a good filing system here, don't get me wrong. But files this old? I've heard of your crime scene photos being sold off to journalists. Ours only get leaked on in basements," Detective Gallagher said.

He'd aimed but hadn't hit his mark. Harri shrugged off the sad insult.

She wasn't going to get anything else out of him.

"Thank you for your help, Detective Gallagher. I won't take any more of your time," she said and stood up, putting her notebook away.

"Sorry I couldn't have been of more use," he said.

Was it Harri's imagination or did he look visibly calmer? As if the tension had been released at the ending of their meeting.

He led her out of the precinct, and they said their final goodbyes in the front lobby. She watched his receding back with a mixture of excitement and trepidation. Could someone be cleaning their tracks? Sure, files went missing, but why put another file in its place? The misstep was in creating the dummy file.

What kind of conspiracy was she dealing with here, anyway? Cops had to be complicit. Who else had access to murder-books? Harri's heart pounded as she headed for the train to the airport.

16

LAX - Los Angeles, CA
DAY 3

Detective Harri Harper walked through the busy airport terminal and joined the disembarked passengers heading toward baggage claim. Eyeing the bathroom sign, she pulled out of the stream of people and found herself at the back of a lengthy line of women waiting to use the restrooms.

Damn, Harri thought. She'd have to wait.

She stepped back into the throng of people and heard a voice calling out her name.

"Harri Harper, Harri! Behind you," Mitzi Jeffries called out.

Harri turned to see Mitzi piling by a family of five, her face red. Like Harri, Mitzi didn't have a carry-on.

"Are you coming back from your interview with Jeremy Evans?" Harri asked when Mitzi caught up to her.

"Boy, am I glad to be back! Spending any amount of time with Jeremy Evans makes me want to take the hottest, soapiest shower ever, maybe with bleach. He's a creeper of the highest order," Mitzi said. "But the deed is done. And I am certain he had nothing to do with our case."

"Not happy to hear our perp isn't behind bars, but at least we can cross him off the list," Harri said.

"Where are you coming from?" Mitzi asked.

"I was up in San Francisco for a meeting with a detective at the SFPD. I wanted to get the murder-book on Rebecca Stevens to corroborate Jane Smith's story. All I found was weirdness." Harri pointed at the signage toward the exit.

They both stepped onto the escalator.

"What do you mean by weirdness?" Mitzi asked.

Harri grasped the moving handrail and shifted her feet uneasily as her breath caught in her throat for a split second. She hated escalators.

"Weirdness?"

"Oh right. The murder-book is gone. Now, that in and of itself is not necessarily a weird thing but the fact there's a replacement file is what's getting to me."

"I don't understand," Mitzi said.

"The LAPD has had murder-books go missing before. Especially for crimes that go back 20 to 30 years. We had water pipes leaking at one of the storage facilities and all the files got destroyed. Those kinds of incidents."

"I've heard of that, but that's not weird."

"Someone created a new replacement file in its place. That's the thing that's bothering me. I don't see a reason for someone to do that. It was a sheet of the basic statistics of the murder with no underlying evidence or support or witness."

"Sounds like a secretary was trying to help."

"That's not the point I'm making. Everything is electronic now. Why wouldn't the secretary or whoever, input the sheet into the computer? It wasn't logged into the system. The database says it's not been digitized, but the sheet presented to me clearly came from the computer. Why wouldn't they log it into the system?"

"Oh, I understand what you're getting at."

"No reason to input it and then print it out to stick in a file without adding it to the database. Something's not right," Harri said.

"Still could be a clerical error."

"True. When taken with the lead detective's attitude toward me, it sent up red flags."

"Was he a jerk?" Mitzi asked.

"First-rate jerk," Harri said. "I spoke to the original detective. He gave me the barest rundown of the basics of the case and made me feel as if I was wasting his precious time. What did it was his relief as I was leaving. His demeanor made me ask why? Why does he not want me to be looking into this case?"

"What kind of detective is he? Maybe the case wasn't investigated properly? Is that kind of attitude typical when working cold cases across departments?" Mitzi asked.

"Most of the detectives I've worked with welcome the help to close old cases. You know that running untested DNA evidence cracks many of these cold cases open. This detective didn't want anyone looking into this case. I felt I'd walked into some odd conspiracy," Harri said and laughed. "I sound paranoid. I recognize that."

The women stepped off the escalator, walked past baggage claim, and outside to the arrival area. Mitzi waved at someone.

Harri squinted her eyes at the glare of the sun against the oncoming windshields and recognized the man walking toward them. For a moment she felt as if the wind had taken her breath. It was a face from long ago. A face she hadn't seen in years.

"Is that Jake Tepesky?" Harri asked.

"Do you know him?" Mitzi asked.

"He was my sister's best friend in high school," Harri said. "You?"

"He's an old colleague of mine that went into private practice. I haven't seen him in a couple of years," Mitzi said.

"Hi Jake!" Mitzi gave the man a big hug.

Jake had improved with age, Harri thought, as he turned his sparkling green eyes to her. He'd grown into quite a distinguished gentleman. His light blonde hair had turned brown and he brushed it to the side. Harri didn't remember his jawline being so sharp. He looked like he'd stepped out of the pages of GQ magazine and was a far cry from the surf bum that had been her sister's best friend.

Jake and Lauren had been inseparable their senior year, going surfing before class every morning. She'd heard Jake joined the FBI soon after graduating college.

She hadn't spoken to him since that fateful fall of Lauren's disappearance. He'd joined the searches her parents had organized after the police had given up on finding her sister.

"Harriet Harper?" Jake asked, his voice a deep baritone.

Harri's stomach did a funny flip-flop.

"It's been a long time, Jake," Harri said.

"It has been," he said.

"I didn't know you were back in LA. Washington too cold for you?" Harri asked, winking.

Jake's intense gaze held her own.

"I'm done with DC," he said.

Harri glanced down, breaking eye contact. Her cheeks reddened.

"I thought you said we couldn't meet today?" Mitzi asked, breaking the silence.

"I shifted my schedule around. With your travel schedule, this was the only time I'd see you this year. I heard from Chester you'd taken over the job of flying around the precincts."

"I sure did," Mitzi answered him.

The first strains of a ringtone playing ABBA's song

Dancing Queen made Mitzi search around her enormous purse.

"It's got to be here somewhere," she muttered to herself. With a look of triumph on her face, she pulled the cellphone out and put it to her ear.

"Mitzi Jeffries," she said.

She listened, a frown forming on her face.

"That's not...I mean I have no jurisdiction..." she said and paused, listening. "Detective Harriet Harper is here with me at the airport, I'm thinking it would be best to talk to her?" She listened some more and handed her phone to Harri.

"Hello?"

"Detective Harper, this is David Swisher. There is a situation unfolding at the El Segundo Police Department. We need you to run interference as we head down there," he said, sounding angry.

"Sure, but who am I running interference with?" Harri asked as she watched Jake talk with Mitzi a few steps away.

"Detective Peter McDonald decided to bring in Christian LeGuerre for questioning of his own volition without checking in with us first. From my sources at the El Segundo Police Department, he already has him sitting in an interrogation cell. Everyone else is out in the field."

"And you are where?"

"Tom and I are inching through rush-hour traffic on the 105 West. Even with our sirens on, we aren't making great time. You're the closest. We need you to slow down the interrogation until we get there. I've attempted to pull jurisdiction on him, but El Segundo is a unique situation. He's our main suspect," David said.

"We can be there in ten minutes," Harri said and hung up, waving her arms to get Mitzi's attention.

"We goin' to go and help?" Mitzi asked.

"He did ask nicely," Harri said and winked.

"Sorry, Jake. Looks like our lunch is going to have to wait," Mitzi said.

"We can wait another year," Jake sighed. "And I got to reconnect with someone I knew long ago," Jake said, his gaze fixed back on Harri.

"Aw shucks, Jake." Harri punched him in the arm.

"How are you ladies planning on getting to El Segundo?" he asked.

"You heard?" Harri asked.

"Your boss talks a little loud," he said. "Better than taking a ride service."

He gestured to a silver Lexus, parked in the red. "I didn't even get a ticket. Getting lucky today," he said.

Harri took the back seat while Mitzi sat on the passenger side. Jake started up the motor and pulled away from the curb. Harri's back slammed into the seat as he pressed on the gas.

"Whoa, Jake," Mitzi said.

"You said ten minutes, didn't you Harri?" Jake asked.

"Yeah," replied Harri.

She breathed in deep. Her emotions at seeing Jake confused her. He was her past like her sister Lauren was. Meeting him again brought so many memories flooding back. Memories that she didn't know what to do with.

Jake's voice interrupted her thoughts. "It was seven minutes, but close enough," he said, flashing his dimples.

Harri forced a smile back. "Thank you for the drive," she said.

Mitzi opened the door and stepped out of the car.

Harri was about to do the same when Jake twisted in his seat.

"Want to grab some lunch sometime?" Jake asked.

"I'd love that," Harri answered, ignoring the warning bells going off. "Where are you located these days?"

"I live in the hills up near Beachwood Canyon," Jake said.

"I'm in Silver Lake. Close enough to make this happen," Harri said with a laugh.

It was well known that people who lived in the myriad neighborhoods of Los Angeles never wanted to travel too far outside of their radius. No one wanted to deal with traffic if they lived in Silver Lake and the person they wanted to meet lived in Santa Monica. They might as well have lived out of state.

"Next week?" Jake asked.

"Call me," Harri said and handed him a business card.

Before he could see her blushing any more than she was, she got out and joined Mitzi.

"This is not going to be fun," Mitzi said.

"It is definitely a shit job," Harri said.

They both put on their best smiles for the uniform on duty as they headed for the front desk.

17

Jane Smith

DAY 3

L ucy Deacon's house did not disappoint. I imagined a
white picket fence with a little green house on a tiny
plot of land right off the main drag. Lucy Deacon did
have a white picket fence, but her house was bright yellow with
white trim. I couldn't think of a more cheerful house if I tried.

I walked up the front lane and knocked on the door. A
petite lady with curly silver hair opened the door within a
minute. Peering over her reading glasses, she gave me the once-
over.

"You're supposed to be dead," she said.

She knew me.

"Who do you think I am?" I asked.

"You're Natalie Peters, aren't you?" She asked. "Or her
little sister? That would fit your age better, I suppose. You
better come on in."

I followed her inside. Her home was as bright and cheerful
inside as the exterior. Lucy painted her walls in bright colors of
red, orange, and pale green. Bookshelves lined the entire back
wall. I wandered over and saw special editions of classics and
little glass knickknacks of all types of birds. Yellow flowered

sofas flanked a white coffee table that held a small white tea set decorated with tiny green vines. Lucy sat on one of the sofas and motioned me to join her. I complied and sat down.

"I'm Lindsey Peters, the little sister," I said. "We disappeared when I was eight-years-old. You knew Natalie?"

"You look so much like her," Lucy said. "I really liked Natalie. That last semester was a difficult one for her, though. When she disappeared, I assumed she ran away from home and took you with her."

She offered me a cup of peppermint tea. The refreshing scent wafted toward my nostrils and relaxed me. I took the tea from her.

"We did run away," I said and took a sip.

"When I saw your names in the paper with those other girls, I feared I'd been wrong. I'm happy to hear that Natalie and you were spared from that horror."

She focused her sharp eyes on me. She wanted to know what I was doing there.

"Thank you for seeing me. I came to ask about a teacher Natalie had, a woman named Barbara. They were close. She helped us that night, but I never heard her last name. My sister refused to talk about anything from that time."

Lucy Deacon sipped her tea.

"What did Barbara look like?"

I closed my eyes, picturing the woman in the driver's seat.

"She had long dark brown hair, parted in the middle. Looked like she was early thirties, maybe?"

"Barbara, hmmm? A Barbara Levinson worked there at that time, but she had to be in her fifties in the early 90s. Could she have been that old?" Lucy asked me.

I opened my eyes.

"No, her neck was smooth. She was a young woman," I said.

"No other teachers by that name worked at El Segundo."

"What about substitute teachers?" I asked.

Lucy pursed her lips. "My memory is quite good, and I don't remember any subs with the name of Barbara back then."

My shoulders stooped a little. This had been my last Hail Mary moment. I didn't have any other leads to follow.

"I can see how disappointed you are," Lucy said, putting her cup down. "What's this about, anyway?" She cocked her head at me. "You really do look quite a bit like Natalie. You've inherited her haunted expression as well."

"Haunted expression? Any idea why?"

Lucy shook her head.

"No, but I've always regretted not doing something for her."

"What do you mean?" I asked.

"Natalie was a student in my science class. She was very inquisitive and interested in the subject matter. She'd come up and ask me what we were studying that day, that sort of thing. One of the few students that showed any interest."

Lucy took another sip of tea.

"As the months progressed, she withdrew into herself. She'd lost a lot of weight and rarely spoke. By the time the last semester arrived, she'd lost any interest in the class. Her grades slipped down to C's and D's. Then she stopped showing up at all."

"She skipped class?" I had never known my type A personality sister to skip an engagement or class.

"It wasn't like Natalie. Her behavior was the clearest indication of some awfulness going on in her private life. I asked her several times if I could help. I even spoke to the guidance counselor about her change. She disappeared two weeks later."

This was the information I had always wanted to know about. The days that led up to our running away.

"Do you know who her closest friends were?" I asked.

"When the school year started, her best friends were Nancy Lyons and Marianne Milnes. I also remember that Melanie Bridgeton, a girl in one of my other classes, was chummy with Natalie as well. But, by the end, she kept to herself. I do remember a big fight between her and Nancy Lyons close to the end of that semester. It stuck in my mind because I was so sorry to see another thing going wrong for her."

I nodded. Natalie never had friends when we lived in Seattle. Some girls tried, but she always rebuffed them.

"Did she have any boyfriends?" I asked.

"Michael Grady, but they were no longer together by the time Natalie and you ran."

"You remember so much." I couldn't help but smile. I sat back on the couch.

"El Segundo High in the 90s was a smaller school. We didn't have as many students and gossip went around. Michael Grady was popular, so the news spread quickly. It's not like that now," she said.

"Was Natalie friends with any other teachers?"

Lucy frowned and placed her cup down on the sunflower coaster. Everything in Lucy's home was cozy and sunny. Her expression didn't match the sunny flowers, though.

"Did I ask the wrong question?" I asked.

"I don't like to spread gossip," Lucy said.

"Anything you can tell me I'd be so appreciative of," I said.

"This happened after Natalie ran away, but I wondered if he had something to do with her change." Lucy leaned forward. "One of the teachers, Paul Adams, had been having an indecent relationship with one of his other students."

"With Natalie?" My stomach churned. Was this it? Was this the reason?

"No. Her name was Clara."

I couldn't help putting my hand on my chest.

"Natalie was in his class, though and I know that she had

been one of his star students. The gossip around the teacher's room was she'd been involved with him and that's what prompted her to run away."

Was he the monster? This teacher. I'd been wrong all this time?

"Now mind you, I had never seen them together and this was gossip. I thought Natalie was smarter than that, but…" she shrugged.

Could Natalie be so afraid of a teacher, though? That didn't fully add up, either.

"In your opinion, could he have been the cause of her change?"

"Honestly, no."

"Really?" I wondered why she even mentioned him to me.

"I wanted to be honest with you with all that was going on back then. I didn't put too much stock in the gossip, though. Clara was also eighteen at the time and they ended up getting married."

"He wasn't a pedophile then?"

"Not in the legal sense."

Ice dripped down my spine and clusters of goose pimples sprouted up and down my arms. Lucy had thrown me a life raft and then taken it away. The monsters were still my family. For one brief second, I felt how it must feel to be free of that knowledge. To be safe. I swallowed the enormous lump in my throat.

"You've given me some names to follow up with. Thank you," I said instead.

My statement pulled Lucy's attention back into the room. She smiled thoughtfully.

"You know, I do remember a woman, in a classroom. With Natalie before the lunch bell went off. She had dark hair parted down the middle."

"A substitute teacher?" I asked.

"Had to be. I don't remember her in school again."

"Do you remember anything about her? Did she call her by name?"

"It was just a flash of memory. I don't remember any sound, voices. They were close together, whispering. Natalie was crying."

"It had to be the woman who helped us."

"I would think so. I'm not sure how you could find her. Record-keeping wasn't so diligent back then."

I deflated. That didn't sound promising.

"Thank you so much for your time, Lucy," I said. I didn't know what else to ask.

"Why are you looking for this teacher? You never mentioned what happened to Natalie?"

"She and I ran away to Seattle. When she went off to college in San Francisco, a car hit her and she died."

"Oh my, that's terrible. I'm so sorry to hear that. I did always hope that she had found some happiness and had managed to overcome whatever she was dealing with."

"She tried her best. She really did," I said and stood up.

"Natalie was a fighter," Lucy said and lifted herself off the couch. "Old bones," she explained. She led me to the door.

"She saved my life. I want to pay her back by bringing to light whatever happened to her. Get her some justice. If I can think of any more questions, would you mind if I came back and asked you?" I asked her.

"I have a question for you, Lindsey," Lucy said as she opened the door.

"Yes?"

"You haven't asked me anything about your brothers," Ms. Deacon said. "Why?"

My heart dropped like a stone.

18

El Segundo, CA

DAY 3

The interior of the El Segundo police building was small compared to the precincts that Harri had worked at with the LAPD. The front lobby was tiny for the number of cops working in this township. The duty officer manning the front desk grimaced when Harri flashed her badge at him. He knew why she was there.

"I need to see Detective Peter McDonald immediately," she said.

"Who's asking?" the officer countered in a clipped tone.

He was going to play that game.

"It's Detective Harri Harper with RHD division with the Ballona Creek Task Force," Harri said.

Mitzi flashed her FBI credentials. "FBI. We need to see him immediately."

"All right hold on please," the officer said and picked up the phone. "You have the cavalry out here," he said to someone on the other end.

It wasn't too long before a cocky, youngish detective pushed through from the bullpen. He was wearing plainclothes with cowboy boots. Harri worked hard not to roll her eyes at his full get-up. He didn't extend a hand to say hello.

"You've heard about me picking up Christian LeGuerre," he said.

"Detective Peter McDonald, I presume?" Mitzi asked.

"That's right."

"What gave you the idea that you could bring Christian LeGuerre in? You'd been told to keep your distance by Detective Tom Bards," Harri said in her most authoritative voice.

Her strategy was to piss him off enough to lose his cool and give the rest of the team enough time to get there.

"El Segundo is not under LAPD jurisdiction. I had every right to pick up a suspect in a case we are investigating. I'm the head detective here," he said, keeping his cool.

His eyes stayed flat.

Harri did not like this man.

"I want to see Christian. Has he called for a lawyer yet?" Harri asked.

"He's only been with us for ten minutes. We're going to sweat him out until we're good and ready for him."

"That's not your call," Harri said.

"Say that again," Detective McDonald said, stepping closer to her.

"Watch yourself, Detective," Mitzi's voice cut through the tension between the two detectives.

"We WILL wait until my team arrives," she said.

"This is my station. You don't get to order me around," Detective McDonald said.

"You don't want your face splashed all over the Los Angeles Times under a headline that you impeded a major crimes investigation, do you?" Harri drawled back.

Detective McDonald stood silent in front of them, his eyes narrowed. To his credit, he kept his mouth shut. Mitzi and Harri stayed shoulder to shoulder and watched him. Detective

McDonald dragged his eyes away from Harri and turned to Mitzi.

"You're the profiler?" he asked.

Harri took note he didn't use Mitzi's name.

Mitzi threw back her head and laughed.

Detective McDonald's face contorted in anger. Mitzi knew what buttons to push, that was for sure.

"Sonny, you're goin' to have to try harder than that."

Harri decided on a different path. "Take me to Christian LeGuerre immediately."

"What happened to waiting on your team?" asked Detective McDonald.

"I changed my mind," Harri said.

"You don't have jurisdiction in the city of El Segundo," he said and crossed his arms across his chest.

"Major Crimes has jurisdiction over all of Los Angeles," Harri said.

"El Segundo is not Los Angeles."

"Why did you bring Christian LeGuerre in for questioning?" Mitzi asked.

"We have uncovered new information in the case of his strangled girlfriend," Detective McDonald said.

"Bullshit," Harri said. She didn't believe a word out of his mouth.

"You need to leave my precinct now," he said, his stance widening and taking up more space. His intimidation tactics were unsubtle.

"Bring me to Christian LeGuerre," Harri said.

"You can watch him through the glass. He needs to be in there for a couple more hours," he said.

With that, he turned on his heels and pushed through the doors to the bullpen.

Mitzi made a face behind his back and rolled her eyes. Harri suppressed a giggle. Mitzi diffused the tension well. They followed him into the bullpen.

Detective McDonald pointed to one of six doors along the back wall.

"You can watch in here."

He opened the door to a tiny room with a one-way mirror along the wall.

Harri, curiosity getting the better of her, walked inside to see what major crimes' main suspect looked like. Christian LeGuerre sat at a small table in a room the same size as the one she stood in. His greasy, black hair was slicked back. His acne-scarred face dripped with perspiration, and his legs twitched. His eyes darted around the room and then suddenly seemed to look right at her, though she knew he couldn't see her, only his reflection.

"How long has he been in there?" Harri asked.

The amount of anxiety rolling off him spoke of longer than a half-hour. She didn't believe a word McDonald had said to her.

"He's acting as if he's been here all day," Mitzi said.

"He hasn't," Detective McDonald said.

"What new information do you have?"

"Our team had an expert take a look at the original case file. He found some aspects of the case that we need to look into," Detective McDonald said.

"Does he know he is a suspect in the '92 disappearances?" Harri asked.

She would not be surprised if he had let that cat out of the bag as he brought him in. McDonald seemed like the kind of cop to mess up another cop's investigation.

"What kind of cop do you think I am?" He asked her, eyes narrowing.

"The kind that would bring in another team's suspect to grandstand for the media on his own behalf," Harri snapped back.

Where in the hell were Bards and Swisher? She didn't want to check the time, but they couldn't stall him much longer. Impatience seemed to blare out of him.

Detective McDonald turned to go.

"Can we get some water?" Harri asked.

He clenched his jaw. "Sure," he said and left.

"We don't have much time left," Mitzi said.

"I know. We did the best we could," Harri said. "What do you think of this one?" Harri gestured to Christian.

"He seems pretty young to have been involved in the '92 disappearances," Mitzi said.

"I was thinking the same thing. He would have been a junior in high school at most back then. He would have made mistakes with all those abductions, wouldn't he?" Harri said.

Mitzi pursed her lips.

"Oh shit," Harri said as the door opened in the interrogation room.

Detective McDonald strode in and pulled up a seat across from Christian.

"I have to get in there," Harri said and rushed to stop McDonald from going too far into his questioning.

"I'm Detective Harper of the RHD Major crimes," she said and sat in the chair next to McDonald. "Do you know why you're here?" she asked Christian.

"No, I don't. And, I want my lawyer," he said.

"Did you hear that?" she asked, directing her question to Detective McDonald.

"A lawyer isn't necessary for this," McDonald said. "I want to ask you a couple of friendly questions about the summer of 1992. You were a junior at El Segundo High School?"

He did exactly what she didn't want him to do.

"He's asked to see his lawyer," Harri said. "This is a violation of his civil rights. Please stop talking, Detective McDonald."

"Yeah, you're not supposed to be asking me any questions without my lawyer," Christian said as he sat back in his seat and crossed his arms over his chest.

Detective McDonald smiled. "After you, Detective Harper."

"I know what you're doing," she hissed.

"Doing my job," he said casually.

He wasn't fazed by her anger.

Detectives Tom Bards and David Swisher pushed through the bullpen doors, the desk officer trailing behind them.

Harri stood and left the room to meet them, McDonald right behind her.

"Tom, David, the suspect asked for a lawyer. This one over here," she jabbed her finger at McDonald, "let the cat out of the bag about the summer of '92."

Detective Bards nodded to the side.

"I'll join you," Detective McDonald said.

Detective Swisher pulled McDonald aside and Detective Bards seized the opportunity to speak only to Harri.

"You're on the Lorraine Benjamin murder. I've cleared it with David. We need to get ahead of this. David emailed you the case file," he said and handed her his keys. "These are for the unmarked we drove here. Go talk to the parents and then come back. I have a feeling we'll be here for a while."

"I'm on it," Harri said, taking the keys.

She motioned for Mitzi to follow her. "Want to go talk to some parents with me?"

"Lorraine Benjamin's parents?"

Harri nodded.

"There's a level of sophistication to the crimes that would be hard for a junior to master," Mitzi said as they stepped out of the precinct.

"I agree. He could be good for Lorraine's murder, though. Her death wasn't on LAPD's radar. Could she be connected to the mummified girls somehow?" Harri wondered aloud as she checked her phone for the case information.

"The methodology of the abuse on the victim's bodies doesn't speak of a teenager with poor impulse control. And after seeing the interaction you had with him in the interrogation room, he isn't the personality type to have done that. He's more of a disorganized mind. I could imagine him strangling Lorraine Benjamin, but not our girls."

"What if he's our follower? And he could be our way to the bully?" Harri argued.

"I was thinking the same thing."

Harri clicked the unlock button on the key fob and searched the parking lot of unmarked cars for the sound of unlocking. Harri clicked again. The sound came from a Dodge four cars down.

"Aha," Harri said.

Once inside, Mitzi wrinkled her nose. "Smells like cigarettes in here."

"I bet it's David. He looks like an unhealthy one," Harri said.

"You're probably right. He's not the pleasant sort," Mitzi added.

The women grinned at each other.

Harri checked her email and got the address for the Benjamins.

"This is going to stir up some trouble," Harri said.

Talking to parents about an open-unsolved of their child was never easy. The wounds never closed. They pulled out of the drive and headed toward downtown El Segundo.

19

The Benjamin House

DAY 3

J udith Benjamin sat next to her husband Henry at the kitchen table across from Detective Harri Harper and FBI Special Agent Mitzi Jeffries. Judith and Henry did their best to be hospitable by offering tea, water, and cookies, but all the treats were left untouched in the middle of the table.

"Are you re-investigating Lorraine's death?" Henry asked.

"We're making inquiries into Christian LeGuerre," Detective Harper said.

"Could you give us some context to his and your daughter's relationship back then?" Agent Jeffries asked.

"We didn't like him at all. The very first time we met him, we knew there was something wrong with him," Judith said.

"Mom, I'm home. I'm going up to study with my friend," Lorraine *said, and Judith stepped out of the kitchen.*

Lorraine, her beautiful, blonde 17-year-old daughter was about to bound up the stairs, with a young man trailing behind her. He had greasy, black hair that was parted in the middle and wore a black heavy metal shirt with saggy, dark blue jeans. This was not the type of guy that

Lorraine had brought home before. Judith didn't like the look of him. He was bad news.

"I think it would be better if you studied in the living room," Judith said.

Lorraine's progress on the stairs slowed. She turned toward her mother, her face reddening.

Judith's heart gave a little tug. She hated not trusting her daughter. The look Lorraine flashed her asked, "How could you not trust me, Mom?"

"What's your name?" Judith asked the young man. She dried her hands off on the dishtowel and held it out.

"M…m… my name is Christian," the greasy boy stuttered.

She gripped his hand in hers. It was limp and sweaty. What in the world was her daughter doing with this guy?

"Are either of you hungry? I could make some grilled cheeses, or we have some fruit in the fridge," Judith offered.

She did not want her daughter to go upstairs with him.

"No, thanks, Mom. I need help with math and Christian is really good," Lorraine said.

They both headed up the stairs and Judith caught a whiff of body odor coming from the boy. He wasn't a boy, though, was he? He looked older maybe 18 or 19. Why did her daughter need to have help with math from someone who looked like that? Judith thought. She didn't want to embarrass her Lorraine in front of her friend, but she promised herself she would talk to her about him as soon as he left.

Judith pulled out of the memory. Tears streamed down her face as she thought of her daughter's smile and the big argument that came after that first encounter with Christian LeGuerre.

"He didn't deserve to be hanging out with Lori. And he's how Lori got pulled into that group of boys," Judith said.

The detective shot the agent a look. They didn't know about the gang then. Heat burned her cheeks. What kind of investigation had the police run, Judith thought? She pressed her cold palms to her cheeks to cool them down.

"What do you mean? What group?" Detective Harper asked.

"The boys who hung out with Danny Peters. Danny provided Christian LeGuerre an alibi for the night that Lorraine was strangled. I never believed him. Those boys lied for each other," she said.

"Were there boys in the group besides Danny and Christian?" Agent Jeffries asked.

"The group was Danny Peters, Christian LeGuerre, Danny's little brother Reece, and Mason Reynolds."

Judith remembered the pack hanging out on her front porch, Lorraine sidled up to Christian.

"Danny Peters was the ringleader. He creeped me out. I wouldn't allow him in the house, but that didn't stop Christian from bringing his boys around and hanging on my doorstep. I think Danny Peters had a thing for Lori, too. I overheard a fight over Lori. It was the only time I saw Christian stand up to Danny."

"How long did Lorraine date Christian?" Detective Harper asked.

"About three or four months," Henry answered her. "If it hadn't been for Christian's father and Danny, Christian LeGuerre would've gone to prison for what he did to our daughter," Henry said flatly.

"What do you mean?" Agent Jeffries asked.

"Danny Peters' father was a local lawyer, a real bully. He worked as GRE's local counsel. GRE is one of the big defense contractors here in the South Bay. Christian LeGuerre's father worked at GRE, as well. Their fathers kept them out of jail. For strangling our beautiful daughter," Judith said, her voice rising a pitch higher.

Judith worked at keeping her anger at bay, but it slipped out despite her best efforts. There was not a day that went by when she didn't wake up thinking, hoping really, that Lorraine was still alive. Then her reality crashed in on her. Her daughter was dead.

"Could you walk us through the day your daughter died?" Detective Harper asked. "I understand this is hard. We know you've gone over this before. We need to hear your story."

"Yes," Henry said.

Judith nodded. It was the best she could do. The sound of their voices lowered and then grew louder. She fought off the urge to scream. She gulped down the knot in her throat with whatever small bit of resolve she could muster.

"Lori told us she had a date with Christian that night. They were going to the movies. She left the house around 6:30 p.m.," she said and stopped.

Judith rubbed her palms against her pants. Pants that Lorraine would have made fun of her for wearing. She choked down a sob at the thought. She nodded to Henry who looked as if he was fighting back tears.

"Lorraine took the same route she always did, walked west on Maple Street. Left on Main Street. The local theater was two blocks from that intersection back then. We heard from Darcy and June, her best friends, about what happened at the theater."

"Did her friends tell you the route that she took?" Agent Jeffries asked.

"No," Judith said. "We'd walked that path multiple times over the years. It's the fastest route."

"Well-lit, too," Henry piped in.

"But no one saw her walk there?" Detective Harper asked.

Judith and Henry exchanged a glance. Were all detectives the damn same? Attempting to keep her voice free of anger, Judith began again.

"Christian's gang was there at the end of the movie,

hanging around. Lori wanted to go home. Christian wanted to walk her home, but she said no. Darcy told me something had happened between Lori and Christian, some sort of fight during the movie. Darcy and June wanted to walk home with her, but she refused them, as well."

Judith stopped and pressed her fist to her lips. If Lorraine had taken them up on their offer, she'd still be alive. She would not cry. She would not cry. The black abyss yawned underneath her.

Henry took over the narrative.

"Lori told them it was only a few blocks home and not to be silly. She waved at them from the corner of Maple and Main Street. She walked east. That was the last time anyone saw her again."

Henry squeezed Judith's hand. He gave her strength as he had for many years.

"The police zeroed in on Christian because of the fight?" Agent Jeffries asked.

"Yes. June Webbley characterized it more as a screaming match at the concession stand. Christian appeared very upset," Judith said. "D...Darcy and June told the police the boys arrived soon after the fight to console Christian."

"The boys?" Detective Harper asked.

"Danny and Reece Peters, and Mason Reynolds," Henry said. "Danny Peters consoled Christian as Lori walked home. They didn't stay long after Lori left. Danny had an old Ford Escort. They all piled into that and drove off. They alibied each other for the entire rest of the night."

Henry's words dripped in pain.

"Do you know what happened to Danny Peters?" Detective Harper asked.

"The whole family died in the Philippines over twenty years ago. The father was on vacation with his two sons. The sisters had been missing a couple of years by then," Judith said.

"A car accident according to the papers," Henry added.

"Is Christian in trouble again? Has he confessed?" Judith asked.

Maybe he'd go to prison another way.

"He's being questioned on another matter," Detective Harper said.

"Are you going to get him this time? Is he finally going to pay for what he did to our daughter?" Judith asked.

The greasy young man that had come in with her daughter flashed again in her memory. Her grief made her nauseous, her stomach contracting in pain again. She should have thrown him out of the house then and there. That was her job as a mother. She should have protected her daughter.

"Will you call us if there is any movement in Lorraine's case?" Judith asked, doubting they ever would.

"Yes, I will. You will be my first phone call," Detective Harper promised.

The other cops made the same promise and broke it soon enough. Judith wanted to believe the earnest woman in front of her, but she dared not hope.

"Our daughter deserves justice."

Tears slid down her cheeks. She swiped at them with the back of her hand.

"We will get it for her," Detective Harper said.

Judith pulled her eyes away from the detective. She refused to hope again. It wouldn't bring Lori back.

20

Jane Smith
DAY 3

I stared at Lucy Deacon. I wasn't sure if I wanted to hear about them.

"My brothers died in a car crash in the Philippines," I said.

"I don't mean about that."

"I don't understand. What could you tell me?" I asked.

"I always thought your brother Danny had something to do with Natalie's breakdown," Lucy said.

My hand gripped the door frame.

"How so?" I asked, my heart thumping.

"The monsters are coming," my dead sister's voice whispered in my mind. I focused back on Lucy and her cheery house.

"Your brother Danny was a senior when Natalie was a sophomore and Reece was a freshman. Reece was reserved and quiet. Danny, however, was a nasty bit of work," she said.

"That's strong language coming from you," I forced a smile.

"All of us teachers knew he was up to something, but none of us could prove it. He was too smart for that. Bullies tend to be easy to catch. Like those football boys that would just throw the weaker boys into the lockers. We saw those coming. But Daniel Peters was something else entirely."

"Did you see him bully other students? What do you mean he was something else entirely?"

Danny skulked in the shadows at home. He kept to the perimeter of all the rooms. That was the clearest memory I had of him. In the shadows, waiting to jump out and scare me. Other than scaring me like that, he didn't have much to do with me.

Any time we ended up in the same room or going down the hallway, we didn't speak. I was an irritation to him, nothing more. My sister was always around when I was home and played with me. She was my family. I barely remembered Reece from back then.

"No, we never caught him at anything."

"Did you call my father?"

"I debated calling him, but after meeting him at the parent conference night, I didn't bother."

"Really? Why? What happened?"

"He was a cold, unfriendly man who didn't care much to hear about Natalie's problems at school. Over the years, I became convinced Natalie's home life was what troubled her."

I nodded. My father barely registered in my memories. My sister kept me away from him after our mother's death. I'd been five at the time and Natalie became my world.

"Did you ever get any indication of what happened after we disappeared? Did Danny change at all?" I asked.

"If anything, he became meaner. We could never catch him at anything, he was too smart. The girls liked him, though. I never did understand why. The bad boy persona, I guess."

"I see."

"It was good your sister got you away from him."

I nodded. "One last thing, I went to El Segundo High

School to find yearbooks that had a picture of my sister Natalie in them, but I couldn't find any from the years she attended. You wouldn't have any of those old yearbooks, would you?" I asked.

Lucy shook her head no. "I had to move houses after my husband died and I ended up tossing a lot of that old stuff. Didn't see the point in lugging them around. Especially as I get on in years."

"Thank you, Lucy," I said and stepped off the last step.

"I hope you're having a happy life," she said.

"I'm searching for it."

"Find it soon. Time goes by and fast."

I nodded but kept my eyes on her well-tended green lawn.

"It's not finished."

"What's not finished? The Ballona Creek case you mean?"

I shouldn't get this nice old lady killed.

"Never mind. Thank you for speaking with me."

She squeezed my hand.

"Don't let it pass you by. Focus on the good parts," she said.

I smiled and turned my back on the cheery little house with the white picket fence.

Lucy Deacon confirmed my suspicions about my brother. Now what, I thought, as I drove toward home, dread and fear making it hard to focus on driving.

"Make it right, make it right," I said aloud, attempting to overcome the pulsating waves of terror wracking my body. I grasped the wheel hard enough for my knuckles to lose their color. The sensation of the steering wheel brought me back to the present moment.

Could my brothers and father have staged their own deaths? And when Natalie resurfaced in San Francisco, they found her and killed her. Then they came for me and Jennifer?

But why? Why couldn't they leave well enough alone?

Unless there was another reason Natalie ran. A reason big enough for them to make sure she stayed silent about it.

Work backward, I thought. Is successfully staging your own death even a possibility? Who would know something about that?

Someone used to finding people, I thought. A Skip tracer. I would hire a Skip tracer. My decision finally brought the panic back under control. I felt more in control.

I am going to find you all, I thought and pressed on the gas.

21

Silver Lake, CA
DAY 3

A phone call interrupted Detective Harri Harper and her typing. She'd spent the last two hours filling out the report for Lorraine Benjamin's parents' interview. She picked her phone up without checking the screen.

"Detective Harri Harper," she said.

"Hi Harri, it's Jake Tepesky. Was wondering if you might want to join me for dinner tonight?" he asked.

Harri smiled despite herself.

"I was planning to work late, but I do need to eat," she said.

"Yes, you do. It was really good to see you today," he said, a sudden wistfulness in his voice.

The memories of him, Lauren, and that summer made her think of salt, sand, and the smell of the wax on the surfboards he and Lauren used. She forced down the sudden lump in her throat.

"Where were you thinking?" she asked.

"What about the Little Birds restaurant? Have you ever been? It's on Franklin, kind of across from the Scientology Celebrity Center and that little village area?" he asked.

"I've driven by a bunch of times. I think I can get there in about an hour," Harri said.

"Great! Can't wait to catch up," he said.

"Me too," Harri said and hung up, cheeks burning.

She'd always considered Jake her sister's best buddy. Jake had the typical southern California surfer good-looks and dated lots of girls that summer. Natalie teased him about being unable to decide on anyone. Harri was more interested in musicians back then and anyway, he was too old for her. But they weren't in school anymore.

Harri left the bullpen, calculating how long it would take her to be presentable. She took stock of her work uniform, black slacks, blue button-down shirt, and her boots. Good enough for an old friend, she thought. Her pace quickened and she rushed to beat traffic.

TRAFFIC MADE Harri fifteen minutes late for the dinner date. Typical for Los Angeles. Harri smoothed her damp palms on her slacks and curiously observed how flustered she'd become in the last ten minutes. Pushing any confusing thoughts aside, she waved at Jake who'd snagged a table at the back of the busy restaurant. The smile he gave her lit up his face and made his eyes twinkle.

Harri beamed back.

"I'm so glad you were able to come tonight," he said.

"Me too," Harri said and sat down across from him. "It's good to see you."

A waitress appeared at their table. "Drinks?" she asked.

They put in their drink orders and waited to speak until she left.

"It's been a long time," Jake said.

"Yes, since that fall. I remember seeing you in one of the search parties, but we didn't speak," she said.

The dark emotions swirling beneath the surface of her life rose up to bring back the memories of that fall: the terror of never seeing her sister again, the thoughts of what could be happening to her, and watching her parents disintegrate in front of her eyes.

"Yes, I remember," he said, his voice low.

"Difficult way to start a dinner," Harri quipped.

"I miss her still," Jake said.

"Every day."

They both looked away.

Harri breathed deep, and plunged in, pushing the pain to the side.

"What made you come back to Los Angeles? I thought you were permanently in Washington, DC?" she asked.

Jake sipped his wine and nodded. "I moved there right after college. I was recruited my senior year and went into training at Quantico the moment I graduated. I've been stationed in Washington, New York, and Miami," he said.

"Ever married?"

Harri watched his face as he worked out how much to reveal.

"I was, but we divorced. Being an FBI agent doesn't fit well into a typical family lifestyle. My wife wanted children, I didn't. We grew apart. It was amicable," Jake said.

Harri noted a catch in his voice. It sounded like there was more to the story than that. Another time, she thought.

"And you? You were on your way to MIT, I heard. How did you end up a police detective?" he asked.

"I lasted a semester in Boston."

"What happened?"

"I couldn't concentrate on any of my physics courses and dropped out before I could fail out. My family fell apart after that fall."

"My mom told me your mother took her own life?"

"Yes. Really, I lost both of my parents the day my sister disappeared."

For the first time in years, tears welled up in Harri's eyes. She hadn't said that aloud before.

"We don't have to talk about this."

"I'm okay. I think about her and them every day. It's been a long time since I've spoken with anyone who actually knew them before."

"I'm sorry I didn't send condolences when your mother passed."

"Honestly, I don't think I would have noticed either way. I was a walking zombie during that time. It's a miracle I graduated from college at all."

"Where did you end up?"

"UCLA. I got a criminal justice degree and went into the Academy after graduation."

"What about your dad?"

"Alcohol took over his life. He's alive, but his mind is full of holes," Harri said.

"Holes?"

"Dementia," Harri said. "How about your family?"

Harri remembered Jake's parents had been divorced, and his mom really struggled to keep them in El Segundo.

"I don't know much about my father these days. We stopped talking during my first year of college and never really reconnected. My mom died of cancer a couple of years back."

"I'm so sorry to hear that."

"Thank you. She was the reason I came back to Los Angeles. I helped take her to her appointments and just spent time with her. I'd grown tired of the BSU (Behavioral Science Unit) and the cases that I was working on. LA was a nice change."

"And you didn't go back?"

"I decided to stay here. I'm still connected at the FBI. I get called in on specific cases or if there's overflow. I also have a consulting practice."

"How does that work?"

"If private clients want my expertise. Specific precincts. Private detectives."

"I see."

Their dinner came and they ate in comfortable silence. A silence developed over years of knowing someone. Jake practically lived at their house during high school.

"I never forgot her," Jake said.

"I'm still trying to find her. I go up every year to Oregon and revisit the case. I interview the same people and see if maybe some little information comes loose. I won't stop until I find her," Harri put down her fork.

"I've checked her case files over the years too, but I couldn't go back there. It was too painful for me," Jake confessed, unable to meet her eyes.

"Want to trade notes? I could use a new perspective on the case from a former profiler," Harri said.

"Can I come with you?" Jake asked.

"Really?" Harri asked.

"Yes. I can't promise it will be any different, but a new set of eyes and ears can't hurt."

Harri smiled at him. He flashed a grin.

"Are you on this Ballona Creek case?" Jake asked.

Harri smiled again, relieved at the change in topic.

"I'm on the task force in a peripheral capacity at the moment. I have a lead that could be a dead-end and is not one of the main threads of the investigation. The case has brought back a lot of memories of that summer. Do you remember much from high school during that time?"

"Yeah, I do. Your mom would not let your sister or you out of the house. I ended up finding another surfing buddy for our morning sessions. I don't know of one girl who wasn't terrified to go outside," he said.

"Did you know a girl named Natalie Peters?"

"I did. She was one of the girls abducted that summer with her little sister? The bodies found in the creek didn't include an eight-year-old though, did they?"

"Have you been asking around about the case?"

"Experts talk," he said.

"I see. What was she like in school? Any rumors swirling around her?"

"That was a long time ago, Harri," he said and sipped his wine. "You know, I do remember girls teasing her about her weight loss. Anorexia wasn't so well understood back then. They called her Skeletor."

"Nice," Harri said.

"Girls can be evil to each other," he said.

"Anything else?"

"She kind of disappeared into herself. Became a ghost."

"That's specific. Were you friends with her?"

"No, but she stuck out. It was hard not to notice her pain," he said.

"Thank you."

"Is she your dead end?"

"Sort of. Anyway, can't talk more about that."

"Fair enough."

"So, did you and Mitzi work together?"

"Yeah, we did. She's a brilliant profiler. Your team couldn't have a better person on the case."

"I love Mitzi, too. I went to Quantico for profiler training and she was my teacher. Interesting stuff."

"With your brain, profiling would be right up your alley," Jake said, and his smile crinkled around his eyes.

Her heart fluttered as their eyes met.

"You put too much stock into my smarts," Harri said.

"Your sister told me your IQ," Jake said. "She was so proud of you."

Harri flushed. "It's not that big of a deal. Not for my kind of work, anyway."

The waitress hovered nearby.

"I think they want us to leave. Do you want to come pick up the case files tonight? I have four banker's boxes filled with copies of the original case file and my notes over the years. September isn't too far off."

"Sure. That would give me enough time to work through all your info," Jake said.

Harri smiled. She remembered the teenager he'd been. The distinguished, intelligent, chiseled man sitting in front of her didn't resemble that teenager anymore. He'd had a carefree love of life back then. None of that existed in the man sitting across from her.

"Why did you really leave the FBI?" Harri asked.

"The job became too hard to handle. I compartmentalized to such a degree that I lost myself. I'd joined the FBI because of Lauren's disappearance."

"Like me then."

Jake nodded and took a sip of wine.

"When I found myself in the BSU, I thought I'd come home. I'd worked years to be considered. I have several degrees in criminal psychology."

"You made it."

"I'd made it. I spent years analyzing the worst that humans can do to each other. In the end, there was a case that broke me. I needed out."

"It's hard to be objective when dealing with the mindless horror of these cases."

"It makes you a great detective," he said. "My ability to inhabit both the minds of a killer and a victim made me an above-average profiler. All the victims are here with me," he said, tapping his head.

They paid for their meal and Harri gave Jake directions to her house.

THEY MADE it to Silver Lake in fifteen minutes. A record, she thought.

As Harri's car pulled up to her garage door, the car's headlights lit up the front of her house. Her front door was ajar.

Harri pulled her gun out of her holster and stepped out of the car.

Jake was next to her in a moment.

"Are you armed?"

"No, I'll call 911," Jake dialed while getting back into the car. "I'm not a hero."

"I'll be right back," she said.

She pushed the door open with her foot; her weapon ready. Scanning her foyer and finding it empty, she flicked the lights on.

"LAPD. Police. Come out slowly. Hands up," she yelled into the space.

She swept the first floor for the intruder. It was empty. She proceeded to the second and third floors in the same fashion.

A splash of red marred her white bedspread.

"I'm armed," she yelled out. "Come out with your hands up."

She kicked the bathroom door open. It too was empty. Scrawled in red on the bathroom mirror were the words COME AND GET ME. The red color didn't match the color of blood and the room didn't reek of iron. It had to be paint. She carefully stepped out of the bathroom and made her way downstairs.

Her hands trembled as she stepped outside.

Her home had been defiled. Someone had penetrated her inner sanctum.

The cavalry had arrived. Jake gestured toward her to one of the officers. She couldn't let this get to her. The intruder wanted her to feel watched, unsafe. She wouldn't let him win.

22

Jane Smith

DAY 3

Memories of my family chased me out of El Segundo. I didn't make it far. Traffic stalled on the 405 North and my car slowed to a crawl.

The thoughts jumbled through my brain at breakneck speed.

My sister's face.

My brother Reece's crying in the bedroom next door.

My brother Danny hovering in the shadows, his eyes glowering.

Don't think of them, Natalie whispered.

Our running out of the house that night. My sister seeing someone behind us and heaving me up into her arms, sobbing.

Jennifer lying dead on the pavement, her eyes staring up into my face.

Natalie's hope blooming as Jennifer read out my family's obituary to the both of us.

My sister Natalie packing to go away to college.

I slammed my palms against the steering wheel. Anger surged past the fear and confusion and blossomed in my chest.

They've taken everything from me. From us.

"Bastards," I said. "I will find you all."

My jaw clicked as I grit my teeth, attempting to control myself. What kind of family had I come from?

The killing kind, Natalie whispered.

A question floated into my mind. How difficult was it to stage an entire family's death? How hard would it be to stay dead?

When Natalie and I fled, we didn't fake our deaths. We disappeared. I later found out that Jennifer was part of an abused-woman underground network and used those resources to help us.

She and her colleagues helped women disappear from untenable lives when the authorities refused to help them. The people in the group gave us our identities, but we'd not been declared dead. That seemed overly complicated. How had my brothers and father pulled it off?

The traffic moved faster, and I focused back on driving. Most people in LA complained about the traffic, but it made me feel like I was part of something. Even when I was alone in my car, driving to my lonely apartment in the middle of the night.

Could I be wrong about this whole thing? My paranoia was fueled by my sister's fear. But Lucy Deacon knew Danny. Knew he was disturbed. Cruel.

It wasn't just me. And, if it wasn't my brothers, who had killed Jennifer and Natalie?

I didn't recognize the man who'd come after us that night. Wouldn't I be able to know my own brother?

Who was that man if he wasn't one of my brothers or my father?

I PULLED off the exit and turned right onto La Cienega Boulevard. I glanced into my rearview mirror and my heart fluttered. Those pair of headlights looked familiar. They were particularly bright with a blue tinge to them. I'd seen them on the freeway and now the car they belonged to was behind me.

"Let's see if I'm paranoid," I said to the car in my rearview mirror.

I turned left on Pico Blvd. Then an immediate right into a smaller street.

I checked my mirror.

The blue headlights did the same. That couldn't be a coincidence.

Sweat ran down my back as I increased my speed and made a sudden left turn onto another residential street and then another left into an alleyway.

I pulled into the nearest empty carport and turned my engine off. I slipped out of my car, and keeping to the wall of the building, I positioned myself to watch the entrance of the alley.

A silver Lexus slowed at the mouth of the alley but didn't drive in. Instead, it drove slowly down the street, slowing down at each new street.

He was looking for my car.

Bastard.

I watched the Lexus take a left and disappear. I waited for a good half hour, barely breathing, my heart pounding. Had he given up or was he out there somewhere, waiting for me to make my move? I had to find another way home, one that wouldn't take me back through the streets I'd come from. The streets he could be staking out, waiting to follow me home.

I slid into my car and mapped out a route I could take home. I sat and waited until the clock turned to 10 p.m. Only then did I pull out and take an alternative route home, my eyes searching for those blue headlights behind me. They never reappeared.

23

Silver Lake, California
THURSDAY, AUGUST 9, 2018 - DAY 4

Harri Harper sat on the front stoop of her home, Jake Tepesky next to her, and waited as the forensic team did its business inside. Jake refused to leave her side the entire night and for that she was grateful. Her anger at the nerve of the perp, however, was becoming harder to control.

Her home was her oasis. It was the only place that she felt safe and comfortable. Now, she would have to work very hard to get that feeling back again. She'd worked enough burglaries in Hollywood division to know that her feeling was standard. An invasion of one's home and privacy was sometimes harder to deal with than anything that was taken from the home. Her situation was a little different since her intruder came to scare her specifically. The red scrawl on the bathroom mirror was to horrify, to prove he could get close. She'd be damned if they would get the best of her in that regard.

"It's paint. not blood," Derek the forensic tech said from behind her.

"I assumed it would be due to its color," she said.

"Good news is maybe we can find whoever bought it. Its

brilliant color must be a unique formulation," Derek nodded. "Let you know as soon as we analyze it. Maybe he made a mistake."

"It's the first mistake he's made," Harri said.

"You think it's connected to the Ballona Creek case?" Jake asked.

"Or to my search for Natalie Peters," Harri said.

She stood up when she recognized Detective Tom Bards behind the wheel of an unmarked cruiser. He parked behind the patrol cars.

"He's the head of the task force," Harri whispered to Jake.

"Surprised?" he asked.

"Very."

"Tom, it's late," Harri said. "Thank you for coming. How did you…"

"I was in the office…got the call. It's a warning for the task force, I believe," Tom said.

"I thought so too, or I hit on something with the Natalie Peters case," Harri said. "This wasn't a burglary. I've found nothing missing."

"Someone with little regard for their safety would attempt to do something like this. Have the techs searched for any bugs or listening devices?" Tom asked.

"Yes, they have. Place was clean. The only thing he left was the paint on the mirror," she said.

"Interesting." Tom turned toward Jake. "Detective Bards," and held out his hand.

Jake shook it.

"Jake Tepesky. I'm an old friend of Harri's," Jake said.

"I'm glad you're here to help Harri out," Tom said. He turned back to Harri. "What have you been working on? The question is why you and why now?"

"My thoughts exactly," Harri said.

Tom looked back up at her house. His eyebrow arched inquisitively.

"Nice place," he said.

"Yep, it is."

Harri fought the urge to explain why she lived in a million-dollar house on a detective's salary. He could come up with his own reasons. She turned to Jake.

"Thank you for staying with me, Jake. You should go home, though. Get some sleep. This is going to take into the morning."

"Got it. If you need anything, call me. I'm ten minutes away," he said.

Harri smiled and nodded.

He opened up his arms and Harri stepped into his embrace without thinking. His warmth felt good and comforting. She closed her eyes and inhaled the scent of soap and some sort of musky cologne. Harri let go first, her cheeks burning.

"See you soon," Jake said.

Harri turned back to Tom as Jake made his way to his car.

"Take me through what you've been up to in the last 48 hours," he said.

"Let me tell you about my fun trip to San Francisco," Harri said.

Tom raised an eyebrow. "Fun?"

Harri described her encounter with Detective Gallagher and how unforthcoming he'd been, how the murder-book had gone missing and a single sheet put in its place while it never was input into the system, and how relieved Gallagher had been on her leaving.

"Detective Gallagher was the original lead on the case, yet he couldn't tell me simple details about it."

"It was years ago, wasn't it?"

"I understand that, but his reaction to my leaving left me with questions.

"This trip attempted to corroborate Jane Smith's story?"

Harri nodded. "Yes. Jane said in her statement that her sister, Natalie, under the alias of Rebecca Stevens, was killed in a hit-and-run."

"You found her."

"Yes. That part of the story checks out. A Rebecca Stevens was indeed killed in a hit-and-run in San Francisco in 1999."

"And Jennifer Stevens?"

Harri looked up, surprised. He'd read her report.

"The woman who Jane Smith said adopted them, a Jennifer Stevens, was killed in a home invasion seven days later, on the day of Rebecca Stevens' funeral."

"Another confirmation."

"Yes. My issue is connecting Rebecca Stevens to Natalie Peters. I've hit a wall."

"No pictures?"

"None. No photographs exist of this woman."

Tom looked up from taking notes. "That's significant."

"It is. I spoke to the Seattle detective in charge of the Jennifer Stevens murder. Originally, he had been unable to find any photographs of either of the two girls, Rebecca or Mary Stevens, which worried him."

"That's something. Did he track any down?"

"No. He couldn't find yearbook pictures, family photos, or any of the usual pictures families keep of each other. He called these girls ghosts. There were photos of Jennifer Stevens. She'd been a defense attorney in family court. Real spitfire."

"So, these women existed, the story she told us is true."

"So far. But I can't connect the girls to Natalie and Lindsey Peters."

"Was their addition with the Ballona Creek girls a mistake then?" Tom wondered aloud.

"They were wrongly lumped with the girls that have been discovered in the grave because they disappeared the same summer. If these girls really are Natalie and Lindsey Peters, then the next connection is Christian LeGuerre."

Tom cocked his head at her. "How so? That's new information."

"I hadn't finished up my report last night. When Mitzi and I spoke with Lorraine Benjamin's parents yesterday, they mentioned that Christian LeGuerre was best friends with Danny Peters and his little brother, Reece. Natalie and Lindsey Peters were long gone when Lorraine Benjamin died, but that's the other connection."

"But Lorraine's death didn't fit the pattern of the Ballona girls," Tom said.

"Judith Benjamin, the mother, feared Danny Peters. She wouldn't let him in the house and talked to her daughter about keeping away from him."

"Do we have another suspect then?"

"No, he died in the Philippines in 1996 with Reece Peters and their father."

"Christian LeGuerre is still our prime suspect then."

"It appears so."

"Thank you for dealing with Detective McDonald yesterday. He threw a nice monkey wrench into the works and we really appreciated your stalling."

"What an unpleasant man."

"That's putting it mildly," Tom said.

Harri smiled at his quip.

"Glad I could help. I'm thinking this intrusion is connected somehow to San Francisco. My brain is not letting go of the inconsistencies."

"Murder-books get damaged often enough," Tom reminded her.

"True, but with Gallagher acting the way he was, my gut is telling me something is there. I need to find the proof of it, though."

"Keep following the trail, Harri. I'll let David know what you've uncovered."

"Thank you, Tom."

"You're going to be okay here tonight?" he asked. "We'll leave a car to watch you for the next twenty-four hours.

"That's not necessary. He's not coming back," Harri shook her head.

"Just in case," Tom said.

Harri didn't think she was going to win that argument. "All right. Thank you. As soon as the techs are done, I'll reset the alarm with a new code and see how he could have gotten in with the old one. Then sleep."

"See you at the download in a couple of hours," he said, checking his watch. "I'll bring David up to speed with your findings for next steps."

They said their goodbyes and she sat down to wait for the techs to leave.

HARRI WALKED BACK into her house at 5:15 a.m. The techs had stayed another hour or so. Her home smelled like a crime scene. Fingerprint powder marred most of the surfaces and the smell of chemicals permeated the air. She would need to get a crime scene cleanup service to come tomorrow and make her home livable again.

First things first. The alarm. How did the bastard get in here? She called the company, and they reported the system had never been turned on.

Cursing herself for making that mistake of not setting it before she ran out to meet Jake, Harri sighed. She reset the code and double-checked with the company it was working. Once that task was complete, she took a blanket out of the closet, brushed her teeth, drank a glass of water, and cocooned herself into the couch.

But sleep would not come. Her thoughts turned to her dinner with Jake. It felt good to reconnect with him again. He was home for her. The thought surprised her. Years had passed without her considering another human in such a way. The thought comforted her and sleep finally came.

24

PAB - Los Angeles, CA
DAY 4

Detective Harri Harper opened the white wrap to her bagel with cream cheese and took a sip of coffee.

Detective Rob Lakin waved a pile of paper at her.

"I picked up your lead sheets, you're welcome." He tossed them on her desk before dropping into his chair.

"You heard the news?" he asked, a big grin on his face.

Harri hadn't a clue what he was speaking of.

"Well? Spill it!"

"I can't believe no one told you yet."

Harri wiped cream cheese off her fingers with a napkin while attempting to swallow through the lump in her throat. What bad news could it be now?

"What is it?"

"The higher-ups didn't much like getting played by Detective McDonald down in El Segundo. David Swisher took the fall for that," Rob said.

"What?"

Harri slept in late that morning and had only arrived five minutes ago, still half asleep.

"What do you mean by fall? Is he off the task force?"

"God, you're slow today."

Getting only two hours of sleep hadn't made for an easy morning. A triple shot of espresso hadn't done anything to help her brain process news any faster, either.

"We don't get the exquisite experience of watching him fumble through this investigation," Rob explained.

David Swisher was gone. No longer on the task force.

"I'm not even sure what to say to that," Harri said.

She polished off the rest of the bagel and gulped down enough coffee to push the whole mass past the lump of anxiety.

"Who's in charge now?"

"Tom Bards. Although, that's not a surprise. He won."

"He did."

"It's time," Rob said.

Harri dragged herself up from the chair and trudged alongside Rob. They left the Cold Case bullpen and walked over to the elevators. Rob punched the down button.

"How's the Charlaine Lewis lead going?" she asked.

The elevator doors slid open and they stepped in.

Harri punched the eighth-floor button. The elevator descended.

"I hit a bunch of dead ends. Pimp didn't give me anything new. He claimed he saw a guy hunched over her body and when he called out, the killer ran away. He couldn't tell me much else because he was high at the time."

"Too high to give a description?"

"Something like that. He didn't seem right to me when we spoke, though. His brain was all jumbled. I'm still convinced Charlaine Lewis belongs in the investigation."

They walked out of the elevator and crossed the hallway to the task force conference room.

Harri's heart skipped a beat. She swallowed the lump down

again. No need for nervousness now. It was a new day and a new start.

HARRI AND ROB opened the doors to find Tom Bards, Jorge Hernandez, and Jackie Render already there. For a difficult case, the tone in the room was strangely chipper. David Swisher hadn't been popular.

Five chairs created a circle in the middle of the room, the whiteboard directly behind the configuration. Tom, Jorge, and Jackie sat in three of the five chairs. Tom waved them over to the remaining seats.

"Have a seat, Harri, Rob. As you all might have heard through the grapevine, David Swisher has been reassigned," Tom said.

Harri found it hard to keep from smiling at that.

"I've been assigned as lead detective on this task force. We've had some interesting developments in the last twenty-four hours. First, we need to discuss the situation with Christian LeGuerre and what happened in El Segundo."

"That's what got David replaced, yes?" Jorge asked, leaning in eagerly anticipating some juicy news.

Harri didn't love gossip, but her curiosity was piqued over the undercurrents of politics that had run through the task force from the very beginning.

"Politics have no place in an investigation like this. That was the problem from the beginning. I'm hoping we can start again. Clean start with good policing."

Tom met each of their eyes, one by one.

"I'm in," Jorge said and flopped his bangs back.

"That's what I'm here for." Jackie smiled.

"Finally," Rob said.

Harri nodded. She didn't trust herself to say anything.

"Detective McDonald and his shenanigans took our

element of surprise. Christian LeGuerre knows what we want from him. He is our prime suspect at this time. We now need to build a case against him."

Tom stood up and moved to the front of the whiteboard.

"What do we know about Christian LeGuerre?" He gestured for them to answer. "I'll write, you call out."

"He knew all our girls. Went to school with them," Harri said.

Tom printed out Christian's name and underneath wrote: Opportunity – school with victims.

"Main suspect in another murder: Lorraine Benjamin," Rob said.

Tom wrote: Experience? Another victim.

"Alibied by Daniel Peters. He also was a classmate of all the victims. And brother of the two girls who ran away," Jackie added.

Tom wrote Daniel Peters on the board above Christian LeGuerre.

"From statements of Lorraine Benjamin's parents, Daniel Peters was the ringleader of their little gang. He was the alpha of the group," Harri added.

"We should add that Daniel Peters died in the Philippines in a car crash in 1996 with his brother, Reece, and father," Jorge said.

Tom added the death information next to Daniel Peters' name.

"These guys still fit Mitzi's profile as it stands," Tom said. "My impression of Christian LeGuerre is that he was a follower, not a leader. His entire being screamed insecure and pathetic at me. We need to place the gang in the vicinity of our disappearances. Re-interview witnesses for sightings of teenage boys."

Tom motioned to someone at the conference room door.

"Speaking of, Mitzi, come on in. I thought you'd left already," he said.

"Catching my plane in two hours. I've finished the report on Jeremy Evans, the plastic bin killer. I'm 99% sure that he had nothing to do with the girls in the creek."

"Glad we can put to rest that avenue of investigation," Tom said.

"He was in Mexico when the first girl went missing. Since we are going under the assumption there are two killers, I dug in deeper to see if he had details on the killings. He did not. I know him well enough to know that he isn't lying about that."

"Any changes to the profile?" Jackie asked.

Mitzi shook her head.

"As of now, the profile I delivered to you still stands. I'm waiting on some more information from the forensic pathologist's report for a clearer timeline on the order of the girls' deaths. The profile will be complete when we uncover who the first victim was. She's the key, I think."

"We still have two Jane Does," Jackie said. "If one of them is the first victim, we need to identify them before that profile will be completed."

"And the Peters girls?" Mitzi asked.

"Neither of the two bodies is that of an eight-year-old girl. Lindsey Peters can't be one of the Jane Does. Harri is working on corroborating the identity of Rebecca Stevens as Natalie Peters," Tom said.

"The Peters family is quite the mystery," Mitzi remarked. "I'll keep in touch to see if you can ferret out the first victim to help me narrow down the profile. Otherwise, I'm off to Maine."

"Thank you for the hard work, Mitzi," Rob said.

"Anytime. Nice to meet all of you," she waved and as she reached the door, she turned one last time.

"Harri, call me about what you find out about the Peters

girls. I can't stop thinking there's something weird there." Mitzi winked and left the room.

"Speaking of Harri, her house was broken into last night. I made copies of the message on the mirror."

Tom handed a copy of the message scrawled on Harri's bathroom mirror to the detectives.

Harri's hand trembled as she received the print-out.

If Tom noticed, he didn't mention it.

"Before we get to that, I wanted to add another connection to Christian and Daniel Peters. Christian LeGuerre's father worked with Franklin Peters at GRE. Neither man had a connection to the dumpsite, but GRE does have contracts with McDougall," Jorge added the information to the board in his barely-legible chicken scrawl.

"Thank you, Jorge. Lots of circumstantial evidence here. We need witness statements to place them in the vicinity," Tom said.

"This must have been unsettling, Harri," Jackie said, pointing to the printout.

"They violated my home, but they made their first mistake." Harri pointed to the letters. "The paint."

Tom pinned his printout to the board.

"I called in some favors down at the lab and expedited the workup. I received their call right before this meeting. The hand-mixed paint was a blend consisting of powdered cadmium red and a specialized walnut oil, both from Europe. I have a detective tracking those. Can't be too many people getting this stuff sent to Southern California."

"Why Harri's home, though?" Rob asked.

"That's the question, isn't it? This brings us to Harri's investigation into Jane Smith's story," Tom said.

Harri cleared her throat and recounted everything she'd been able to confirm of Jane's story, her strange meeting with

Detective Gallagher, and her conversation with Detective Larrabee.

"I also confirmed the Peters family deaths through the death certificates issued in the Philippines."

"What happened to the bodies?" Jorge asked.

"Cremated in the Philippines and buried here," Harri said.

"When did Charlaine Lewis die?" Tom asked Rob.

"Charlaine Lewis died in 1998. I spoke to her pimp, a Lucky Charles, and he recalled a man hunched over her body. He was not able to make ID because he was high at the time. I'm not even sure he saw what he said at all. But the carving on the chest is the same drawing as the mummified girls. The forensic pathologist confirmed the drawing was almost exact and made with a similar weapon.

"The Peters brothers were dead by 1998," Harri said.

"He could have found another partner," Jackie said. "Someone he could initiate into the fantasy that reminded him of Danny."

"I watched the tape and Christian did not come off like a bully. If you had said boo, he'd have jumped out of his seat in a second," Rob said.

"I agree with Jackie about him finding another sociopath to partner up with. This new partnership could explain why Charlaine Lewis' death was less theatrical in nature, while also having identifying characteristics similar to the Ballona Creek girls. The new sociopath enjoys strangling women, while the follower exacts his fantasy on the dead body," Tom said.

"How should we approach the case of Jane Smith?" Harri asked.

"If Jane Smith is Lindsey Peters, then she is central to our investigation. Her brother could very well be our original killer. A fifteen-year-old running away from home with her eight-year-old sister tells us that something was going down in that home," Tom said.

"Could Natalie Peters have seen something?" Rob asked.

"Hang on. Could Natalie Peters be our victim one?" Harri asked. "Sociopathic tendencies can be seen at home first. The family always knows."

"We need to prove that Jane is who she says she is. Keep working on getting that documentation, Harri."

Tom paused and glanced up to the board. "And Natalie Peters. Her hit-and-run. Can we tie Christian LeGuerre to it?"

Harri scribbled her to-do-list in her notebook. She looked up when he had finished.

"What about the other boy in the Peters' gang?" Harri asked.

"Mason Reynolds? See what you can dig up on him too," he said.

Tom turned to Jorge.

"Jorge, set up a surveillance detail for Christian LeGuerre with whatever uniforms we have available. He's been rattled by Detective McDonald and could contact his partner."

"On it," Jorge said.

Tom scribbled a note into his book.

"Rob, I'd like you to keep working on the Charlaine Lewis case. I'm hoping there is some biological evidence that our killer left behind that hasn't yet been tested. Unfortunately, the forensic pathologist has not been able to find any biologicals on the mummies. Also, please dive into Michael LeGuerre, Christian's dad, in light of his connection to Franklin Peters."

Tom turned to Jackie. "We need to identify our two last girls."

"I'm down to a hundred girls," Jackie said.

"Great work, Jackie," Tom said.

He cleared his throat.

"The case is moving forward due to all of your hard work. We will bring these girls home and bring their killers to justice." His voice was gruff and filled with emotion. "I know these kinds of cases are marathons and not sprints. Keep up the good work."

With those words of encouragement, the team disbanded and Harri followed her colleagues out the door.

Tom Bards taking over the case was more than she could have ever hoped for. A renewed vigor surged through Harri at the prospect of seeking justice for the victims without getting mired in too much politics. She hoped this situation could last for the duration of the case. A small smile played on her face.

"You look pleased," Rob said.

"I am," Harri said but didn't elaborate.

It would be bad form to gloat.

25

Jane Smith

DAY 4

O ne of my IT colleagues put me in touch with a skip tracer named Frank Ahrens. Mr. Ahrens had been amused to find out that I wanted to learn how to fake my own death and have it stick. We agreed to meet first thing in the morning.

His office was in a nondescript building off Hollywood Boulevard. The office was professional looking and made me breathe a bit easier. When I first approached my friend about skip tracers, she'd told me about numerous shady operations. This one, she'd promised me, was legit. The money spent on the waiting room was evidence this was not a fly-by-night operation.

I checked my phone. I was five minutes early for the meeting. I smiled at the dark-haired older woman sitting behind the reception desk. A brass nameplate in front of her stated her name as Mrs. Flowers.

"You must be Jane Smith?" Mrs. Flowers asked.

Her eyebrow raised at my name; I was sure.

"Yes. I'm a little early," I smiled.

"Would you like some coffee or tea?" she asked.

"No, I'm fine. Thank you," I said and sat down on the leather mid-century modern sofa.

A man with an 80s style mustache came out of a door to my left with a big grin on his face. He was big, 6-foot-four at least, and had a dominating air about him. His eyes, however, were kind and friendly. He held out his hand to me.

"Hi, Frank Ahrens at your service. You must be Jane Smith. Is that really your name?" he asked with a twinkle in his eye.

"No. My real name is Lindsey Peters," I said.

I waited to see if he recognized the name, but he didn't. He laughed a full belly laugh and brought me back to his large office overlooking the Capitol records building.

"Thank you for agreeing to meet with me. I know it's a strange request, Mr. Ahrens," I said.

"Call me Frank. Why do you want to fake your death?" he asked.

"I don't, exactly."

He raised his eyebrow at me and pursed his lips.

"It's not for me. Let me explain. I have family members who supposedly died twenty-two years ago. I want to know how they could have faked their death certificates and managed to stay dead all these years," I said.

Frank leaned over. "Tell me more. Pseudo-cide is a very difficult thing to get right and pull off. How long ago did these deaths supposedly happen?" he asked.

"They died in 1996 in the Philippines," I said.

"Ah. Okay, that makes more sense. The Philippines are known for their death certificate enterprises. So, what exactly happened?"

"According to the papers, my father and my two brothers died in a fiery car crash in the Philippines, while they were on vacation in 1996. Their death certificates were filed, and their ashes were sent home to Southern California."

"Why do you believe they are still alive?" Frank asked.

"I believe I saw my younger brother at Trader Joe's a few days ago."

"Did you go up and ask him?"

"I couldn't. Things were complicated between us. Can you help me? Is it possible to fake three deaths?"

I couldn't tell him the whole story. He wouldn't want to help a supposed fugitive and crazy person.

Frank cocked his head at me, watching me.

"This was in 1996?"

"Yes," I said.

"That right there is good reason to believe they were successful. 1996 was pre-internet days for most of the country," Frank explained. "Faking your own death today is very difficult to do because people tend to keep the same hobbies and friends. After a time, they want to have pieces of their old life back and get back on the internet."

"You mean like Facebook?"

"Exactly. Social media is a killer. The only way to stay dead is if you actually become a totally different person and hopefully in a small country that has no extradition for criminals," Frank said.

"What if they came back to Southern California?"

"That would be risky. What if someone recognized them like you just did?"

Frank sat back thoughtfully.

"These kinds of schemes need money."

"My family was well-off. My dad was a lawyer."

"For this to be successful, the money couldn't just be hanging out in the accounts. Do you know where the family money went after they died? Did it go to you?"

"No. It didn't."

I pushed the lump in my throat down. I didn't want to tell him the whole story but also didn't want to lie to him.

"That's the first thing I'd look into. Where did the money

go? Did it go into offshore accounts? Or go to the state? Why didn't you get the money?"

"I'd run away. No one knew where I was."

That was the truth.

"A good way to see if your family stayed dead is if the state of California seized the money and it's stayed there. Have family members come forward to get it? Or is it still there?" he asked.

"We had no other family. My mother's parents were dead. She was an only child. My father's parents were dead as well. He was an only child, grandparents were dead and long gone," I said.

"The money is the first step. The death certificates will probably be a dead-end because of how long ago it was. The players who helped them back then are most likely out of business by now."

"How would someone fake their death today?"

"Imagine it was you. You would go to the Philippines and hire a fixer. They have people at the local morgues that trade in human remains. One of those poor souls would become you and be cremated in your place."

"Is that when the death certificate is created?"

"Correct. And a story is then placed in the local paper of a car crash involving a United States citizen. Then you bugger off to the small country of your choice."

"And that all takes money?"

"That's right. Now, first place I go is the internet. I look at a web browser to see what country the now newly deceased has been researching. Then we analyze their social media accounts. Check their besties' phone records. People can't leave their old life alone," he said.

"But there was no internet back then?"

I didn't get my first email until 1998 at least.

"That's why in your case I'd start with the money," Frank said.

I nodded. Biting my lip, I dared to ask the hard question.

"Is it totally crazy to think that if my brothers were successful they could change their appearance?"

"Are you talking about plastic surgery?" he asked.

"I know that sounds very James Bond," I said.

My cheeks reddened. The last thing I wanted to do was come off as a crazy conspiracy theorist.

"If somebody really wants to stay dead and inhabit this new persona, then absolutely plastic surgery is a possibility. Nothing is too far out if you have the money," he said. "Money makes this sustainable for the long term."

"Have you seen that before?"

"In fact, I have. It was an insurance fraud case. He had his nose and cheeks done."

"How did you catch him?"

"He contacted his mom." He grinned at me.

I shook my head in disbelief.

"Really?"

"It's very hard to leave your old life."

"It sounds like it. How much would you charge to find the money trail?"

My heart felt like it was tripping over itself in excitement. I liked feeling in more control.

"I have a retainer of $2000. I bill day-to-day but let me take a crack at it and see. Usually, this kind of case takes at least a couple of days."

"You're that good?"

"Yes." He grinned at me.

"Great. Do you take credit, cash, or check?" I asked.

He held up his hand. "Let me get their information first. Your brother's names?" he asked.

"Daniel Peters and Reece Peters. Father's name was Franklin Peters."

I gave him our old address in El Segundo as well as my mother's maiden name. I couldn't remember anyone's birth dates.

"I'll get started on this today."

He shook my hand and said, "If they are alive, I'll find them." He rubbed his hands together. "I love a challenge."

He took me out to the front office and told Mrs. Flowers to take payment from me as a retainer.

"I'll give you a call tomorrow and let you know how it's looking," he said.

I smiled. I felt lighter than I had in a long time. My next move was to speak with Detective Harper.

26

PAB - Los Angeles, CA
DAY 4

D etective Harri Harper threw herself back in her office chair. All of her intel about Detective Peter Gallagher was coming back unremarkable. The few contacts she had up at the San Francisco Police Department all agreed he was a run-of-the-mill detective. Her investigation on the disappearing murder-book wasn't helping her theory, either. She chewed on the back of her pen as she contemplated the next steps. Even the missing murder-book had been explained.

A broken pipe destroyed the records room at the storage facility where Rebecca Stevens's murder-book resided. The officer in charge of records remembered several clerks attempting to recreate the basic files of the damaged murder-books. He remembered Rebecca Stevens's file since it was one of five that were almost unreadable. The ink had run, and the pages stuck together.

Harri couldn't believe that Peter Gallagher had told the truth about that.

"Dammit," Harri slammed her pen down on her desk.

Harri wanted to believe in a bigger conspiracy, but the facts were facts. Her last Hail Mary was a phone call she was waiting for from Detective Benji Okinawa, an old friend from the Academy who also worked with the SFPD. She hoped he could give her some dirt on Gallagher. She would not let go of her feeling that something was up with that guy.

"I hope you're doing better than I am," she said, with a flourish of her arm.

"I'm definitely not making as much noise as you are," Rob said, arching his eyebrow. "Although I'm not doing much better myself."

"Where are you at right now?"

"I have no biologicals to test on the Charlaine Lewis case."

"Really? The perp had experience then."

"Yes. There was no sperm or outside DNA found on her. No skin under her nails. The perp wore gloves."

"What do you have?" she asked.

Rob had even less than she did.

"The knife. I think he used it to carve the eyes on her chest. It connects to the kind of knife used on the mummified remains."

"That's something then."

Rob shrugged. "Barely."

"Was I crazy to think that Gallagher was shady?" she asked, the pen back in her mouth.

Rob shrugged. He picked up his file again. "I have to find something in this. It's all here."

"I guess my gut was wrong," Harri said, still bothered by the massive dead-end she'd hit.

"But your brain isn't. It found a discrepancy. You haven't figured out what the importance of it is. That's what the gut is. It's your physical reaction to something the brain doesn't fully understand yet."

Harri was buoyed by that. She knew it was the truth, but discouragement was always around the corner on cold cases. A detective had to push through them.

Harri nodded. "I still have to connect Rebecca Stevens to Natalie Peters definitively. I've hit dead-ends there, too."

"Speaking of, how are you doing on the Peters family deaths?" Rob asked.

"I've received notice there should be death certificates for the family in Manila. I can't exhume any bodies to match DNA to Jane Smith because they were cremated."

"Oh? In the Philippines?"

"Supposedly. The ashes are buried in the South Bay."

"Who brought them back here?"

"Good point," Harri said and scribbled down the question.

"Philippines, hey? An unusual vacation destination for back then," Rob said.

"It's an island. It's tropical, I think."

"This reminds me of an article I read in the Independent about the Philippines. They have a growing industry around faking deaths, but not sure if it's relevant since our case was decades ago. They died in 1996, right?"

"That's right. When was the article from?"

"2017."

"That's Jane Smith's theory, too," Harri said.

"It's an avenue to explore," Rob said.

Harri's cellphone rang. She lunged at the phone sitting on top of the files on her desk. Papers cascaded off her desk, hit the garbage can, and knocked it over.

"Dammit," she hissed.

She clicked it on to answer. "Harri speaking."

"Hey Harri, how you doing?"

It was Benji.

"Benji! Thanks for calling me back. LA is hot and smoggy,

you know? How's San Fran?" Harri asked, attempting to pat old coffee off the carpet with a handful of used napkins. She righted the trash can and saved some pages from the dripping coffee.

"I love it here. Don't miss the smog," he said.

"Wife and kids?" she asked as she threw the twice dirty napkins in the garbage and pulled her seat up.

"All good. This isn't a hey-how-are-you call is it, Harri?"

"No. I have a question about another cop. Are you in a place where you can talk freely?" Harri sat down. She turned to Rob who was barely holding in his laughter.

"Yeah, I am. Aren't you on the Ballona Creek task force?"

She flipped Rob off.

"How do you know that?"

"News travels," Benji said.

"I see. Peter Gallagher. What do you know about him?"

She turned back to her desk.

"Pete. He's a Southern California boy, too."

That piqued Harri's interest.

"Did he go to the Academy down here?"

"No. I mean, he grew up in the South Bay. Manhattan Beach, I think. He did his training up here."

"Southbay, do you know anything about his family?" she asked.

"He's mentioned his father worked in weapons of mass destruction. He thought it was pretty funny."

"Like GRE?"

"Yeah, companies like that. Not sure if that was the exact one, though."

Harri noted down the basics.

"Are you friends with him?" she asked.

"We play ball on the same team, but otherwise we don't talk much. He runs with vice and robbery, you know those guys," he said.

Harri knew exactly the kind of guys he was talking about. She didn't need any other description.

"Thank you. You've been so helpful," she said.

"Anytime, Harri," he said.

There was a pause for a second and then, "September is coming up. Are you going back up to Oregon again?"

"Yeah, like every year," she said.

At the Academy, she'd confided in Benji the real reason she became a cop. Benji had joined her in the search almost every year until he had his first kid. She appreciated his help over the years.

"Good luck. I hope you find her," he said.

"Thank you," Harri said. "That means a lot to me."

She hung up the phone and turned to Rob, a grin spreading across her face

"Your mood has changed," Rob said.

"Detective Peter Gallagher is a Southbay boy. He's from Manhattan Beach. Guess what else?"

Rob motioned for her to continue.

"His family is in the weapons of mass destruction business. Remind you of someone?"

"Like Christian LeGuerre's father," Rob said.

"That's right. Christian LeGuerre was in a gang. The Peters brothers and one last kid, a Mason Reynolds. I bet you, he's still somewhere in the South Bay."

She noticed she held her cellphone in a death-grip and dropped it on her desk. She stacked the files she'd been working on to the side to unearth her keyboard.

Harri fired up her computer and logged into the DMV database. She bounced in her seat getting rid of her nervous energy. Finally, some sort of lead.

She typed in Mason Reynolds and watched the search results propagate. Ten entries in the Los Angeles area showed up. Only one name corresponded with an address in the South

Bay. She clicked on the Mason Reynolds living in Manhattan Beach. A picture of a blond man in his late thirties popped up on her screen.

"Mason Reynolds lives in Manhattan Beach," Harri observed.

Of course, he does. Manhattan Beach was filled with bros like Danny Peters' little gang of miscreants.

"Most people stay near home most of their lives," Rob pointed out.

"True," Harri said.

She jotted down his address and telephone number. "I have a lead. Hello, Mason Reynolds."

Her stomach dropped toward the ground as butterflies rushed up through her body. She recognized the feeling from her last case when she'd stumbled upon the piece of evidence that brought her to her perp. She grabbed her jacket and keys. Her cellphone buzzed again.

"Detective Harri Harper?" a woman's voice asked.

"This is she," Harri said.

"This is Lindsey Peters."

Harri finally recognized the voice.

"You aren't going by Jane Smith anymore?"

"No. I've reclaimed my name. I'm downstairs at the desk. Can I come up and talk to you?"

"Sure, let me come get you," Harri said and clicked off.

She threw her jacket back on her chair.

"She's here?"

"That's right."

Rob stood up. "This should be interesting."

"Hope so."

Harri followed Rob out of the bullpen.

"I'll go find a conference room we can use," Rob said. "I think Conference Room Five is available. It's on the sixth floor."

"Great. I want to lead the interview."

"That will work. I'll take notes."

Harri walked toward the corridor as Rob turned toward operations.

27

Interrogation Room
DAY 4

Detectives Harri Harper and Rob Lakin sat across the small table from Lindsey Peters AKA Jane Smith in the largest interrogation room Rob could find. They didn't want to create any unnecessary pressure on Lindsey yet wanted to make sure the conversation was recorded.

"Interview with Jane Smith alias of Lindsey Peters commencing at 1:30 p.m. on August 9, 2018. Detective Harriet Harper and Detective Rob Lakin conducting the interview."

Harri noticed the woman's new appearance. Lindsey Peters was determined, a fierce gleam in her eye and the shifty fear she had come in with at first was gone.

"Lindsey, you requested this meeting. Do you have any new information for us?" Harri asked.

"Yes. My brothers did not die in the Philippines," Lindsey said.

"Do you have any evidence supporting that claim?"

"Sort of. I know you didn't believe me when I said I was Lindsey Peters. But I know who I am. I know my own story. I wanted to find someone to corroborate what I knew to be true so you would believe me." Lindsey lifted her shoulders and squared her chest.

Harri admired the woman for her self-assuredness.

"We have been unable to prove you are Lindsey Peters. But we are not giving up, yet."

Lindsey leaned in.

"You have been investigating my sister and Jennifer's death," she said.

"I have. I went up to San Francisco to speak with Detective Peter Gallagher who was the lead detective on your sister's case," Harri offered.

"And? Have you found anything?"

"You first. What makes you think that your brothers are still alive?" Harri asked.

Rob looked up from his note-taking to watch Lindsey's face.

"I found and interviewed a retired teacher who knew my sister and my brothers."

Harri didn't like the fact this woman was investigating, too.

"Interviewed? We must ask you not to interfere with our investigation."

"I know you didn't believe me and my story. I'm trying to find a way to change that," Lindsey said.

Harri caught Rob's eye. She registered Rob's barely perceptible nod. Let her talk, he was saying.

"What did she have to say?" Harri asked.

"She intimated to me that something was happening between my sister and my older brother Danny. According to her, Danny was a unique kind of bully. The teachers could never catch him at anything, but the students were terrified of him. My younger brother followed Danny around, but was harmless to her knowledge."

"Did she see him abusing her?"

"Not directly."

"Then that's hearsay."

"That gives you a path to follow though, doesn't it?"

"And what's her name?"

"Lucy Deacon."

Lindsey wrote down the address on the notebook to the right of her and pushed it toward them.

"We'll speak to her," Harri said. "Why do you think your brothers are still alive?"

Harri hoped that her voice was level and neutral.

"I'm being followed."

"Followed?" Harri asked.

Cracks showed in Lindsey's demeanor. "I'm not paranoid. One of Jennifer's friends was a retired CIA agent. Per Jennifer's request, he taught my sister and me evasive tactics. One of them was noticing when we were being followed. Another was losing the shadow. I've kept a low profile since my family's deaths. I've lived this long because of it. Since I came into your precinct, I've noticed a tail. I'm being followed. Is it the LAPD?"

"It's not us," Harri said. "I've been the only one following up on you. I didn't order any surveillance; you can rest assured."

"Then it's someone else. Someone who has killed everyone I've loved," Lindsey said.

Harri watched her struggle to keep her composure

"Is that why you think your brothers are still alive?"

"I think I might have seen Reece at the grocery store last week," Lindsey confessed.

Harri leaned in. This was something new.

"Are you sure?"

Lindsey deflated somewhat.

"I don't know. I think so? The last time I saw either of my brothers was decades ago. But," she paused, "he has my eyes."

"Your eyes?"

"The color. The pale blue is unique. I haven't seen any other person with that shade until the man at Trader Joes."

Harri had never seen eyes exactly like Lindsey's, either.

"Did you speak to him?" Harri asked.

"No, I ran away. I was terrified." She sat, biting her lip. "Who else knows that I came forward? Is it in any accessible files?"

"The detectives on the task force," Harri said.

"But did you put it in any computer files?" she asked again.

"Yes," Rob said.

"I see," was all she said, deep in thought.

"We don't know where you live, remember?" Harri reminded her.

"Right," Lindsey said, fear flickering in her eyes.

"Anyway, I talked to a skip tracer about the faking a death thing. He believes the way to prove they didn't die was to follow the money trail. We had no other relatives, so what happened to the money? Apparently, it takes money to purchase believable death certificates. If we find the money, we can catch them."

Harri saw that Rob was as skeptical about this as she was. She didn't want to lose Lindsey's trust, so she skirted the issue.

"Can I ask you some questions about your sister's hit-and-run?" Harri asked, hoping the change in topic would pull her back.

"I didn't go with Jennifer because I didn't want to see Natalie like that. I don't know how helpful I can be," Lindsey said.

"Did Jennifer tell you anything about the detective she spoke to?" Harri asked.

"She didn't speak much after that trip. Natalie's death devastated both of us. Then six days later Jennifer was gone," she said, her voice dropping.

By the look in her eyes, Harri knew that she was going back

in time again. To that terrible night when she lost her adoptive mother, as well.

"She didn't talk about the case or the detective?" Harri prodded.

Lindsey shook her head.

"One last question. The night of Jennifer's death, you mentioned a man coming after the both of you. Did you recognize the man?"

"Not really. It was so dark that night. I only caught a glimpse of his face. He looked familiar, but I couldn't be certain it was one of them."

Lindsey stopped talking and rubbed her face with her hands. She was nervous. Why?

"What's bothering you?" Harri asked.

"I know this sounds nuts, but I spoke to the skip tracer about this and he assured me he'd seen it before."

Harri caught Rob's eye. This should be good.

"With enough money and need, he's seen people undergo plastic surgery. With enough money, of course." Lindsey reddened.

"Plastic surgery?" Rob asked.

"Yes." Lindsey stood her ground.

"That's a bit far-fetched," Harri said.

"It is, but this case is crazy. I mean, mummies?"

Lindsey sat back and folded her arms across her chest.

Harri didn't have a good answer for her.

"We can check out your claims. We'll see where they take us," Harri said instead.

"That's all I'm asking. I wanted to let you know," Lindsey nodded.

"As far as your safety concerns," Harri began.

Lindsey put her hand up to stop her. "I'm going to keep being as vigilant as I have been. I will let you know if I see anything out of the ordinary. If someone is tracking my movements in the police department, then it wouldn't be very smart for me to have that same police department knowing my every move."

"You don't trust the police?" Harri asked.

"I don't trust anyone."

"Then why come to us?" Rob cut in.

"Because I want justice for all of us," Lindsey said, straightening her back and lifting her chin.

The interview was over.

"You're still not going to tell us where you live?" Harri asked.

"What do you think?"

"Thank you for coming in and talking to us," Rob said.

Harri followed his lead and stopped asking any more questions.

They led Lindsey out of the PAB and said their goodbyes. They watched as she hurried along Second Street, shoulders slumped forward and her back curved, then up toward the Disney Hall.

Foreboding descended on Harri. Lindsey was in danger, Harri felt it in her bones. She believed the woman when she spoke of being followed. If her brothers were somehow alive, they would go after her. Harri agreed with Lindsey on that. She couldn't think why Christian LeGuerre would. This case became stranger and stranger with each new twist.

Rob interrupted her thoughts. "She's a strange character."

"I would be too if even half of what she has said is true," Harri said.

Lindsey's last words had struck her. Her wanting justice for all the lives these killers had destroyed. Harri, all the detectives, and uniforms working the case wanted that.

"I'll help you track some of this down," Rob said.

"You're better with the money angle. Want to work on that

while I go whole hog on those death certificates? Do you think she saw Reece Peters?" Harri asked as they headed back inside.

"Her eye color is unique. I don't think I've ever met anyone with that shade," he observed.

"Me either," she said. "If they did fake their deaths, this is going to be one doozy of a case."

"It already is. If they are alive, how much you want to bet Christian LeGuerre knows something about that."

"They wouldn't dare come back here," Harri said.

"Why not? That's what trips all these fake death people up. Contacting friends and family. Coming back home. No place like home, am I right?" He winked at Harri.

She nodded, her mind racing with the possibilities.

28

Lindsey Peters (Jane Smith)
DAY 4

Standing in line at the West Hollywood branch of the Los Angeles Public Library, I scanned the faces of all the people present. It was an old habit, a handy one at times like this. I swore I'd go into hiding, but a book I'd been waiting on finally had arrived. And I was happy to be out of the house. I breathed in deep. The smell of books calmed me.

My favorite place in the world when I was a kid was the El Segundo Library. My sister Natalie took me there every Saturday morning for storytime and the library became my childhood refuge. I hoped I wasn't making a mistake by coming here, but I smiled despite my fear.

My apartment was a couple of blocks away from this branch. I tended to check books out online and go pick them up here. I'd been researching serial killers, sociopaths, and all other types of deviants to try to protect myself from my brothers by knowing exactly who the enemy was. I'd come up with a cover story of being a thriller writer researching a book. No one had questioned me thus far.

A young librarian with pale pink hair motioned me to come over to her station when it was my turn. The woman rocked old granny, punk style. She wore glasses, a button-down sweater over a pale-yellow gingham dress adorned with little pearls, and bright red lipstick. I liked her style immediately and wished I could be friends with her.

Don't be silly, my inner voice said. You can't have friends, remember, it whispered.

"Hi," she said.

I put the books down and gave her my library card.

She scanned my card and looked through the books. "Light reading you've got here," she remarked, picking up a book on how to disappear successfully.

The others were written by FBI profilers about their biggest serial killer cases.

"I'm researching a book. I'm a thriller writer," I explained.

"That is so cool, have you been published yet?" she asked.

"No, not yet. I'm just working on my first manuscript," I said.

"That's really cool," she said. "I hope you get some really scary stories out of this one," she said and checked the books out.

Scary stories, indeed, I thought. If only she knew.

I smiled and took my card back. I slipped the books into my backpack and took another look behind for anyone taking any interest in me. No one looked up from their work. Safe for now, I thought.

"Have a great day," I said.

She smiled back at me and I left. It had been a long time since I had such a warm interaction with a human being, and I missed it. I wanted a life again.

29

Conference Room - Los Angeles, CA
DAY 4

Detective Harri Harper was in the middle of researching the thriving fake death certificate trade in the Philippines when her cell phone rang. Detective Larrabee's name showed up on her phone screen.

"Hi Detective Larrabee, do you have anything for me?" she asked.

"I'm downstairs in receiving," he said.

"Wait, you're here? In Los Angeles?" she asked.

"Indeed, I am. After sending a mountain-load of paperwork to the powers that be, they okayed me to bring my box of evidence to you. Are you in the building?"

"I'm coming right down," she said.

"Thank you, Detective."

She raced to the elevator, her heart thumping with excitement. He found something big, otherwise, why would he be here?

Harri punched the down elevator button, jumping from foot to foot getting her nervous energy out. Breathe, she reminded herself. She stopped moving and focused on calming down all the way to the lobby.

She filled in the sign-in sheet for Detective Larrabee and found a rugged, Washington mountain man standing in the near-empty lobby. He had to be in his sixties with deep tan skin, salt-and-pepper hair, and wearing cowboy boots.

"It's so very nice to meet you, Detective Larrabee," she said, extending her hand.

He pumped her arm with his right hand while holding an evidence box.

"Is that what I think it is?" Harri pointed at the box.

"Yes, ma'am," he said. "It's been a lot of years, but at least one of the puzzle pieces fit somewhere."

Harri entered an empty conference room, with the detective right behind her. Detective Larrabee unsealed the evidence box and pulled out a stack of plastic evidence bags.

"I talked to one of Jennifer's old friends, a woman named Lila Jasper. She had the lockbox Jennifer had entrusted to her of the girls' real identities."

He fanned out the evidence baggies. Harri saw the birth certificates of Lindsey and Natalie Peters. Two passports and photos of the girls growing up.

"Let me go grab the files we've collected on the girls and the head of the task force," she said and ran out of the room.

It took her five minutes to get the files from her desk, and another ten minutes to bring Tom Bards from his office.

"I have proof that Natalie Peters was Rebecca Stevens. Please come meet Detective Larrabee from Seattle PD," Harri said.

"Good work, Harri," he said.

"It was all Detective Larrabee," she said.

Tom followed Harri back into the conference room.

"Detective Larrabee, this is Detective Tom Bards. He's head of the task force."

The two men shook hands and Harri pulled out the photo of Natalie Peters from the newspaper.

"Thank you so much for bringing this down to us, Detective Larrabee," Tom said.

He stared at the photo she held. The photo of Natalie and Lindsey surrounding a pretty blonde woman must've been taken the first year they had arrived in Washington. Natalie Peters was Rebecca Stevens.

"The girls ran away after all," Harri said almost to herself.

"The mystery of the missing pictures has been solved," Detective Larrabee said. "Looks to me like they were in hiding and that someone found Natalie and came after Lindsey, too. It's the first real lead I have in clearing that woman's name. I never felt right about pinning the killing on her."

"I'm not seeing any diaries or personal writings?" Harri asked.

"This was all there was," Detective Larrabee said. "I was hoping for some living trust documents or some sort of explanation of the girls' situation."

"That would help all of us, wouldn't it?" Tom quipped.

"Yes, it would have," Detective Larrabee said.

"Lindsey will be happy to have these back," Harri said.

"I can't imagine how she's been surviving all these years," Detective Larrabee said.

Tom pulled out his phone and took pictures of each one of the evidence bags.

"I'll put these in the files. We will go through the correct paper channels if this goes to court," Tom said.

As he finished up, Harri turned to Detective Larrabee. "How long are you staying in Los Angeles?"

"I'm back on a plane tomorrow morning. I wanted to bring these down myself to see if you could tell me about the kind of investigation you've got going on. I always find it's better to talk to cops face-to-face than over the phone," he said.

"Tom is in charge of the task force and can better gauge what we can share and what we can't," Harri said.

Tom straightened and pocketed his smartphone.

"We're working on the Ballona Creek case."

"I assumed you were," Detective Larrabee said.

"The Peters family has become central to our investigation. We needed to find what happened to the sisters. You helped us with that. Thank you."

"Is someone in their family a suspect?" Detective Larrabee asked.

"They are dead. But one of their friends is our prime suspect."

Harri noticed Tom didn't mention Christian's name or the theory they weren't really dead.

"Did the girls run from their own family then?" Detective Larrabee asked.

"We believe so. Lindsey has stated as much to us," Harri nodded.

"You're sharing a lot with me," Detective Larrabee observed.

"Every detective has a case they can't let go of. I have a couple of those myself. I want to help you close your case as much as I want us to close this case," Tom said. "You connected the girls to our case."

"I really appreciate that," Larrabee said.

"Did you ever come across a Danny or Reece Peters in your investigation?" Harri asked. She knew it was an extremely long shot, but figured she had to cover all her bases.

"No, those names never came up in the Jennifer Stevens case," Detective Larrabee said.

"Was there any physical evidence collected at the Jennifer Stevens' crime scene that was unaccounted for?" Tom asked.

"As I told Detective Harper here, there had been a lot of people in and out of that house, because the funeral had been that day. We have four or five fingerprints that have not been accounted for, but we can pinpoint that they were left that day," he said.

"How?"

"The maid had come the day before to clean the place up. Swore she wiped down the surfaces that we got the fingerprints off of."

"Could you have your lab send those fingerprints down here? We'll check them against our suspect," Tom said.

"Sure thing."

"I'm not holding out hope, but sometimes we get lucky," Tom said. "Thank you for bringing these down for us and great work, Detective."

Tom left Harri and Detective Larrabee sitting at the table.

Harri sat staring at the picture of Natalie and Lindsey and Jennifer. Natalie did look haunted. She wouldn't look at the camera. Her eyes were downcast, and she was extremely thin. What had those boys done to her?

"I'm not an emotional man but finding those images after all this time made me take a beat," Detective Larrabee said.

"I can only imagine. Had you talked to her friend before?" Harri asked.

"Yes, we did, but she held the lockbox back from us back then. After all the years that had gone by, she thought there was no point in keeping Jennifer's secrets anymore," he said.

"Jennifer must've been quite a woman to have taken those girls in," Harri said.

"From everything I've dug up about her, she was quite the character," he said.

Harri stood up and so did Detective Larrabee.

"If you need anything else, have any questions, or want to run anything by me, I'm staying with my son in Pasadena. Snuck in a family visit while down here."

He handed her his business card with a phone number and

an address written on the back. "This is their number, in case you have to find me immediately."

They shook hands and Harri led him out of the PAB. Detective Larrabee sauntered off into the late Los Angeles sun and Harri went back upstairs, suddenly extremely tired.

Lindsey Peters was telling the truth, and they had run from real monsters. Harri blanched at how scared the girls must have been, and when one of them went to the cops, they were not believed. She had not believed her.

Guilt sucker-punched her in the gut.

She hadn't believed a victim.

But she hadn't given up on corroborating her story, either. It was a consolation, but only a small one.

On one hand, they were getting close to finding out what happened all those years ago. On the other hand, they most likely blew Lindsey's cover and put her in mortal danger.

30

Beachwood Canyon

DAY 4

arri Harper reached her desk and found a message from Jake Tepesky waiting for her.

"I guess I didn't scare you off," Harri said to herself as she listened to his message. She picked up her phone and dialed his number. "Hi, it's Harri."

"Hey there, you up for maybe grabbing some dinner? Or I could cook something here and you can bring those boxes over," he said.

Harri hesitated. The direction of the investigation had heated up enough that she didn't want to lose any momentum. On the other hand, she wanted to see Jake. She had some questions of her own to ask him.

"Sure, I have to eat. I need to get back on shift later, so maybe we grab something quick at your house?"

"I'm a pretty good cook now," he said.

Harri laughed, remembering how that was a going joke with her sister Lauren and him in high school. Jake's ultimate goal had been to live on doughnuts and breakfast burritos.

"I'll see you in forty-five minutes," she said.

She got off the phone and informed Rob of her plans.

"New boyfriend?" Rob's voice was high, imitating a girl's.

"Old friend from high school actually," Harri said.

"Uh-huh," Rob said.

He winked at her and focused back on his work.

"It's not like that," Harri said although she blushed.

Maybe it was and she hadn't fully taken stock of her feelings. They were too complicated with the trip to Oregon and the current case. Even so, a smile played on her face. She was looking forward to seeing him. He made her remember happier times.

The drive home was fast, her sinking feeling familiar. It had been the same feeling she had coming to her parents' home after Lauren disappeared. And now, each time she drove up her own driveway, that same feeling came back.

Dread, she thought, as she walked up her steps. She needed to scrub the intruder out of her home and fast. Otherwise, she'd have to sell and move on. Home was too important to her survival.

Harri opened up her door and disengaged her alarm. Her home still smelled of fingerprint powder. She opened all the windows on the first floor to air it out, before moving on upstairs.

Calling the cleanup crew was the first priority, she thought and made a reminder on her phone. She then proceeded up to the second-floor library to retrieve twenty years' worth of case files on Lauren's disappearance.

She carried six banker's boxes down to her car and caught her reflection in the hall mirror. Presentable enough, she thought and smoothed down her hair. This was how she looked tonight. Harri was about to engage the alarm again when she remembered all the open windows.

"Damn," she said and went back through the house closing

them back up again. She engaged the alarm and checked her watch. Twenty minutes late wasn't too bad.

She mapped Jake's Beachwood Canyon address and drove over. He had done well for himself. Harri parked in front of a three-level Mediterranean home with a gnarly amount of stairs. She called Jake.

"Hi, are you here?" he asked.

"Sure am, but you didn't tell me about your stairs. I have six very heavy banker's boxes in my car waiting for you to take them up," she said.

Jake laughed. "I'm coming down."

Harri shut off the engine and stepped out of the car. She opened the trunk but didn't take any of the boxes out. Jake appeared on the bottom steps, a wide grin on his face.

"You made it," he said.

"This is going to be quite the workout," Harri said, gesturing to her trunk filled with boxes.

"I won't have to go jogging tomorrow morning," he said and grabbed the nearest box.

Harri found the lightest box and followed Jake up the three levels of winding stairs. Catching her breath wasn't the easiest thing when she reached the top. Harri was a lot more out of shape than she realized. Jake opened the front door and dropped his box on his dining table. She put hers next to his. He motioned to a jug of water.

"Help yourself. I'll get the rest."

"Are you sure?" Harri asked.

"Absolutely. I know you have to be back on duty, so wine is out of the question. I can make some tea or coffee when I get back."

He bounded down the stairs again for the rest of the boxes as Harri poured herself a glass of water. Jake was back in no time at all. He must've run up the stairs. She watched him, amused as he fought to catch his breath.

"Is that some wheezing I hear coming out of you?" she asked, laughing.

"Stairs are rough. And, I have more to get."

He disappeared again and each time he brought a box in, it took him longer to come back.

Jake looked a little pale after the last box. He flopped down and guzzled the rest of the water in the jug.

Harri gave him time to recover before saying anything.

"Can I get you more water?" Harri asked.

"I'm good," he sputtered. "Heavy boxes…"

"Take your time," Harri said.

She sat back in her chair and checked out Jake's house. She could see into the living room and the kitchen. The kitchen hadn't been modernized and appeared original. The living room looked cozy even if it had a fifteen-foot ceiling. The over-sized sectional flanked the fireplace. Bookcases took up the visible walls.

"I like your house. It's cozy. Did you decorate yourself?"

"Absolutely. I'm all about comfort. I want my home to be a home, if you know what I mean."

"I do."

"Ok, I can breathe again. I hope you're okay with chicken and salad leftovers. I planned a feast, but a client called at the last minute and I couldn't get down to the market."

"Leftovers sound great. I'll definitely take you up on the offer of coffee as well."

"Excellent," Jake said and groaned as he rose from the chair.

Harri followed him into the kitchen where he pulled out a roast chicken and a bowl of salad.

"These leftovers are serious. I'm impressed," Harri said.

"I'm a reformed man. I've evolved since high school."

He grinned at her, and Harri's heart skipped a beat. She ignored it.

"I can set the table," Harri offered.

Jake pointed to the cupboard near her head. "Plates are up there," he said.

Jake warmed up the chicken as Harri set the table. They were eating within minutes. The coffee Jake made was equally delicious.

Harri smiled. "I really needed this today. Thank you, Jake."

"My pleasure. It's been great catching up. I thought speaking with you would be incredibly painful."

"Uh, thanks," Harri broke in.

"You know what I mean," Jake said.

"I know. It's been great though," Harri nodded.

"It has been. It's been good to catch up," Jake said.

His look was intense enough to make her focus on her coffee. Harri changed the subject.

"Our case broke in my direction today. I can't go into particulars, but my lead is central to the Ballona Creek case."

"That's a big break," Jake said.

"It is," she smiled. "Would you mind if I asked you a question about your expertise?"

"I'll help in any way I can."

"What personality type abuses their own sister?"

"This must be about Natalie and Lindsey Peters?"

"Did Mitzi consult you on the profile?"

"She did. I still have my security clearances and credentials with the BSU. You can share case details with me. I'm listed as one of the profilers on this case."

"I didn't know that," Harri said, relieved. "Natalie and Lindsey Peters ran away from home because of their older brother Danny. At least, that's the direction we are going in right now. Could an eighteen-year-old develop enough skills to abuse his sister and get away with it?"

"I agree with Mitzi's profile of a sociopath and a follower. However, the more I thought about the profile, I'm still not sure an eighteen-year-old could pull off that large number of abductions in such a short period without making a mistake. The lack of mistakes is what troubles me. Have you considered the sociopath could be the father, and both of the brothers were followers? That makes more sense to me," he said.

Harri sat back, deep in thought.

"The care and patience successful abductions take are monumental. Without being sloppy, that is. Patience is not what eighteen-year-old boys are known for," Jake said.

"That's why Natalie didn't go talk to her father about her brother. I wondered if the father was absent, but if he was one of the perpetrators that could cause her to disappear like that."

"Exactly," he said.

Harri sipped the last of her coffee. Silence fell between them.

"You still surf anymore?" she asked, knowing she'd have to leave soon.

"I haven't surfed since Lauren disappeared," he said.

"Really?"

That surprised her. Surfing was all Jake cared about when she knew him.

"Lauren and I surfed together. We fell in love with the ocean at the same time. We started as sophomores, remember? That's ancient to start surfing here. Other surfers made fun of us, but we kept at it. We grew closer. Every time I see the water, I see Lauren's face."

"I can't tell you the last time I went to the beach," Harri confessed. "I feel Lauren there, too."

He took her hand and squeezed it. "Give me the date and I'll be there," he said.

"For September?" Harri asked.

Jake nodded.

"I usually leave the weekend before she disappeared and

stay for two weeks. Interview everyone and hope I can get any new leads. If I keep at it, eventually someone is going to say something they've been holding back from me."

"Have you uncovered new leads that way?" he asked.

"I have. They are all in the files. I'm hoping you can suss out some new leads."

"I'll dig into the files tomorrow."

"Are you really coming up with me?" she asked.

"Yes, I am."

Jake held her hands in his and looked into her eyes. "I want to bring her home as badly as you do," he said.

His touch sent a shiver up her arm and into her body. Harri fought back tears.

"Thank you," she said.

"Always," he said.

He let her hands go. It was time for Harri to go back to work.

"Let's not talk about Lauren's case until you've read through all the files. I don't want to color your impressions," Harri said.

"I agree. Once I'm done, I'll give you a call. Maybe, we can meet for dinner and go over all the theories. Best to do that before we leave," he said.

"Before I go, I apologize for my tone yesterday about staying at your place. You were kind to offer. I don't want him to win," she said.

Jake pulled her into a hug and held her tight. "I figured as much," he said into her hair.

Harri basked in his warm embrace. When he pulled away, she missed his warmth.

He walked down the stairs with her.

"You're a glutton for punishment," she said.

"I like being a gentleman," he said.

"I like that you're a gentleman," Harri beamed.

They said their goodbyes and Harri got into the car. He watched as she drove away down the narrow street.

She looked back in her rearview mirror to see him still standing there, watching as she drove away.

31

PAB - Los Angeles, CA
FRIDAY, AUGUST 10, 2018 - DAY 5

Detective Harri Harper swung her purse underneath her desk. She took stock of her workstation. Two old coffee cups and a granola bar sat nestled among the stacks of files and binders, obscuring her mouse and keyboard. She threw the old coffee out into her trashcan and placed her new cup in the empty spot. Her stomach grumbled. Dinner hadn't been enough to keep her going through the night. The granola bar wasn't too appetizing, though. She checked the time. 11 p.m. She would have to find something to eat.

She flopped into her chair instead. Her mind wandered to Jake and their dinner, but she pulled herself back.

"Focus," she muttered to herself.

She grabbed the first file she didn't recognize and when she saw its contents, she smiled. One of her uniforms tracked down the Peters' death certificates.

"Good job, Officer Reyes," she said.

She scanned the contents. Each of the three death certificates said the same thing, death from blunt force trauma due to vehicular collision. The original police report had been appended to Franklin Peters' certificate. Harri read through the document for inconsistencies.

Multiple spectators witnessed a rental car driven by an older white man, Franklin Peters, crash head-on with a small red Fiat traveling the opposite direction. No names were listed as witnesses, Harri noted.

The three males were transported to the local hospital where they were pronounced dead. The coroner's name was listed as Jose Atia. The police report listed the head detective as Joven Rodriguez from a regional police station. Finding the original detective was a long shot, but worth a try.

Harri looked up the time in Manila. It was two o'clock in the afternoon the next day. Working night hours had some benefits.

Harri dialed the phone number listed on the police report. A voice responded in Tagalog.

"Do you speak English?" Harri asked.

"Yes, some," the voice answered.

"Can I speak to a Detective Jose Atia?" she asked.

"No officer working here," was the answer.

"What about a detective assigned to a foreign crime, American deaths?" Harri asked.

"Hold please," the voice said.

A cheery song played on the hold line. Harri waited several minutes before a man picked up the line.

"Hello, Detective Marcus Buado speaking." He answered in much clearer English.

"My name is Detective Harriet Harper of the Los Angeles Police Department. I'm looking into the 1996 vehicular deaths of three members of the Peters family, Franklin Peters, the father, and his sons Daniel and Reece Peters."

"1996 was a long time ago," Detective Buado said.

"Do you have a liaison at your police department that takes care of Americans who die in car crashes?" she asked.

"You're speaking to him. What kind of information are you looking for?" he asked.

"I'm trying to determine if they actually died," she said.

"Death kits," Detective Buado said. "It's a booming business here for sure. Life insurance scams have been going on here since the '80s. Not sure how I can help on a case from so many years ago, though."

"I found the police report attached to the father's death certificate with Jose Atia's name listed as lead investigator. Do you know him?"

"No, I don't, but I could ask around," he said. "Could you email me the original file?? It will save me some time."

He dictated an email address to her.

"Will do, Detective Buado."

"Also, I'll have one of our insurance investigators contact you. Their division has more resources than mine does."

"By resources, I'm assuming you mean money?" Harri asked as she used her smartphone scanner app to photocopy the documents and send them to her LAPD email address.

"That's correct."

"I see. Please have them reach out to me," she said.

She opened her email on her desktop computer and found the email she'd forwarded to herself. She typed in his email address and pressed send.

"I just emailed you a scan of the police file. It only contained one page."

"I'll give you a call if I find anything," Detective Buado said.

"Thanks," she said and hung up the phone.

Harri flipped open her notebook and read over her notes from earlier. She'd come to the same conclusion as Lindsey Peters. She would follow the money trail. Harri's research found professional death kits available through fixers in the Philippines for $30,000 per individual. And if Lindsey was right about her brother changing his appearance, facial reconstruction surgery would cost a pretty penny for the three men as well. Over $90,000 in cash was a significant sum to track.

Harri didn't have the experience of investigating a money trail that far back, but she assumed probate court records were the place to start. If the entire estate was sent there, that meant the money was still sitting in the state coffers.

If not, then someone claimed that money.

Now, if they had siphoned the money off into offshore accounts before their "deaths" then there wouldn't be much of an estate to find.

A forensic accountant was who she needed to call. She checked the time. It was past one o'clock in the morning. She'd make those calls later in the morning before her interviews with Natalie's high school friends.

Harri stood up and grabbed her jacket. Two questions were nagging her.

Why did Natalie run that night? If she'd been abused for months before, why that night?

She hoped some of her friends might have the answers to that.

The other big question she needed to answer was: If the brothers and father faked their deaths, why wait until 1996?

She rubbed her eyes. It was time to go home.

Harri pulled her purse out from below her desk and left the empty bullpen. She walked down the deserted hallway, the building around her silent. Not many cops left at this hour.

She entered the elevator and pushed the button for the lobby. She leaned against the wall; eyes closed. What had happened in 1996 to spook them?

The elevator lurched to a stop. Harri's eyes flew open. Jackie Render walked in.

"You're here late."

"You too," Jackie said. "I messed up. I was supposed to be home about an hour ago. My daughter was waiting for me."

"Aren't your kids in bed now?" Harri asked.

Jackie had a 10-year-old girl and a 15-year-old girl.

"My oldest is having boy problems and can't sleep. I promised her I'd be home in the next half hour," Jackie said.

"I'm sorry."

"Me, too." Jackie bit her lip.

"I'll walk out with you."

"Case have you spooked?" Jackie asked.

She didn't sound like she was kidding.

"You too?"

Jackie nodded.

They made it out of the building in less than five minutes.

"Which parking lot are you in?" Jackie asked.

They stepped out into the cool night air. No one was in sight. Isn't it August in LA? Is the night air cool?

"The usual one on Main Street," Harri said.

"Me too," Jackie said.

They walked the pathway toward Main.

Harri shivered. The day had been hot and dry, and the air was now cool and muggy. She wished she'd brought her jacket.

"I think that Natalie Peters is the key to crack this open," Jackie said.

"I agree," Harri said. "I scheduled interviews with Natalie's high school friends tomorrow and her boyfriend at the time. I'm working on a timeline of when the abuse started."

They reached Jackie's car. "Good luck, I'll see you at the meeting tomorrow," Jackie said.

"Drive safe," Harri said.

Jackie opened the door to her BMW.

Harri waved goodbye and headed for her car. She rubbed the bleariness out of her eyes. Home. She wanted her bed.

'FIND ME' scrawled on her bathroom mirror flashed in her mind.

Harri shook off the image. Her home would be her sanctuary again. They weren't going to take that away from her. Mind made up; she drove out of the parking lot.

She would reclaim what was hers.

32

Silver Lake, CA

DAY 5

Detective Harri Harper, still wearing her bathrobe, woke up in her bedroom to her alarm blaring at 6 a.m. At least, she'd managed to shower before passing out.

Yesterday, the cleaners brought her home back to the way it was before the intrusion. They also took down her bathroom mirror at her request. She'd get a new one. A fancy one to replace the one that had been defiled.

She dressed for the day and ate her usual breakfast of toast and coffee. The download meeting started at 8 a.m. She'd told Tom Bards she'd like to skip it to go start her interviews with Natalie's high school friends. First on the list, Nancy Lyons, Natalie's best friend. Nancy was a stay-at-home mom and Harri wanted to catch her before her day started.

Harri gulped the last sip of coffee, grabbed her keys, and set the alarm with her new code. She glanced around the space and smiled.

This was her home.

Her sanctuary.

She closed her eyes and imagined the light filtering into her living room, the red Gerbera daisies on the coffee table. Her sister, Lauren's laughter sounded in her ears. Lauren loved Gerbera daisies. They reminded her of a rainbow sun, she'd always said.

Harri opened her eyes and smiled. She'd found the Gerbera daisies on her front stoop with a note from Jake last night. He'd had her smiling more in the last week than she'd done in ages. It felt strange but in a good way. She breathed the fresh air and took in the deep blue of the sky. It was a gorgeous morning. She clicked her car open and slid inside. If she was lucky, she'd miss the morning traffic going south.

AN HOUR AND A HALF LATER, Harri turned onto Sheldon Street and inched forward until she found the number on the curb.

No one from the task force had spoken to Nancy Lyons yet, which Harri was glad about. Nancy would be fresh and unguarded. Harri hadn't called first to schedule a meeting either for this same reason.

Nancy Lyons' home was on a small cul-de-sac street lined with tall trees. It was a pretty little neighborhood like the rest of El Segundo. The horrors of what happened to the mummi- fied girls and the Peters sisters were unimaginable on this sunny street in front of this Martha Stewart-like pale blue house. Harri parked a few houses away.

Harri lifted the ring of the brass knocker and knocked three times.

A dark-haired woman with a baby on her hip opened the door. "May I help you?" she asked, fear crossing her face.

Harri pulled out her LAPD badge.

"Are you Nancy Lyons?" she asked. "I'd love to talk with you about an old friend of yours."

"Oh, thank god," the woman said, holding her hand to her

chest. "I thought something happened to my husband. Yes, I'm Nancy Lyons. Please, come inside."

Nancy's brown eyes twinkled as she stood aside to let Harri in. She kissed her child on its downy soft hair. The baby looked angelic with the same brown eyes and rosy cheeks.

"So cute! How old is she?" Harri asked.

"He's a boy," Nancy laughed.

"Oh gosh, so sorry," Harri said as she entered a bright, decorative living room.

"It's his hair. It's so beautiful and curly, I haven't had the heart to cut it. Everyone thinks he's a girl," Nancy explained.

"I can understand why," Harri said.

Nancy led Harri through the living room and motioned for her to sit at a kitchen table filled with the detritus of breakfast. Nancy strapped her baby into his highchair.

"Mind if I keep feeding him?" Nancy asked.

"Please, go ahead."

Harri opened her notebook as Nancy picked up a baby spoon and a bowl of orange mush.

"You were friends with Natalie Peters?" Harri asked.

She watched the woman out of the corner of her eye.

"I wondered if that's who you were here about," Nancy said.

Harri took note of her nonchalance. She wasn't sure if she bought it. Time to drop a bomb.

"Her sister indicated that you were her best friend in high school."

Nancy's hand froze in front of her baby's face. There it was.

"Wait, they are alive? But the paper said their bodies were found in Ballona Creek?" Nancy asked, pulling her eyes from her son to Harri's.

"The newspaper ran the story before all the forensics were in. The girls ran away from home in the summer of 1992.

Their father reported them missing and they got lumped with the other missing girls.

"That makes sense," Nancy said.

Harri cocked her head.

Nancy sounded calm but her body language spoke of stress. Her back had noticeably stiffened and she kept touching her face.

"I mean, Natalie running away. She was really troubled that last semester," she explained.

"Do you know why? Did she ever tell you what was happening to her?"

"She never spoke about it. I asked her so many times. But she always pushed me away. She lost a lot of weight that semester and turned her back on me. Natalie broke up with her boyfriend, stopped going out, and kept to herself," Nancy said.

"Do you remember her boyfriend's name?" Harri asked.

Nancy swiped at her hair again with the back of her hand. Her eyes blinked several times. What was she lying to Harri about?

"Michael Grady," Nancy said and finished giving her baby the last of the orange goop.

Harri wrote the name down.

"What kind of relationship did Natalie have with her brother Danny Peters?" Harri asked.

Nancy looked relieved to be moving off the boyfriend. Interesting.

"Natalie hated him. Danny beat her up all the time. He was a nasty bully, especially after their mom passed."

"When did their mom die?"

"The mom passed when Natalie was eleven and Danny was fourteen, I think. Their dad wasn't around much, and the family disintegrated."

"In what way?" Harri asked.

"I mean Danny. He went off the rails. Danny was always popular and got a lot of attention. After the mom died, he got mean. Danny stayed popular, but he brutalized kids less popular and weaker than him," Nancy said.

She wiped her baby's face and took him out of his seat.

"What about Reece?" Harri asked.

"You know, I don't really remember Reece that well. He was younger than us. I remember Reece had the most piercing blue eyes I'd ever seen. Same as little Lindsey's. They were like glassy blue diamonds. Reece was a gorgeous kid, but quiet and shy. I think Danny was bullying him, too."

"Around what date did Natalie start not eating and pulling away?" Harri asked.

"About two months before she disappeared. I remember the day so clearly. I walked over to her house to get her. We always walked to school together. Natalie sat on the front step, bawling her eyes out."

Nancy's words flowed now. She had gotten into a groove in the interview. Harri didn't see the stress and lying signs she'd seen when speaking about Michael Grady. Hopefully, Michael could help her understand why.

The baby gave a small cry and wiggled in his mother's arms.

"Do you mind if we move into the living room? I can put him down. It will be easier to talk."

"Of course," Harri said.

They shifted to the sunny living room filled with house-plants. The pale yellow of the walls and upholstery played well with the green of the plants.

Harri smiled as she watched Nancy place her son amongst his toys.

She sat on the edge of a loveseat and turned back to Harri. "She wouldn't tell me what was wrong, but I'd never seen her so afraid before. After she disappeared, rumors started circulating about a teacher having a relationship with another girl at the school. His name was Paul Adams, I think. I wondered if he had anything to do with her running until all the other girls started disappearing. Then, I thought the worst like everyone was."

"Why did you wonder about Paul Adams?" Harri asked.

"He and Natalie argued the week before. She was bitching about how he was treating her unfairly. When I asked for specifics, she clammed up."

Nancy stared at her son. "That day with her crying on the steps was the turning point in our friendship."

"Do you remember the exact date?" Harri asked.

"Oh gosh, I would have to look at a calendar. It was a Monday, around seven weeks before she disappeared," Nancy said.

"Does Michael Grady still live in El Segundo?" Harri asked.

"Last I heard, Michael lived down in Hermosa Beach. He's a lawyer now. He did very well for himself," Nancy replied.

Harri detected a hint of wistfulness.

"If Lindsey is alive, is Natalie alive too?"

"Unfortunately, Natalie was killed in a hit-and-run years ago," Harri said.

"Oh," Nancy said. "Oh, I'm sorry to hear that. I wasn't a very good friend to her in the end. We were only fourteen at the time, but it's not an excuse. Back then, there wasn't much information about anorexia or depression. I wish I could have helped her in some way."

"Was there anybody else in school that Natalie Peters was close to? Maybe a teacher?"

Nancy shook her head.

"I don't remember. I was seeing someone and was too self-involved to notice. I'm sorry. I don't think I'll be able to help much more."

"I understand. Thank you for meeting with me. If something turns up, can I come back if I need more details or insight?" Harri asked.

"Absolutely. I'd love to help in any way that I can," Nancy said.

Harri stood up to go.

"One last thing. Did Natalie ever mention rape?" Harri asked.

Her bluntness made Nancy glance up, brow furrowed.

"No, she never mentioned it. That doesn't mean it didn't happen. The amount of trauma she went through those last weeks, I honestly wouldn't be surprised."

Her baby howled and Harri knew it was time to go.

"I'll show myself out," Harri said.

"Thank you for telling me about Natalie. My heart ached to know she'd been found like that in Ballona Creek. Not saying dying young from a hit-and-run isn't horrifying enough, but the alternative…" Nancy's voice faded to quiet.

Harri understood what she was trying to say.

"Thank you for your time," Harri said and walked through the small home to the front door.

Her heart beat in excitement, and she breathed in deep to catch her breath. She was on the right track. She felt it in her gut. She had the name of a teacher, Paul Adams, and her boyfriend, Michael Grady. More importantly, Harri was convinced Natalie knew something about the disappearances of the other girls. Maybe, Natalie had talked to her boyfriend about what she'd seen. She needed to speak to Michael Grady.

Harri checked the time. It was only 10 o'clock. If Michael Grady was a lawyer, he'd be in his office by now. Harri got in her car and looked up Michael Grady's office in Hermosa Beach. At this hour, she'd be there in fifteen minutes. Harri started the car, mind racing.

33

Lindsey Peters (AKA Jane Smith)
DAY 5

I activated my security system, came out of my door, locked the three deadbolts, and bounded down the steps. Crossing the street was the punk rock librarian. Today she wore cat-eye glasses, a pale blue cardigan over a red-flowered dress straight out of the 1950s. She was focused on her phone and hadn't seen me yet, which saved me from saying anything. I scurried toward the garage when the librarian caught sight of me and smiled.

"Hi there. How's the writing going?" she asked.

I stood there, mouth slightly agape. She knew where I lived. Then another thought struck me. My hand fluttered to my wig. I had the blond ponytail on today and I couldn't remember if the last time I'd seen her I was wearing the dark-haired bob. I forced my mouth to move.

"Oh, you know, it's always difficult to sit down to write, but once I get going, I'm good. The books have been very useful," I said.

This was West Hollywood and lots of people dressed up and wore wigs. I hoped. That's what I would say if she asked.

"So how does one disappear?" she asked.

My face flushed.

"M…m…most people don't do it successfully apparently," I said. "In most cases, the disappeared can't let go of their old lives."

"Is that how they get caught?"

"Yes, they end up contacting an old friend or parent or an ex-lover and blow their cover. After they spend an enormous amount of money on fake papers."

"Figures," she said. "I'm Marjorie by the way. Do you live here?"

My heart beat faster. I wanted to tell her the truth. *You can't do that*, my sister's voice sounded in my ear.

But she's a librarian, I reasoned. She'd probably seen my address when they scanned my card anyway. I didn't want to lie anymore. I didn't want to be weird or strange.

"My name is Jane. And yes, I do live here," I said.

The truth sounded exhilarating. I hoped I wouldn't regret that. *You will*, my sister's voice chastised me.

"I have more books coming so I'll see you next week," I said.

My face grew heated. That sounded desperate.

"Excellent, I'll see you then," she said and smiled.

Marjorie waved goodbye and walked up the street. Her name suited her perfectly.

A small smile played across my face as I headed to the underground parking space where my car sat waiting for me. I stopped. I should take the subway instead, or the bus into Hollywood. Public transport kept me nimble in case I needed to lose a tail. Disappearing was harder in a car.

I SAT in Frank Ahrens waiting room ready for my 10 a.m. meeting, surprised he'd found something so quickly. My coworker had praised his speed and expertise and she hadn't been wrong. My leg pumped up and down as I fought to not bite my lip. The cookies and coffee Mrs. Flowers, his secretary, had brought me hadn't helped my nerves much. Sugar had made the willies in my stomach all that much worse.

Finally, Frank Ahrens opened the door to his office and motioned me inside.

"I wasn't expecting to hear from you so soon," I said.

"I'm that good, Ma'am," he said.

He sat down behind his desk. "Since this was 1996, I used more human psychology to get the information I needed than the usual deep dive into electronic records."

I took the only other available seat.

"Human psychology?" I asked.

"When you call someone on the phone and ask for their manager and sound convincing and get information out of them," he said.

He handed me a folder. I opened it to find bank statements and account printouts inside, all under the name of Jasper Inc.

"Is this where all of my father's money went to?" I asked.

"You got it. Your father acted like a good small-town citizen and used the local bank for all his finances. The nice lady had no problems talking to me about an account closed long ago," he said.

"Really? I thought privacy laws would stop anyone talking about a former client?"

"Your documentation as his only surviving relative helped my case immensely. Glad those detectives found your birth certificate. They gave us access to the closed account."

He raised his eyebrow at me waiting for an explanation as to why LAPD sent him my birth certificate and passport. I kept my mouth shut.

"Banks keep records going back quite a long time. I was initially worried about the time frame. We got lucky, I suppose," he finished.

I looked over the documents. "I'm not seeing what I'm supposed to be seeing," I said.

"From these financial statements, your family was bankrupt by the date of their deaths. The house and the cars were sold off by the bank to cover the mortgage and the outstanding debts that your father had accrued."

My shoulders sank. "There was no money for this ruse then?" I furrowed my brow in confusion.

"If you look closer at the transaction dates, you will see your father siphoned money out of his personal accounts for two weeks previous to their deaths. All told, your father moved close to $825,000 into a corporation called Jasper Inc."

"That's a lot of money," I said, as the willies returned. This was real. They were alive.

"Enough money to buy a professional death package, decent plastic surgery, and a cushion to start a new life. Invest whatever was left and they would not want for much," he said.

I shuffled through the sheets and found the Cayman bank the money went to.

"Did you get the account number of where the money was wired to?" I asked.

"The banks in the Cayman Islands are not willing to give information even to an heir of an estate. Only the account holder has access to that kind of information. I hit a dead-end there."

"Is the account open still?"

"Yes. I believe your theory is right. Someone in your family is alive and using that money."

I stared down at the sheets in my lap. My proof that my family was crooked. Responsible for this in some way. Natalie had been right to be worried. My heart beat like a stampede of wild horses fleeing danger. It took over all my senses.

One of them was alive. Or all of them.

They had gotten to my sister. Followed Jennifer home and came after me.

I clenched my jaw. They had taken away so much.

"You all right?" Frank asked.

"I'm taking it all in. Is there a way to move forward? To find who they are now?"

"If they had been smart, they would have stayed out of this country and bought an identity off some poor soul in a non-extradition third world country and lived out their days hanging out on the beach," he said.

"They came back to Southern California. I'm sure of it," I said.

He shot me another look.

I wanted to tell him the truth, but I couldn't bring myself to do it.

Frank took a beat and nodded. He acknowledged my need to not fill him in on everything yet.

"I can work with that. The papers had to be good enough for them to get in through the border. Only a few individuals are that good. I'll ask around, see who was working back then."

"Thank you very much, Frank. I'm still shocked this is real," I said and stood up to go.

"Do you need any water? You're looking a bit green around the edges."

"I'm fine. I need some air."

My hands shook noticeably, and I stuffed them into my jeans' pockets. I pictured my sister's face, and the world shifted and not in a good way. My journey out of the building was a blur. One minute I was making my explanation to Frank, the next I was stepping out onto the sidewalk.

Pain brought me back to the present moment. Someone yanked my ponytail hard and my head snapped back. My wig came off in his hand.

"What the hell?" a man's voice exclaimed behind me.

He grabbed me by my short hair before I could react. The unseen attacker pulled me into an alleyway.

My training took over.

I swung my body around. I grabbed the hand holding my ponytail and pressed it hard against my head. I flung myself forward to face my attacker.

Clasping my hands together on my head and pressing as hard as I could, I kicked the man in the groin twice.

Hearing him groan, I whipped my left arm out and jammed the back of the man's head into my uplifted knee.

Bam.

Bam.

Crunch.

His nose broke against my knee. Wetness seeped into my jeans. He released his grip on me.

I punched him on the right side of his face.

He doubled over. "Bitch," he groaned. He was recovering.

I didn't stick around to hear more. My body buzzed with adrenaline. My legs pumped underneath, but I didn't move.

Until I did.

I shot off like a rocket down the small alleyway to the street and toward Hollywood Boulevard. The busy streets cloaked my movement.

I swung left without looking behind me. Between his groin and his broken nose, he wouldn't be as fast as I was.

I sprinted in and out of pedestrians, cursing myself while also proud I'd escaped his clutches.

Detective Harper would hear from me.

They knew I was coming for them. Good. I was ready. I'd track them down first.

34

Hermosa Beach, CA
DAY 5

etective Harri Harper was having a good morning. Michael Grady's law offices were off the main drag in Hermosa Beach and he had no court appearances scheduled today. Michael's secretary squeezed Harri in between two appointments and she sat in his gorgeous well-appointed designer waiting room overlooking the ocean, waiting for him to emerge. Harri didn't wait long.

He appeared several minutes later, all windswept blonde hair and warm brown eyes. Michael Grady was a prototypical SoCal surfer and reminded her of Jake Tepesky from back in the day. The tan on Michael's face showed he spent a lot of time in the water.

"Detective Harper, hello. Michael Grady," he said and pumped her hand.

"Thank you for taking the time to see me. I'm here to talk about Natalie Peters," she said.

His face turned into a grimace.

"I wondered what the LAPD wanted with me. I worried one of my clients ran afoul again," he said and laughed.

"You're a defense attorney?" Harri asked.

"That's right. My bread and butter. There's no way I'd be able to afford this office and my lifestyle if I was working at the prosecutor's office," he said.

"Defending criminals pays well," Harri remarked.

He cracked a grin.

"Oh, you cops. Tsk. Tsk," he said. "Innocent until proven guilty."

He offered her one of the leather armchairs overlooking the Pacific Ocean. She took it and he sat in the one opposite.

"What would you like to know about Natalie Peters?" Michael asked, his face drawn sharp.

"I spoke to Nancy Lyons earlier and she mentioned that Natalie and you were dating around the time she ran away."

"Ran away?" Michael asked.

Good, he caught that, she thought.

"That's correct."

"She wasn't one of the Ballona Creek girls? The papers were wrong?"

"That's correct."

"I'm surprised you divulged such sensitive information," he said.

"I want the honesty to go both ways," Harri said.

Their eyes met.

Harri needed him to be honest with her.

"What do you want to know?" he asked. "Did Nancy tell you what happened between us?"

Ah, so there it was. The lie Nancy Lyons told her that Michael was about to expose.

"No, she didn't. I wondered though," Harri said

"In all frankness, I'm surprised Nancy mentioned me at all."

"Were you the one Nancy got involved with?"

Michael threw up his hands. "Not my proudest moment. Yes, Nancy and I hooked up."

"Hooked up or started dating?"

"Dating. Nancy and Natalie had been best friends since like fourth grade. I started dating Natalie the first month of her freshman year. Natalie had a wicked sense of humor and was gorgeous. She was full of life. God, she was something else."

His eyes dropped to his hands.

"Then everything changed," he said.

"Around what time did this change occur?"

"More like why. She went on a family trip and when she came back, she refused to let me touch her."

"A family trip?"

"A weekend away more like. She cried every time I saw her that first week back. Then, she stopped talking to me altogether."

He surprised Harri with his reaction for a girl from high school that he'd dumped for her best friend.

"I was a 15-year-old kid, and I didn't know how to handle something like that. I went and talked to Nancy about it."

"And one thing led to another?" Harri finished for him.

"Yes. When Natalie found out, the look in her eyes. I'll never forget the hurt," he said.

"Tell me more about this family trip. When did she go and where?"

"I would say about two months before she disappeared."

"End of March?"

"Yes, around then. I remember it being rainy and wondering why in the world anyone would want to go to the Salton Sea."

"Hold on, they went on their family trip to the Salton Sea?" Harri asked, her heart tumbling in her chest.

"That's right," he said, looking down at his hands. "I really hurt her."

"She ever mention what happened at the Salton Sea?"

Michael shook his head.

"I tried asking at the beginning. She freaked out on me. Crying hysterically and shaking. I didn't dare ask again."

"How did Natalie find out about you and Nancy?"

"I told her. I felt bad going behind her back. Especially with her best friend. She had already lost a lot of weight in those first three weeks back. She skipped class all the time, stopped washing her hair, and taking care of herself. She was a different person."

"What did she say when you told her?" Harri asked.

"She gave me that awful look, shrugged, and told me it was for the best," Michael said.

"A 14-year-old girl finding out her boyfriend was cheating on her with her best friend and she just shrugged?"

"Looking back at it now, I can see how troubled she was," Michael said.

His face appeared stricken.

"Nancy mentioned a teacher named Paul Adams. Do you remember him?" Harri asked.

"Yes right, that guy. He ended up having some sort of relationship with a senior that year. She was 18 at the time, and he wasn't her teacher, but still. There was an uproar."

"Did Natalie have any dealings with Paul Adams?"

"If you're thinking he's the reason why she went all crazy and weird, I want to stop you right there. It wasn't Paul Adams. There was something hinky going on with that family," Michael said, leaning toward her, his arms gripping the handrests.

"Did Natalie tell you that?" Harri asked.

"I knew it. Her brother Danny terrified Natalie. He bullied and beat on all of his siblings."

"Did you know Danny?"

"Sure did. Danny and I fought several months into school. I told him I'd kill him if he touched her again."

"What did he say to that?"

"He laughed at me. He was a strong son-of-a-bitch. I assumed her father was either fully involved or totally absent. I begged her not to go to the Salton Sea, but she said she had no choice. And she had to protect Lindsey," Michael said, his eyes cast down.

Harri stayed silent.

"I was fully out of my depth back then. But I've been a lawyer for years now. I can tell you now that Natalie acted like other rape victims I've encountered. The women fold into themselves."

He stopped and retrieved a small bottle of water from a mini-fridge. He drank it down in a single gulp.

"I defended my first and last rapist twelve years ago. I did my best defending him, but he was guilty as sin and was convicted. When his accuser took the stand, her manner hit me so hard, it left me speechless. It was like seeing Natalie again like she'd been those last weeks. I pulled myself together and finished the case. He was convicted and I've never taken a rape case again. I'm convinced Natalie was raped on that Salton Sea trip."

"Did she tell you where they stayed?" Harri asked.

He shook his head no and checked his watch.

"Unfortunately, my next client is waiting for me," Michael motioned to the door.

Harri stood up and shook his hand. He'd given her the key to this case.

"Thank you, Michael. You've helped me so much."

Michael stared out onto the sparkling water of the Pacific Ocean. He barely heard her.

Harri left his office, said thank you to the secretary, and left the building.

It took all her resolve not to sprint back to her car. Her heart pounded in her chest, a full flock of butterflies' wings beating against the walls of her stomach.

Michael had given her the key to the case. Harri was sure that Danny Peters had raped Natalie at the Salton Sea.

Natalie was the true first victim like Mitzi spoke about in her profile. Harri knew it, but how could she prove it? Was there a way she could prove the beginning of all of this was the Salton Sea?

She didn't know much about the Salton Sea except it was in the middle of nowhere and had cheap real estate. A perfect place to take girls and make them into mummies.

Her questioning of Mason Reynolds would be much more on point now. She gunned the engine and thought about calling Tom or Rob to tell them the news. Or she could get a more exact location from Mason and call them then. Happy with that decision, she headed toward Manhattan Beach.

35

Manhattan Beach, CA
DAY 5

Detective Harri Harper pulled up to the pale gray beach bungalow at 1820 21st Street in Manhattan Beach; the address she'd found for Mason Reynolds last night. Harri parked her unmarked car beside his driveway and was about to get out when her cell phone rang.

The number was Lindsey Peters, she took the call.

"Hi Lindsey, I was going to call you today," Harri said.

There was a lot of sound coming from the other end and hard breathing.

"Detective Harper, this is Lindsey Peters. A man attacked me when I came out of my skip tracer's office," she said in between pants.

"Attacked? Are you okay? Are you in the hospital?"

"I damaged him more than he did me. He pulled my hair and pushed me into an alleyway. I broke his nose and kicked him in the groin. I've practiced for such an attack all my life."

"Go to the nearest police station and fill out a report. Where are you?"

"Isn't calling you and reporting it enough?"

"There needs to be an official report on file. Where are you?" Harri asked again.

"I'm at the Hollywood Boulevard Metro station," Lindsey said.

"Go to the Hollywood division station on Wilcox. It's a couple of blocks down from where you are. Report it as an attempted abduction and make an official statement. Did you get a good look at your attacker's face?"

"If you're asking me if he was one of my brothers, I don't think so. I didn't recognize the guy, but then again, I only got a fast flash of him. He had dirty blond hair, tan skin, wearing a dark blue polo shirt, I think."

Her description wasn't specific enough to help identify the man, Harri thought.

"I'm in the South Bay right now following some leads, but when I get back into the city we can meet back at the PAB?"

"Sure, I can take the Metro down there," Lindsey said.

"Are you okay to travel?"

"Yes. He might've pulled a couple of strands of hair out of my head, but otherwise, I'm fine. I'm shaken, though. I know for certain my brothers are alive, and they now know I am here in Los Angeles helping with your investigation," Lindsey said.

A beat-up Nissan Sentra pulled into the driveway of Mason Reynolds' home, catching Harri's attention. A man with dirty blond hair, blood smeared across his nose and cheeks, wearing a dark blue polo shirt opened the door and gingerly rose to his feet.

The man was in pain.

"I can't believe it," Harri said, pulling out her badge.

This man wasn't going to come with her without a fight, she thought. He looked mean even in his battered shape.

"What?" Lindsey asked

"I found your attacker. I'll call you," Harri said.

She threw her phone on the passenger seat and unholstered

her firearm, clicking her safety off. Badge in left hand and gun in her right, she pushed the car door open.

"LAPD get your hands up in the air," she called out, as she maneuvered around her car door.

The man whipped his eyes to her and her badge.

Harri recognized Mason Reynolds from his driver's license.

"Mason Reynolds put your hands up in the air," she yelled again.

Mason's face screwed into a scowl. He ducked back into his car, slamming his driver's door shut.

He was going to run, she thought. Not having a good shot on him, she instead shot out his back tire.

That didn't stop him. He floored the gas and reversed out of the driveway, hitting her unmarked car in the process.

Harri scrambled back into the car. She turned the key and placed the emergency light on the roof. She threw her badge down on the seat and re-holstered her weapon.

Driving in pursuit, she called for backup.

"12-4-347 to Dispatch, I am in pursuit of a suspect in a 241. Give me backup and airship. 21st Street and Sepulveda. Heading toward Sepulveda, Manhattan Beach," she said into the radio.

Mason turned right onto Sepulveda.

"Suspect heading north on Sepulveda. Maroon Nissan Sentra four-door, damage to front right fender, license plate two-Peter-Omega-Larry three-four-nine," Harri said, keeping her eyes on Mason's car.

"Any unit in the vicinity, 347 is in pursuit of a suspect in a 241. Any unit code three assist and airship with the supervisor," the dispatcher crackled over the radio.

. . .

HARRI WEAVED in and out of traffic, keeping her unmarked car at 35 miles an hour. Mason sped away faster, his back side swerving from the shot-out rear tire.

It was only 11:30 in the morning and the traffic was light but going any faster on this stretch was dangerous. She didn't push it but kept her siren blaring. Cars pulled over to the side in front of her.

Thank you, citizens, she thought.

"I am now on Sepulveda and Marine Drive, heading north at high speed," she said.

Out of the rearview mirror, she saw two cruisers joining the chase behind her.

The dispatcher's voice crackled over the radio sending out the information to the other units in pursuit.

Harri focused on her driving as she scanned the side roads for any cars that might get hit. She hated car chases. Los Angeles was known for them, but this was only her second one. Her fear for any bystanders pushed her over the shaky threshold of an adrenaline rush. The whump, whump, whump of a helicopter above her wasn't helping her nerves either.

Out of the corner of her eye, she watched a minivan pull out of a side street, seemingly unaware of the maroon Nissan speeding directly at it.

Harri saw the baby on board sticker and her heart dropped.

"Oh God, no," she screamed as the Nissan Sentra crashed into the driver's side of the van.

The vehicles careened out of control in opposite directions. White airbags exploded out of the steering columns.

The maroon Nissan hit a telephone pole. Harri wasn't sure if anyone could survive that hit. The minivan spun out into oncoming traffic.

A Lexus braked, but was going too fast and collided head-on with the van. Cars behind the Lexus swerved left and right to avoid the devastating crash.

Harri drove up to the crash and positioned her cruiser to block all traffic coming from the south. Her first priority was the innocent victims brought down by Mason Reynolds' reckless driving. Two kids in the backseat were screaming from their car seats.

Harri picked up her radio. "I need an ambulance at Sepulveda and Main. Car chase vehicle crashed into a minivan."

Harri hoped and prayed they were okay.

The mother lay against the deflated airbag, not moving.

This was a disaster, Harri thought, as she heard the operator call for emergency assistance.

36

South Bay, CA
DAY 5

Detective Harry Harper stood off to the side as the first responders worked on getting the mother out of the minivan.

A firefighter wielding the jaws of life cut through the ceiling of the minivan. The buckled frame of the van trapped the mother inside. Her kids miraculously seemed unharmed. The medics took them to the hospital anyway to rule out internal injuries due to the severity of the crash.

A uniformed EMT, supervisor emblazoned on his lapels, motioned for Harri to come closer.

"Are you the officer in charge here?" the supervisor asked.

"Yes, I am. Detective Harri Harper," she said.

She stuck out her hand and he shook it.

"EMS supervisor Gavin James," he said. "This is a bad one."

"Unfortunately, the driver of the Nissan Sentra took off before I could apprehend him. I attempted to keep it slow, but he had other ideas."

Harri explained and then felt foolish for doing so. He was not the person she needed to answer to.

"Car chases in Los Angeles," he said, shaking his head.

She felt the same way. The city was the worst place for such reckless driving. And yet, criminals always felt that they would somehow get away unharmed.

"Do you have any new information on the driver of the Nissan?" Harri asked.

She had chosen to stay with the mother and the kids to make sure they had the best care. She'd checked on the firemen and ambulance workers getting Mason out and knew that she would get an update as soon as they had one for her.

"The gentleman in the Nissan Sentra appears to have a broken neck. He has not regained consciousness since we pulled him out of his vehicle. He's being taken to Manhattan Beach General with a police escort. We were very careful moving him, but it doesn't look good for him."

"What about the mother in the minivan?" she asked.

"It's taken us a while to get her out, but she is speaking. From everything that she's told us, sounds like a lot of broken bones and contusions. We'll know better when we get her out."

Just as he was finishing speaking, a cheer went up as the men finally got the van's roof off. Four EMS responders pulled the mother out onto a waiting stretcher.

Harri and the supervisor watched as the EMS swarmed around. Supervisor James joined his crew. Harri stood back and waited. Flashing lights grabbed her attention, and she looked over to see a line of uniforms holding media at bay.

Great, she thought. How did the media get here so fast?

Her heart pitter-pattered in her chest like a canary fluttering in its cage inside a coal mine.

The media wouldn't be interested in a bad car crash. Not here in LA.

Why were they here? Was it the car chase? Or did they know something about their case?

Her phone rang.

"Detective Harri Harper," she answered.

"It's Tom."

"It's really bad, Tom."

"What happened?"

"I was in pursuit of Mason Reynolds," Harri started.

Tom cut in. "Why?"

"Lindsey Peters called. Told me she'd been attacked."

Harri observed the reporters shooting questions at the uniforms.

"Mason Reynolds?"

"I sent her to the Hollywood Station to fill out a police report."

"How did you get onto Mason Reynolds?"

"He was on my list of witnesses to speak to today. I went to Mason's house to question him. When he got out of the car, I saw his broken nose and he matched the description that Lindsey had given me as the man who attempted to abduct her in the alleyway."

The media circus was getting bigger. What the hell was going on?

"And? Did you speak to him?"

"No, I didn't get to. I presented myself as an LAPD officer. He ran," Harri said. "He jumped into his car and peeled out."

"You followed?"

"I did. I drove slow but did follow in pursuit."

"He knew you were after him?"

"Yes," Harri said. "There is a media circus down here. Have you heard anything?"

"I'm sure we'll find out soon enough." His voice sounded noticeably tighter.

Harri wondered if Richard Byrne had leaked to the media again.

"Anyway, he hit a minivan. I spoke to the EMT supervisor a second ago. Mason has not regained consciousness nor is it looking good for him. They think he has a broken neck."

"What about the people in the minivan?" he asked.

"I'm waiting to hear about her, but she's speaking, and her kids are safe and at the hospital."

Harri heard someone in the background. "Hold on a second, Harri."

The phone fell silent. He'd put her on hold.

Tom clicked back over.

"The media found out we have a prime suspect and that someone involved with the case went on a car chase in the South Bay. It's all over the news."

"How is that possible? We hadn't put him on our board until late yesterday," Harri said.

"People above me are dealing with that. We have a situation though," Tom said.

"What kind of situation?"

"You need to get back to the PAB. We need to follow procedure now and have you interviewed by IA."

Harri's heart thrashed against her chest. The canary was attempting to break out of its cage. Her hand drifted over her heart as she gulped down a breath.

"Are you saying there is disciplinary action against me for what happened today?"

"That's not what I'm saying. A man might be dead, and bystanders were involved. We need this to go through the proper channels."

"Do I need to have my rep with me?"

Cold fingers raked down her spine.

"I honestly don't think so, but if you feel like you need to protect yourself, I understand."

"I will. Thanks," Harri said and hung up.

She steeled herself. Get it together, a voice hissed inside her head.

The EMT supervisor walked back to her.

Harri nodded at him. "You have news?"

"We brought the mother to Manhattan General like her kids. She has broken bones and contusions with a slight concussion, but she's lucid and talking. We think she's in better shape than we first thought."

"Thank you so very much, Supervisor James," Harri said. "Everything here seems to be under control."

She gestured to the detectives standing near the uniforms on the left side of the median. "Traffic division is here. You can coordinate whatever you need with them."

They shook hands and Harri turned to go. A thought struck her. This was the perfect opportunity to search Mason's house for evidence he was connected to the Ballona Creek girls.

She called Tom Bards back.

"Sir, we need a search warrant for Mason Reynolds' house. Can we use the attack on Lindsey Peters as his connection to our case? He might not wake up," she reminded him.

"I know a judge we can contact," he said.

BOOM.

BOOM.

A plume of smoke and fire exploded into the sky south of the crash. Everyone including bystanders, media, cops, and EMT's stopped and turned to see from which direction it came.

"What was that?" Tom asked.

"An explosion," Harri said.

Her heart dropped like a stone. She sprinted back into her car to get on the radio. The operator was calling all units to the address she had on Mason Reynolds.

"It's Mason Reynolds' house. Someone blew it up," she said.

"I'm on my way," Tom barked and hung up.

Firefighters all around her sprang into action. In a whirl of sirens and lights and fast-moving vehicles, all emergency personnel that was not needed at the car crash scene raced to Mason Reynold's house while support staff helped to direct traffic and get the cars off the road.

One of the Traffic Division detectives waved Harri off. She raced down Sepulveda, back to Mason's house, and all her imagined smoldering evidence. It took her five minutes to make it back to his address.

THE SMALL HOUSE was in flames. Four fire trucks sprayed water on both the left and the right sides.

Harri flashed her badge as she ran up to one of the nearest firefighters.

"Is anybody inside?" she asked.

Mason's files didn't mention anything about kids or a wife. Harri hoped he didn't have pets or a girlfriend inside that house.

"Due to the explosion, we haven't been able to get inside to check. By the time we arrived, the whole place was engulfed in flames. It's an old house and dry enough that I'm not sacrificing any of my men to get inside."

"So, containment?"

"Right We don't want the whole street going up in flames," the firefighter said.

One of the firemen shouted, as licks of fire started hitting a tree that was in the backyard of the house and the fireman ran off to help.

Harri watched as potential evidence went up in flames in front of her. She prayed that there was nobody inside. The day had turned into one of horror, although if the mother and kids survived the crash, she'd be thanking all her lucky stars. Mason Reynolds wasn't going to get so lucky. The explosion told her they were on the right track.

"Tom," she said after she had dialed his number again.

"It's gonna take me about an hour to get down there," he said.

Harri checked the time and it was already 3:30 in the afternoon. The entire City of Los Angeles would be gridlocked in traffic for another four hours.

"I can stay here and coordinate with the firefighters and local police if you give me that authority. I don't think there's going to be anything we can use. The firefighter said the explosion took the entire house down with it," she said.

"Copy that, I'm turning around and seeing what I can do from the PAB."

"I'll keep you apprised of the changing situation as it happens," she said.

She saw two detectives coming at her from a Manhattan Beach Police squad car.

"Going to talk to the locals now," she said and clicked off.

"My name is Detective Harri Harper. I was attempting to interview this suspect in a case that falls under major crimes of the LAPD," she said as an introduction.

"Major crimes? Is this the Ballona Creek Girls case?" The older man asked.

"It is. The man who lived in this house, Mason Reynolds, was a witness as well as a potential suspect. He attacked a woman in Hollywood earlier this morning. I identified myself as an officer and he drove off. A car chase ensued.

"This explosion is connected to the disaster on Sepulveda Boulevard that we've been dealing with for the last three hours?" the other man asked.

They hadn't even introduced themselves, Harri thought.

"And you are?"

"I'm Detective Corrigan and this is Detective Harrington," the older man said pointing to the younger. "Looks like we're going to be on this case, so it seems we will be working together."

If they're detectives, why were they in a squad car?

"I'm going to refer you to the head of the task force, Detective Tom Bards. His number is 323-555-9605," she said, and Detective Corrigan took down the number.

"We welcome all the help you can give us."

The detectives nodded without saying anything else. They moved on to talk to the firefighters who had finally gotten a handle on the flames.

Harri shook her head and sat on the hood of the car waiting for more information.

SEVERAL HOURS LATER, the firefighters put out every small ember that had basically burned Mason Reynolds' house to the ground. There was hardly anything left of the home.

Detective Corrigan and Detective Harrington had taken statements from all the neighbors. From what Harri overheard, the detectives had struck out since most of the neighbors weren't home when the fire broke out. Apparently, this was a working-class neighborhood where everybody was gone during the day. It was a perfect place to do a perfect crime.

If this was Danny Peters, he was good, Harri thought.

Tom gave her the go-ahead to come back to the PAB. Harri hadn't eaten all day and her head was swimming. She found a protein bar in her bag from the day before and ate it, trying to keep the dizziness at bay.

She wanted to shower because she smelled of smoke and sweat, but she wasn't going to get that lucky. Tom requested she come in right away. No one made IA wait.

Harri decided not to even ask if she could go home and instead, after saying her goodbyes to the two detectives and lots of the firemen, pulled away from the curb and started her journey toward downtown, her excitement from the day gone completely. Exhaustion and worry had replaced it.

37

PAB - Los Angeles, CA
DAY 5

Detective Harri Harper pulled into her usual space at the downtown PAB parking structure when her phone rang. She didn't recognize the number but picked it up anyway.

"Detective Harper?" a man's voice asked.

"Speaking," Harri replied.

"This is EMT James. We met at the crash site on Sepulveda Blvd. I wanted to inform you that one of the drivers in the crash, Mason Reynolds, died on the way to the hospital."

Harri's heart dropped.

"Thank you for the info." She clicked off the call and stepped out of her car, barely breathing.

Her actions resulted in another human being's death. As a cop, she knew that was inevitable. In her years on the force, Harri had never taken another's life. She'd been proud of that statistic. Now, she had to deal with the knowledge that she had and also deal with the consequences.

Harri walked to the office in a daze, replaying the entire day's events. Each step, she'd followed protocol.

Mason Reynolds attacked Lindsey Peters; she was sure of

that. She'd announced herself to him and he'd chosen to run. Those were the facts.

His choice to start a high-speed chase on busy streets.

His choice to run.

She'd pursued him as slowly as she could per protocol.

Maybe it wouldn't have mattered much, anyway. One of Mason Reynold's neighbors characterized him as a prepper, stockpiling weapons and creating a backyard bunker stored with food and supplies, per Detective Corrigan.

Firefighters found the bunker after all-clear for booby traps or extra explosives from the investigative team.

The neighbor had been right.

The only good news was no one died in the fiery explosion. The house had been empty.

HARRI ARRIVED in the task force conference room so deep in thought that she stepped back in surprise when she walked inside, having no idea of how she'd gotten there.

The entire task force was assembled. Everyone looked exhausted and stressed. The case was going well, but this kind of setback never played well in the media or with the higher-ups. Quiet investigations were the best investigations.

"You've had quite the day," Jackie Bender said.

"And it's not over," Harri said. "Mason Reynolds died on the way to the hospital."

Tom motioned to her to join him at the front of the room.

Harri complied.

She put her backpack down at her feet and turned to the team, wiping her sweaty palms on her dirty slacks. She met Rob's eyes.

He nodded at her.

She took a deep breath. Her heart sprang to life, fluttering nervously.

"I believe Natalie Peters was raped, most likely by Danny Peters, on a family trip to the Salton Sea. That's where it all began." Her voice was steady and sure.

That got everyone's attention.

HARRI FILLED them in on her interviews with Nancy Lyons and Michael Grady. She spent time discussing Michael's revelations about the trip and Natalie's behavior after it. When she finished, the question she expected came from Tom Bards.

"Did you believe him?" Tom asked.

"I did. He confessed that he and Nancy started a relationship soon after a traumatized and shocked Natalie came back from that Salton Sea trip, something that Nancy didn't mention when I interviewed her. It clicked as true."

"But Nancy didn't mention this trip?"

"No, she didn't. But I knew she wasn't telling me the entire story. He filled in the blanks."

"He's only speculating on the rape, though. She didn't specifically tell him that she'd been raped by her brother," Rob prodded.

"That's correct, but her behavior is consistent with that of a traumatized rape victim," Harri countered.

"I can attest to that as well," Jackie said. "Her behavior is textbook."

"For now, let's go on the assumption that an assault happened on this trip to the Salton Sea. Did Michael have any idea where they stayed?"

"No," Harri said.

She gulped down the lump in her throat. Her legs wobbled beneath her. She needed to sit. She gestured to the chair.

"I need to sit." Before anyone could say anything, she pulled the chair over to her and slumped into it.

"Then you proceeded to the Mason Reynolds' residence?" Tom asked.

"Yes. Michael Grady's office was five minutes away from Mason's residence. As I drove down there, I received a call from Lindsey Peters. A man attacked Lindsey as she left her skip tracer's office. The man yanked her ponytail and dragged her into the alleyway. Unfortunately for him, Lindsey Peters is some sort of black belt in Krav Maga and she kicked the bejesus out of him, breaking his nose and injuring his groin area."

"Good woman," Jackie said.

Harri nodded. "Lindsey described the man in general terms."

"You were at Mason's house at this point?" Tom asked.

"Yes, parked at the curb in front of his house."

Rob leaned over and handed her a bottle of water.

Harri hadn't realized how thirsty she was until she saw the bottle. She grabbed it from him and drank it down in gulps. The cool water calmed her dry throat. She licked her lips.

"A Nissan Sentra pulled into the driveway. A man matching Lindsey's description stepped out of the car, his nose bloodied and walking funny. I pulled my badge and gun and ordered him to put his hands up. He jumped back into his car and took off down the street. I managed to shoot out one tire."

"Didn't stop him, did it?"

"No."

"You never communicated with him beyond that?" Tom asked.

"I did not, he didn't say a word to me. I called for backup and followed him," Harri said.

A record of her call and the ensuing police presence would back her story up.

"How did the accident happen?"

"The woman driving the minivan pulled out of a side

street. She didn't see the Nissan Sentra. He T-boned her driver's side," Harri said.

Harri leaned back in her chair. Her story was almost complete. By the look on both Rob's and Jackie's faces, she was missing an important piece of the puzzle.

"What are you all not telling me?" Harri asked, biting her lip down, forcing back tears.

"Due to the accident, an IA investigation has been opened," Tom said.

"Right, I know that. I...I...also received a phone call from the EMT supervisor right before this meeting. Mason Reynolds died on the way to the hospital," Harri said.

"Damn," Rob said. It was the first thing he'd said since the download began.

This didn't make anybody in the room happy. A viable suspect was gone, and the IA investigation became more serious.

"Wish we could have searched his house. Whoever set the fire knew what they were doing. There was nothing left. The firefighter's preliminary investigation found no human remains in the house. At least, that's good news," Harri said.

"We have a bigger problem," Jorge said as he took the floor.

Harri closed her eyes and waited for the bad news to come.

"I dug into Mason Reynolds' life this morning," Jorge began.

"Is this what you all are looking so serious about?" Harri couldn't help but ask.

"He has an alibi for the summer of 1992. I spoke to his parents when I couldn't reach him."

"Of course, he does," Harri muttered.

Jorge held up his hand. "It's pretty legit. Mason was having a lot of behavioral problems in high school. His parents sent him to a military-style camp for troubled teens up in the Redwoods past San Francisco."

"He could have flown in, drove in. San Francisco isn't that far away," Harri countered.

"I checked the map. The camp is in the middle of nowhere. I have a call into the camp."

"I've called some witnesses we've been interviewing. No one saw Mason Reynolds that summer. It was common knowledge he'd been sent to military school," Tom said.

"When did he get back to town?" Harri asked.

Her heart somersaulted all over her chest. A silent scream sounded in her head. He was involved. He had to be. Why had he grabbed Lindsey if he wasn't?

"He returned on September 10, 1992," Jorge said, reading off his copious notes.

"That's exact," Harri remarked.

"Right? I asked about that. The parents had the paperwork because there was some sort of dispute over the amount they owed the camp. The Reynolds took the camp to court. The father sounded militant. He would have those records."

"Why did Mason Reynolds run? The bigger question is why attack Lindsey Peters all the way in Hollywood?" Harri asked.

"He's still in contact with the Peters brothers?" Jackie asked.

"What about this explanation," Tom interjected. "Mason Reynolds has an alibi for that particular summer. He's in the clear on those abductions. What if Danny Peters asked him to take care of his sister? There'd be no connection coming back at him."

"That doesn't make sense either, though. Why would Danny Peters out himself like this? Danny Peters has success-fully stayed dead for over twenty years," Harri said. "If he exposed himself like that, he had a bigger reason."

"This could be a distraction. Muddy up the waters as it were," Jorge said.

"He's still in play in the Lorraine Benjamin case though, isn't he?" Harri asked. "He could have assisted in her murder. Mason was in the same gang. The boys started without him, but he wanted in. He could be culpable in crimes we haven't uncovered yet. If the gang got away with the mummified girls, then why would they stop?"

"Christian LeGuerre, Mason Reynolds, and the Peters brothers were all in the same gang. Were they all involved in the killings? Could they keep a secret like that for so many years?" Tom asked.

"That's a good enough reason to run from the police. Mason must have known Christian LeGuerre was brought in for questioning. Did he think that Christian turned him in?"

"Why attack Lindsey? She doesn't know anything. Her sister ran away, and they were gone for all the subsequent crimes. They were in hiding themselves. It doesn't fit." Tom said.

Before the conversation could continue, a knock sounded on the door. Lieutenant Violet Sanford popped her head in.

"Harri, I need you to come with me. IA is ready to take your statement," she said.

Harri stood up on unsteady feet. Her lack of eating throughout the day made her feel faint and the stress made her heart thump faster.

Harri clutched her chest and breathed in deep. You can get through this, she thought. She grabbed her backpack and joined Violet in the hallway.

"You haven't cleaned up yet, have you?" Violet asked.

"I smell like smoke, don't I?" Harri asked.

"You do," she said. "IA won't wait, though."

Harri steeled herself. Jorge's information on Mason Reynolds rattled her. She didn't believe he was an innocent man and doubted the new information would have changed the outcome of the day. Mason Reynolds assaulted Lindsey Peters. He had run with no provocation. Harri took a deep breath. She had followed protocol at each step. She hoped that would matter.

Violet led Harri to a smaller interrogation room. Of course, IA would want to record the interview. Detective Moss and Detective Gerhard were already there and waiting.

She knew them by sight but had been lucky enough to only see them in the hallways. No one liked Internal Affairs detectives, but she heard they were fair. Well, as far as Internal Affairs detectives could be. Harri lifted her chin. She had nothing to hide.

AFTER AN HOUR of IA grilling and Harri telling her story three times, the IA detectives dismissed her. Exhausted, she dragged herself from the conference room back to the cold case bullpen. She opened her drawer and found an old bottle of seltzer water. She drank it greedily as she searched the drawer for another protein bar but came up short.

Rob sat back in his chair and waited for her gulps to subside.

She stopped drinking. "What?"

"How did it go?"

"As expected, I have nothing to hide. I went over my actions numerous times. What they do now is out of my control," she said.

"You didn't miss much from the meeting. We kept going over the Lindsey Peters attack. We don't have a good theory on that yet," he said.

Rob knew her well enough to focus on the investigation, instead of grilling her about IA. She appreciated that from him.

"Lindsey said she'd meet me here after giving her statement to Hollywood division. Let me call her and see if she's still there," Harri said.

"Lindsey has her own skip tracer?" Rob asked.

He took a big bite of a donut and washed it down with an iced latte.

"Have another one of those?" Harri asked, her stomach rumbling.

Rob nodded and tossed her a Dunkin Donuts bag. She peeked inside and found a Boston Cream. Her mouth watered. She pulled it out and bit in, savoring the sugar and chocolate. She welcomed the sugar rush.

"She does," Harri said. "Whatever the skip tracer is finding triggered her brothers to send Mason Reynolds after her. It's the only explanation I've come up with."

The phone buzzed on her desk. "Maybe this is her." And, in fact, it was.

"Want to join me?" Harri asked.

"It's better that I do. Most likely, you'll be benched by IA while they finish the investigation of what happened in the South Bay. I should be the point on this," Rob said.

Harri nodded and lifted herself from her chair with quite a bit of effort. Her lower back ached and she caught the whiff of body odor and charred plastic coming off her hair.

But Lindsey was waiting.

38

PAB - Los Angeles, CA
DAY 5

Detective Harri Harper shuffled after Rob Lakin as they exited the elevator. Lindsey, her shoulders hunched, stood to the right of the intake desk. Rob signed her in as Harri approached the young woman.

"Lindsey are you all right?" Harri asked.

Lindsey's blond ponytail was askew and Harri saw the short hair underneath. The woman wore a wig. Harri wondered if her hair was real. Lindsey wore a long-sleeved black t-shirt and black yoga pants reminding Harri of the stereotypical yoga mom. Lindsey was anything but that.

Her brilliant blue eyes flashed at Harri.

Harri wondered what she really looked like when she was not in disguise.

"I will be when you find my brothers. They're after me." Her mouth was set in a thin line.

Lindsey was made of steel, Harri thought.

Then the younger woman's chin trembled.

Or she was barely keeping it together.

Harri understood that feeling well.

"Let's go to a conference room," Harri said and motioned to the elevator.

They brought her to the nearest available conference room located on the second floor. Harri and Rob sat down at one end of the table, Lindsey took the other side.

Lindsey placed a narrow envelope on the table and slid it toward them.

"This is why I think that man attacked me," Lindsey said.

"Are you hurt?" Rob asked.

Harri hadn't noticed Lindsey moving any differently in the short time they'd been together.

Lindsey averted her eyes and pulled her wig off. She ran her fingers through her short pixie cut and rubbed her head.

"My scalp hurts." Lindsey massaged the side of her head. "The wig came off in his hand. I'd been stunned by some news and didn't react quick enough. He grabbed me by my real hair and yanked."

Rob's look of shock mirrored Harri's own. She hadn't expected Lindsey to reveal herself like that to them.

"You were in disguise?" he asked.

"I'm always in disguise."

"Did you report the attempted abduction to the police?" Rob asked, getting back his composure.

Lindsey was hellbent on surviving. Harri fully understood that now.

"I did as Detective Harper asked. I'm not sure the officer who took my statement believed me, though. I don't have any bruises or scratches on me."

"But, he took your statement down," Harri pressed her.

Lindsey's description of her attacker and the damage she did to him had to match Harri's statement on Mason Reynolds' condition before the chase.

"He did. I described the man and the moves I did to escape

him. His injuries, if you find him, will correspond with my given statement."

"How did you get away from him?" Rob asked.

"I am in one of the master levels of Krav Maga. I've been doing that kind of self-defense training since I was ten-years-old," Lindsey stopped and laughed.

"My sister was right. The training kept me alive." Her blazing blue eyes met Harri's.

Harri cocked her head at the woman.

"We can't protect you if you keep refusing to tell us where you live," Harri reminded her.

"Are you going to open it?" Lindsey asked.

Harri picked up the envelope and opened it. A single copy of a financial record was inside. Harri noted the name of the skip tracer whose work she held in her hand. Ahrens Corp. She'd heard of him. He was one of the best.

"What is this?" Harri asked.

"It's where the family money went to fund my father and brothers' fake deaths in the Philippines," she said.

"Have you ever heard of a Jasper Inc.?" Harri asked as she read through the skip tracer's work.

"No. I was eight when we left, remember. The transfers began several years later. The skip tracer couldn't make any more headway with the Cayman Islands bank that this account was created in."

"Is it still active and open?" Rob asked.

He had more experience with financial documents and the working of offshore banks.

"Yes. He was able to check that," Lindsey said.

Another reason to believe the brothers were alive, Harri thought. The father as well.

Lindsey pulled on her sleeve.

Harri watched her move as she sought to hide the bruise on her wrist.

"Did the officer who took your statement take pictures of your bruises?" Harri watched Lindsey's face.

The woman dropped both hands into her lap.

"He didn't notice. Neither did I honestly," she mumbled.

Rob shot her the back-off-for-now look.

"Why do you think your father would have gone along with this?" Harri asked.

"He could have been involved," Lindsey said.

"In what?" Rob asked.

"What they did to those girls," Lindsey said.

Harri and Rob exchanged a glance. They both thought her father was involved as well even though the team's entire investigative theory centered around the gang of boys. Mitzi had said the main sociopath would need to be calm, exacting, and patient. Qualities that most teenage boys did not have developed yet.

"This is the reason you think the man attacked you?" Rob asked.

Lindsey nodded and rubbed her head again.

"Do you want any water or…" Harri trailed off.

Lindsey shook her head. "No, thanks."

Rob steered them back. "How did they find you?" Rob asked. "How did they know?"

"The skip tracer must have tripped an alarm at the Cayman bank. They staked out his place." She gnawed on her lip.

Lindsey didn't make those kinds of errors in judgment, Harri thought.

"I left myself exposed."

"Lindsey…" Rob began.

Lindsey shook her head furiously. "I keep making mistakes. I come here. I'm followed. I go to the skip tracer, they find me."

"It's not your fault."

"You don't understand. I have some serious disappearing and tracking skills. I first noticed my tail after coming here to speak to the police. I lost that tail."

"I'm not sure how to take that," Harri said.

"I'm not a lunatic. Anything but. The man waited for me outside. How did he know I'd be there? At that time? An alarm was tripped."

Harri raised an eyebrow at that.

Lindsey shrugged her shoulders.

"My story has checked out so far, hasn't it?"

It had checked out. She was right about that.

"If you haven't yet heard on the news, the man who I believe attacked you died on his way to the hospital. He refused to be brought in and ran. He died due to injuries from a car crash. Nothing you did," Harri said.

Rob shot her a watch-what-you-tell-the-witness glare. He didn't want Harri to give out too much information. Harri felt Lindsey should know.

"Did you get his phone?" Lindsey asked.

Harri frowned.

"No, I didn't. It should be with his belongings with the police down in Hermosa Beach. Why his phone?" Harri asked.

"Because he could have sent pictures of me to my brothers. They don't know what I look like. If he has pictures of me, then they're one step closer to me," Lindsey said.

Harri sat back in her seat. She hadn't thought of that angle.

"We can provide you with police protection," Rob said.

"Is that why you came here, Lindsey? You could have emailed us this information. What are you not telling us?"

Lindsey stiffened and looked down.

"I came to make sure you were looking for my brothers. I can't do this alone and you are the LAPD."

"What about protection?" Rob asked.

"I don't want it. I can handle myself."

Even if that was the case, which seeing how she dispatched Mason Reynolds was more true than not, Harri worried they were missing something.

"We're cops. It's what we do."

Lindsey stood up to go.

"Find my brothers. That's the most important thing right now."

"Thank you for filling out the report and coming in," Rob said.

Lindsey nodded but kept her eyes on Harri. "It's too bad he's dead. He could have told us who hired him."

"Why do you think he was hired?"

"He wasn't the man that came after me at Jennifer's. And he didn't have my eyes," she stated simply. "I'm going underground for a while. Here's a new phone number where you can reach me."

"Are you dumping the phone we have for you?" Harri asked.

Lindsey pulled out a card with a phone number on it.

"This is the number for the new burner. I've gotten rid of the one I used to call the skip tracer in case it was compromised."

"Is that really necessary?" Rob asked.

Harri heard the skepticism in his voice.

"Yes. Please keep this number between the two of you until you catch them. I don't want to end up dead."

Harri stood up and took the card from her.

"Oh, one last thing. Please check on Mr. Ahrens. I'm worried I put him in harm's way. His address is in the documents I gave you."

"Thank you for coming in, Lindsey," Rob said. "And giving us this."

"Find out who is using that money. The only way I will be safe is if you unmask who my brothers became," she said.

With that, she squared her shoulders. "I don't want to be afraid anymore." Lindsey's voice trembled as she spoke.

They stood in awkward silence.

"Be safe," Harri said.

Lindsey nodded.

A feeling of overwhelm washed over Harri. She hoped they were making the right decision and letting the woman go off on her own.

Apparently, Rob was thinking along the same lines. "What if Detective Harper takes you home," he suggested.

"Absolutely not. I don't want anyone to know where I live." Lindsey shook her head.

"We can protect you." He tried one last time.

Lindsey gave them a sad smile. "Not from them, you can't," she said.

"I'm calling it a day," Harri said to Rob.

She turned to Lindsey. "I'll walk you out of the building."

"I'll start looking into Jasper Inc.," Rob said as they left the conference room.

Harri waved bye to Rob and the two women walked in silence to the elevator.

"Why do you smell like burnt plastic?" Lindsey asked.

"The man who attacked you, his house blew up soon after he was in the accident," Harri explained.

"It's horrifying that they are capable of anything," Lindsey said.

39

PAB - Los Angeles, CA
MONDAY, AUGUST 13, 2018 - DAY 8

R ob had been right, Harri Harper thought, as she sat on desk duty for the third day. Violet, her lieutenant, had promised her that the investigation would be swift, but Harri was itching to get back out into the field.

She wanted on the Christian LeGuerre stakeout but wasn't allowed in the field. She worried about Lindsey as well. Lindsey hadn't contacted her since they had spoken two days ago either and that concerned her.

She'd spent most of her time tracking down where the Peters family stayed in the Salton Sea back in '92. She called all the motels open back then, but no one kept records that far back.

She'd spoken to several old-timers, but no one remembered the Peters family. She'd contacted the newer resorts and hotels and hit dead-ends there, too.

Her phone calls with the Philippines hadn't ended well, either. Apparently, their record-keeping was atrocious, and they didn't have death certificates on file for the Peters brothers or Franklin Peters, the father. That line of investigation was effectively stalled.

In the last twenty-four hours, Harri dived deep into Franklin Peters, Lindsey's father. He had been a lawyer with the same big weapons defense company as Christian LeGuerre's father. The family lived in a nice house, in a good neighborhood, and everyone said he was an upstanding citizen.

After hours of searching, she'd finally found his former secretary through an article on Franklin Peters' philanthropy through an El Segundo charity. The woman had been with him in the photo and something about her demeanor told Harri she wasn't a fan of her boss.

After several phone calls, Harri finally reached her and set up a meeting. Even though she was on desk duty, she figured this type of interview would be okay to do. Really, she wanted out of the chair. Everyone else was too busy.

The task force was gathering evidence to charge Christian LeGuerre officially. Jackie Render had finally identified the last mummified remains of the two girls. They had been runaways living on Hollywood Boulevard. Their victim profiles matched that of Charlaine Lewis. Rob was sure that Charlaine was also a victim of the Peters family.

The change of victimology concerned the team enough to contact Mitzi Jeffries for a modification to the profile. It felt like they were in the one-step-forward-two steps-behind part of the investigation.

The firefighters determined an arsonist poured accelerant throughout Mason Reynolds's house and set it on fire as Harri dealt with the aftermath of her chase.

Harri's frustration at doing nothing hit its peak. She couldn't take one more second of this. She stood up to get more coffee when Violet appeared in the bullpen. Harri's heart leapt. IA had made a decision.

She followed Violet into her office.

"Is there any news?" Harri asked.

"There is. You've been cleared in the vehicular homicide

on Sepulveda. They've deemed it reckless driving by a suspect fleeing a police interview. You're all good to get back to the task force."

Harri jumped out of her seat. "Thank you, Violet."

"You have somewhere to be?" Violet asked.

"A character witness interview with Franklin Peters' secretary from the early 90s. I've spent days calling her and was waiting to get the okay to set up the interview."

Violet cracked a smile. "Don't let me hold you," she said.

Harri flew out of her office, and the moment she returned to her desk she called Marcy Walker again and changed the meeting to today. They agreed on a coffee shop in mid-Wilshire. Harri hung up and checked the time. She had forty-five minutes to get there. She'd barely make it. Harri grabbed her backpack, her excitement growing.

MARCY WALKER WAS NOT what Harri had expected. The woman in the photo from the early 90s was petite with brown hair and sharp eyes, dwarfed by Franklin Peters' height. The woman sitting at the table looking over at Harri almost seemed like someone else completely. This woman was ripped. Marcy appeared in her late 50s, maybe early 60s, but there was not one piece of her body that wasn't hard muscle.

"Thank you so much for meeting with me, Ms. Walker," Harri said.

She sat down across from the woman at the table in the corner of the coffee shop and recovered her notebook from her bag. Harri smoothed down a piece of her hair and smiled.

"I'm a bit flustered from the drive over here. I might have broken some traffic laws," Harri said.

"Oh," was all Marcy said.

Harri noticed a hesitancy about her. Before she could reassure the woman, Marcy directed her gaze at Harri.

"Your phone call was startling but didn't surprise me. Any time I think of Franklin Peters, I know I dodged a bullet," she said.

"I think you just might have. Before we begin, do you mind my asking how you've gotten so strong? I hit my 40s last year and I have to pass those physical tests. What's your secret?".

Marcy visibly relaxed as Harri hoped she would

"I do CrossFit four times a week and eat a lot of protein," she replied.

"You must feel amazing."

"I do, thank you. I promised myself I would never be bullied again. After I left that job back in the 90s, I refocused on myself. I started several businesses and really got myself in shape. I needed to feel strong in every way."

Harri leaned in, her pen at the ready. "By that job, do you mean the job with Franklin Peters?"

"Exactly. That man was a brute. I survived two years and I still don't know how. I held my ground one day and spit in his face. I quit and never looked back."

There was a determination in Marcy's eyes that Harri recognized. It's probably what helped propel her out of that situation.

"I'm so glad I found you. I've been researching Franklin Peters for days and nowhere does it mention this side of him."

"He had a very good mask. He'd turn on the charm, but there was something cold, hard, and mean in his eyes."

"Franklin was a difficult boss?"

"He loved torturing and manipulating me throughout the day. He took sick pleasure out of making me do things over and over again and yelling at me that I had done things wrong. He made me a nervous wreck. Almost."

Marcy shredded her napkin into thin strips while biting down at her lip. She noticed the mess she'd made and swiped it into her lap.

"But I had an amazing boyfriend at that time and he really pushed me to stand up for myself. To not let him steamroll me. It took me weeks, but I did finally get up the courage to quit. On the day he threw a stapler at my head."

"He didn't?"

"He did," Marcy stated flatly.

"Did you report him to HR?" Harri asked.

Marcy threw back her head and laughed.

"Oh honey, things didn't work like that back then."

"I'm sorry. I can't even imagine how angry…"

Marcy snorted.

"I developed a strong survival instinct. I'm thankful for it now."

Marcy sipped her latte, her gaze distant.

Harri changed course. "What about his children?"

"That older boy, Danny, was just like his father. If they hadn't all died in the Philippines, they would have been in the papers for some sort of crimes. Mark my words, that whole family was bad news," she said.

"Did you know any of the girls? Natalie Peters ever come in to see her father? Or Lindsey Peters, the younger one?" Harri asked.

"I never heard hide nor hair of them. In fact, I didn't even know he had two girls until the news of their disappearance came out."

"Really? There weren't any family pictures in his office?"

"Nope. Not a one. He never spoke of them, either. The only reason I knew Danny was because he would come by the office asking for money all the damn time," Marcy said with disgust in her voice.

"As his secretary, did you ever book a trip to the Salton Sea for the entire family?" Harri asked.

"No. Franklin owned property out there, though. I remember having to do the paperwork to complete the sale.

It was on a huge tract of land, like a compound," Marcy said.

"Did he ever mention his interest in the Salton Sea?"

"Not to me. It's far out and secluded, though. He wanted to be far out there."

"Any reason why?"

"He wanted privacy."

"That's what he said?"

"Yes. Those exact words."

Harri sat back.

There it was.

The missing piece.

They took the girls to the compound. It was in the middle of nowhere, then they had all the time in the world to do whatever they wanted.

"I know this was so many years ago. But do you remember the address?" Harri asked.

"Not the address. It had a strange name. Like you know, those cutesy, funny desert names like sagebrush or tumbleweed. Look for a name like that. It was about ten minutes off the main boulevard. Close enough to town for supplies, but far enough for privacy. I remember he was very specific about needing privacy," Marcy said. "This is about those poor girls at Ballona Creek, isn't it?"

"I can't really get into that," Harri said while nodding.

"Thank you. I figured it had to be something big and horrible like that. He was an ugly, scary man."

"What did you think of their deaths in the Philippines?" Harri asked.

"Outside of relief, not much. More like good riddance."

"If I told you we were looking into whether they'd faked their deaths over there, what would you say?"

Marcy sat back thoughtfully.

"I would tell you if there is any man who would do that it would be him," she said.

"Did you ever have any dealings with Jasper Inc.?"

Marcy shook her head. "Name doesn't ring a bell."

Harri took note of that. Her face must have shown disappointment because Marcy frowned.

"Should I have heard of that?"

"Not necessarily."

"They terrified me. Over the years, I came to understand how traumatizing that experience had been for me. I've never had a boss again. I swore to myself I'd never put myself into that kind of danger again."

"Danger? What do you mean? Were you afraid he would hurt you?"

"It wasn't anything so concrete. Any time I was in his office, something felt off. Kind of like your body telling you to flee, but your brain wasn't picking up the signal. Then one day I did and told him no and suddenly a metal stapler whizzed past my head, barely missing my face."

"There was a book about that," Harri said.

"Right, now what was it called?"

Marcy closed her eyes. She sat silent for a moment. Her eyes popped open and a smile crossed her face.

"The Gift of Fear. That's what it was. The author talked about how women had a sense when they were in danger and to make sure to listen to that sense. I feared that man any time he was within five feet of me. I have no idea how those daughters survived in his presence."

"Did anyone else feel this way about him?"

"All the girls I spoke to kept their distance from him. But the people in charge loved him. He was a damn good lawyer which meant that back then, he was untouchable in the company." Marcy's face glistened with sweat. The memories were not pleasant for her.

"Thank you for meeting with me about such a traumatizing time. This interview helped our case tremendously."

"Well, I'm glad I could help. Now go, so I can forget all about this again." Her mouth set in a grimace. "I remembered the name. Rancho Honolulu."

"Seriously?"

"Yes."

Harri grinned and gathered her things. She was almost out the door when she waved back to a pensive Marcy, still sitting at the table, lost in the past.

Harri used her shoulder to get the door open and was on the phone with Tom Bards before she left the coffee shop.

"He owned a property out in the Salton Sea. I finished interviewing his old secretary. He was the alpha. The boys could have been under his spell. Franklin Peters is our main guy."

She listened as he relayed the information to Jackie and Jorge.

"Find the address, Harri," he said.

"On it, boss," Harri said.

She slammed her car door shut and smiled. They were so close to catching them. Getting justice for the girls, for Natalie, Lindsey, and Jennifer. And the girls they didn't yet know about.

She sped toward downtown and the Hall of Records.

40

Lindsey Peters (AKA Jane Smith)

I'd managed to stay in my apartment for two days, catching up on some coding work I'd gotten from San Francisco. By the third day, I needed to get out of the house. I'd convinced myself that taking a walk around the block wouldn't expose me too much. I put on my most covered-up disguise, adding a baseball cap pulled low over my eyes, and set off.

The air was fresh and the street green. I needed this reprieve. I'd walked all the way around the block back to my street when I saw it. As per usual, I scanned for idling cars or strangers loitering where they weren't supposed to. The street was empty.

As I walked by a streetlight, I noticed a missing person's flyer. My legs trembled beneath me and my breath caught. I knew her. The punk rock young grandma. It was Marjorie, the librarian from the local library. The only person who knew where I lived. And now she'd gone missing? That couldn't be a coincidence, could it? My mind ping-ponged through all sorts of theories.

No one would have known that we'd met on the street by

accident. It's not like she'd mention it to anyone. Why would she? My paranoia was getting to me.

I willed my legs to move. I stumbled toward my apartment, my mind racing. The flyer said she'd gone missing over twenty-four hours ago, soon after I'd seen her on her walk. This was Los Angeles, a big city. Crime happened.

Not to librarians though, I reasoned. That's not right. Anyone could find themselves in trouble.

The pain in my gut told me this wasn't random. Had my brothers found me? They would have come after me then and not someone I barely knew. I shouldn't go home now, though. What if someone was watching to see where I lived?

You didn't see anyone though, the voice in my head said. I stood, unsure. What if I asked around at the library? Maybe she'd turned up already.

I checked the time. The library was open for another couple of hours. I'd ask around. I turned on my heel and walked the way back I'd come. I took a right toward Robertson and the library.

The smell of books calmed me as I stepped up to the front desk. I didn't want to appear too weird when asking about Marjorie, so I smiled and tried to act normal. But a smile was inappropriate. And what in the world was normal, anyway? I ended up nodding to a male librarian I'd never seen before.

"May I help you?" he asked.

"I saw a missing flyer for one of your librarians, Marjorie. I...I knew her. Has she been found yet?" I asked.

"No, she hasn't," he said.

"Did she disappear during the day?" I asked.

He nodded at the person directly behind me and frowned.

"Why do you want to know?" he asked. "Do you have any books to check out?"

"No, I don't have books. Marjorie was kind to me. Can I help search for her? Is there a Facebook group or someplace I can volunteer to help in any way? Are the police involved already?"

"Marjorie went missing on one of her daily lunch walks. The head librarian called the police yesterday. I don't have any more information past that," he said.

Someone cleared their throat behind me. The librarian looked over my shoulder again. I wasn't going to get anything else out of him.

"Thank you," I said.

I left the library, my thoughts jumbled. This couldn't have anything to do with me, could it? She knew where I lived? She knew I wore a wig? I bit my lip hard enough that I tasted blood. I was being paranoid.

This could be a tragic accident that befell the young woman.

What if it wasn't though, Natalie's voice whispered.

Could I help her in any way?

I didn't figure out the answer on my walk home. I double-backed several times and circled the block to make sure no one watched my progress.

When I was sure I hadn't been followed, I entered my apartment and locked myself in. I'd made it.

I drank a glass of water, my mind spinning. Should I do something? Or stay put?

She'd been so kind.

What if her meeting me spelled her doom?

41

PAB - Los Angeles, CA
DAY 8

Detective Harri Harper knocked twice on Detective Tom Bards' office door.

"Come on in," he said and looked up from piles of files. "Save me."

"Funny. I have a lead. I've come across Franklin Peters' secret hideaway," Harri said excitedly.

"How sure are you it's THE hideaway?" Tom asked.

"I tracked down the property records of the compound outside of the Salton Sea," she said, excitement seeping out of her.

"Is it still in the Peters family?" he asked, her excitement contagious.

"Indirectly. Guess who it's registered to?"

"Hmmm, Jasper Inc., perhaps?"

"Excellent guess, boss," Harri nodded.

Her knee gyrated up and down. She used all her might to still her body. It was not easy. Electricity had replaced her blood.

"Any word on who controls Jasper Inc.?" Tom asked.

"Another shell company. In fact, a string of shell companies owns Jasper Inc."

Tom's eyebrow raised. "A string?"

Harri nodded

"I used Rob's forensic accountant. He went down the rabbit hole in discovering all about Jasper Inc. He's still digging down to the owner. The connection is solid, though. And the compound is in use. Satellite imagery from Google maps shows trucks. Someone lives there," Harri said.

"That's a bit too circumstantial. We haven't connected Jasper Inc. to the Ballona Creek case yet," Tom said.

"We have something else tying a certain cop's house break-in to the Salton Sea environs."

Tom stopped fiddling with his papers and leaned in. "Tell me that paint was his mistake."

"Exactly. The lab tech on the break-in called me before I came to you. The paint analysis indicated a type of salt compound in the hand-mixed paint. This particular salt compound can only be found in and near the Salton Sea."

"Is that too specific?" Tom asked, steepling his fingers under his chin.

"The Salton Sea is unique in high salinity as well as mineral make-up due to fertilizers, its place in the desert, and the Colorado River. That is more solid than coincidence."

"For your break-in. That doesn't point a finger to the specific compound."

"I was working on Lindsey Peters' story. She connects with Jasper Inc. Could we get the search warrant on finding the red paint from my break-in?"

"That tie-in could work because of the lab results and family money. I know a judge who would go for a preliminary search warrant," Tom said.

"I was hoping as much. The residence falls under the jurisdiction of the Imperial Valley Sheriff's Department. Rob and I could go out there to serve the warrant with the sheriff's deputies? Do you know of anyone out there that could expedite this?"

"Lieutenant Richard Byrne does, I think," Tom said.

Harri flinched at the name.

Tom noticed her reaction but said nothing.

Harri checked her cellphone as Tom made the call. Her leg pumped up and down. She didn't want to be in the office to hear this phone call. She mouthed bathroom at Tom and left his office. She wasn't sure if superstition drove her out of there, but she was taking no chances.

This lead was it. The big one. Her gut told her she'd found them. Harri opened the bathroom door. It was empty. Relieved, she splashed cold water on her face to bring her jitters down. Tom wouldn't mention she'd been the one to find the property, would he? He didn't seem like someone who played politics. She hoped she was right.

Harri walked back to his office and found him pacing. That didn't look promising.

"Judge or Richard?" Harri asked.

"Judge gave us the go-ahead. Richard is calling his friend right now. His friend is the sheriff over there and Richard jumped to help," he said.

"Why are you pacing then?" Harri asked.

"I've got a bad feeling about something, but I can't put my finger on it. We're missing something."

"On this Salton Sea angle?" Harri asked, confused.

She wasn't entirely seeing his concern.

"I'm not sure. We haven't had much luck on Christian LeGuerre." He pursed his lips. "We are missing something, aren't we?"

The phone rang and Tom jumped to answer it.

"Hello? Yes, thank you. I'm waiting for the call from Imperial Valley to send it over to them. This will be a joint affair," he said and listened some more. "Thank you, Judge." Tom hung up and turned back to Harri.

"Once Richard's sheriff gets back to us, we can coordinate the search warrant with them."

"Do you think we'll get it this afternoon?"

Tom's mood unsettled her and squashed her excitement on the lead.

"That's what Richard was going to push for," he said.

Harri checked the time.

"Can I take Rob Lakin with me? If we leave now, we could make it there in about four and a half hours," she said.

"Yes. Make sure you have enough officers with you. Can't be too careful about the middle of nowhere locations," Tom said.

She stood up to leave when both of their cell phones started buzzing. They looked at each other. Harri picked up her cell as Tom picked up his.

"Detective Harri Harper speaking," she said.

"Christian LeGuerre. He's dead. We found him dead inside the house about ten minutes ago," Jackie Render said.

Harri's heart dropped.

"Wasn't he under surveillance?"

Harri and Tom stared at each other, each listening to a different version of the same story.

"Yes."

"There's been no movement in his house for the last two days, but each shift thought he was in hiding and scared. His not leaving his house for 48 hours didn't sound any alarms for our surveillance teams. I came down to execute the arrest warrant and we found him dead."

"Thanks for letting me know," she said.

She hung up and turned to Tom. His face was fixed in a grimace.

"Christian LeGuerre," she said.

"I knew something was off. What a shitshow," he said, his shoulders slumped. "We need the Salton Sea lead to pan out. If it doesn't, Christian's death will force an evaluation of our team and we won't come out looking too good. We've had too many missteps. Find me something out there. A man was murdered while under surveillance? This is unbelievable." He scratched his head. "Shit."

Harri had never seen Tom Bards this upset. The man kept himself stoic and focused on the task ahead.

"We have to find this killer," he said to Harri.

"I'm leaving right now." Harri rushed back to the cold case bullpen.

Rob sat slumped in his chair, staring off into space, wearing a look of forlorn resignation.

"I volunteered you to come with me to the Salton Sea to execute a search warrant on Franklin Peters' ranch."

His eyebrow raised. He sat up straighter and whistled.

"Hope this pans out because we are a very unhappy team right now," he said.

"Right, agreed. We're leaving now," she said.

He grabbed his jacket and they headed toward the elevators.

"Salton Sea is damn hot right now," Rob grumbled.

He checked the temperature on his phone and groaned. He showed the screen to Harri. The temp out there was 110°F.

"It takes four hours to get there. It'll cool down by then," Harri said.

"Wishful thinking, lady," Rob said.

"I agree. But this is the place. It's got to be. It makes sense with Mitzi's profile. Natalie was victim number one."

The adrenaline was back and pumping. Her gut told her this was it.

42

Salton Sea, CA

DAY 8

T he trip out to El Centro in the Imperial Valley was in its fourth hour and they were still an hour out. It had been a mostly silent ride.

After the first hour, Rob turned on the radio to a country station and hummed along to the song playing. Harri didn't recognize the song or singer. She'd never been a country music fan. Rob drove and rules were rules. The driver chose the music. Harri tuned the music out and stared at the barren landscape out the window, lost in her thoughts.

The desert held no beauty for Harri. She'd grown up in Southern California and her family had done the requisite trips to Palm Springs and surrounding areas. She hated the heat and the dryness. Folks talked of the brilliant colors of the desert, but she didn't see it. She loved the forests, dampness. and the green lushness of the Pacific Northwest.

Rob wasn't a fan of the desert either, she knew. The heat made him ill.

The sky turned dusky.

"We aren't going to make it in daylight," Harri said.

"We have another forty miles," he said. "The good news is we've given the Sheriff's Department enough time to track down whatever judges live out here and get that signed warrant." He grinned at her.

HALF AN HOUR LATER, Rob pulled into a parking spot in front of the Imperial Valley Sheriff's Department station. Harri couldn't wait to stretch her legs. She jumped out and lifted her arms into the sky. Her back cracked. She rolled her neck and rubbed her sore shoulders. Rob wasn't in much better shape.

Harri's jitters made her excited at the beginning of their journey. Now, she was starved and exhausted. Not the best way to start this part of the investigation.

Harri followed Rob inside where two deputies waited.

"Hi there, I'm Sheriff's Deputy James Garcia," a short man with a mustache said.

"And I'm Sheriff's Deputy Julian Vega," said the short man who stood next to him.

He, however, did not have a mustache. They both had dark hair and bronze skin. Anyone living out here would look this weathered, thought Harri.

"I'm Detective Harri Harper and this is my colleague, Detective Robert Lakin. Took us a while to get here," she said.

"The warrant came in twenty minutes ago," Deputy Julian Vega said.

"Good timing on my part then," Rob said.

"This property is a good forty-five minutes away, past Rancho Las Palmas," Vega said.

"I've never heard of Rancho Las Palmas. Is that a popular site to visit?" Harri asked.

"Rancho Las Palmas was famous in the 1930s. It was the

closest resort-like structure to the biggest oasis near the Salton Sea. The little house is empty now, but a lot of hikers go up there to check the ruins out. A Hollywood mogul owned the property back then. He and his friends enjoyed all the nature," Deputy Garcia said.

By his tone, Harri inferred he didn't think much of Hollywood people and their friends.

"Have either of you been called out to Rancho Honolulu," she asked.

"No, we checked when your call came in. Rancho Honolulu is squeaky clean."

"Why would anybody call it Honolulu?" Rob asked.

Rob and Harri followed the deputies to the door.

"On the west side of the Salton Sea, there's a whole community of streets named after the Hawaiian Islands," Sheriff's Deputy James Garcia said as he motioned toward an SUV parked next to their dusty unmarked car.

"We need an all-terrain vehicle. Most of the streets around here are paved up to a point, then turn into dirt. Your unmarked won't make it on some of these unpaved streets," he said dryly.

"Works for us," Harri said.

"We need more backup," Rob said. "Who do you have available?"

"Why do we need more men?" Deputy Garcia asked.

"What are you not telling us? Isn't this a standard search warrant?" Deputy Vega asked.

Harri stopped walking and checked in with Rob. He nodded.

"We're working on the assumption that the owner of the Honolulu killed five girls."

"The Ballona Creek murders?" Deputy Vega asked.

"Yes," Harri said.

"We have two blue suits that will be following us," Deputy Vega said and pointed to a cruiser pulling into the lot.

Harri nodded and hopped into the backseat. Rob got in on the other side.

"Is this man dangerous?" Deputy Garcia asked.

"We're not sure of anything," she said. "The Honolulu property is in the name of a corporation holding the money of the suspects. Through this search warrant, we hope to connect them to a break-in and police intimidation."

No one talked much through the thirty-minute ride to Rancho Honolulu. The shortwave radio crackled often, but Harri paid it no attention. She stared into the growing evening and the poverty and desolation of the small broken-down homes and salt-encrusted trailers that peppered the beach of the Salton Sea.

"The Sea has receded a lot in recent years," Rob observed.

Harri glanced at him. Maybe she'd been wrong about his not liking the desert.

"It will keep receding. Not sure if there's going to be much left here in the next fifteen years," Deputy Vega said. "Not with the kind of global warming we got here."

"Just last month the temp hit 125°," Deputy Garcia said. "That's hot even for us."

"That's the Rancho Las Palmas," Deputy Vega pointed out to a cluster of palm trees up a hill.

The contrast of the palm trees against the bare red hills was almost pretty. What worried Harri was the fast-approaching darkness. Serving a search warrant at night was not advised under most circumstances. Too many variables and things go wrong.

Deputy Vega checked the map.

"Take a left up here," he said to Deputy Garcia.

Deputy Garcia complied.

"Your car would've definitely not made it up here," Deputy Vega remarked.

The SUV jostled back and forth on the uneven and rocky road. They drove down the pothole-filled dirt road for another ten minutes.

The Peters family had all the isolation they wanted here, Harri thought. No way could anybody hear a woman scream out here. Even if a victim escaped, the desert would kill her within hours when the sun came out.

Deputy Garcia pulled up to an outcropping of four buildings and parked. Rancho Honolulu was as broken down as its closest neighbors. The main building's front consisted of two windows and a door. A dusty beat-up truck with gigantic tires sat next to a rusted Mercedes from the 1970s. Light streamed from the window to the right.

Harri checked the sky. They had another ten minutes of daylight.

"Are we ready?" Harri asked, a sense of urgency in her voice.

"I'm finishing up reading the warrant. We're looking for red paint?" Deputy Garcia asked.

"That's right," Rob said. "Or the unique materials to make up the paint. Like powdered pigment."

"All right. Hope this one will be easy," Deputy Vega said and opened the driver's door.

Harri readied her weapon and opened her door.

Rob did the same.

Harri's stomach dropped. Something didn't feel right, but she was unsure of what. She inched away from the car, all senses firing.

Deputy Garcia waved at the blue suits to stay inside. He took the lead up the drive, Deputy Vega at his side.

A curtain shifted.

Time stopped.

Harri made out the barrel of a gun against the curtain. Firearm in hand, she shouted, "Gun. Take cover!"

Pop.

Pop.

Gunshots rang out. Harri dropped to the ground.

43

Lindsey

DAY 8

I'd finally run out of food and I needed to eat before my women's defense class tonight. Not wanting to chance a supermarket visit, I'd decided on some Italian takeout from up the street for dinner. I'd gone up to Santa Monica Boulevard to pick it up and got back to my apartment without incident. Being cooped up inside the house was not doing wonders for my mood. Getting out even for such a small amount of time provided a bit of relief.

I put my takeout on the dining room table along with my keys and illegally-bought taser and did my usual search. My apartment was empty. Good. I returned to the living room. My stomach grumbled. The smell of the pasta Bolognese made my mouth water. With Marjorie on my mind, I turned to the kitchen when a knock sounded on my door.

No one ever knocked on my door.

I froze, unsure of what to do. I did not want to open my door. If I made no sound, they'd go away.

"LAPD. I know you're home, I saw you come in," a man's voice said from the other side.

I tiptoed through my living room and peeked into my peephole. An LAPD badge filled the viewer. I didn't have a secondary exit. No way I could leave now.

"What do you need, officer?" I asked, my heart thumping hard.

"Are you going to open the door?"

"I don't have to unless you have a warrant," I said.

"I'm here about Marjorie Wilson, the missing librarian," he said.

Damn, I thought. He followed me from the library. Or the cops were canvassing the neighborhood. I pursed my lips. I didn't know anything.

"I don't have any information about Marjorie Wilson," I said.

"Then you knew her," the cop asked.

Guilt pierced through me. Why was I feeling guilty? It wasn't my fault that she'd disappeared. Was it?

"Show me your badge again," I said.

The man held the badge up to the peephole and I read the number on the badge. It was authentic. It looked just like Detective Harper's. I undid the deadbolt and chain and cracked the door open.

"I only met Marjorie a couple of times. I don't really know her," I said.

The cop looked like a male version of Detective Harper in black pants, a button-down shirt, a blazer. He nodded and wrote something in his little book. He looked to be in his mid-to-late 40s. He kept his gaze on his notebook and I couldn't see his eyes.

"I see. When was the last time you saw her?"

"Several days ago. She walked down this street toward the library."

"It's good to be careful these days," he said, motioning to my door.

His eyes met mine. It wasn't Reece.

"Especially with Marjorie's disappearance. But, I am the police. Are you going to let me in?"

"I don't have any other information to give you. We said hi a dozen times, that's about it," I said. "What's your name, Officer?"

"My name's Detective Peter McDonald."

44

Harri

DAY - 8

H arri Harper swore to herself as she ate dirt. The uniformed officers in the patrol car opened fire on the house in the direction of where the bullets came from. Harri, Rob, and the deputies were caught in the crossfire.

"Rob, you hit?" she called out, keeping her eyes closed to protect them from the dirt.

"No, you?" he called back from somewhere to her left.

"I'm in one piece," she said. "We need to use the car for cover."

She opened her eyes when there was a lull in the gunfire. To her right, she saw Sheriff Deputy Garcia down, a hit to his head. No way he was getting up again.

Sheriff Deputy Julian Vega crawled toward the SUV they'd driven in. Good idea, she thought. Without lifting her body off the ground, she crawled on all fours as fast as she could toward the car. From the sounds coming from Rob's direction, he did the same.

A gunshot pinged a foot away from her head.

She froze and took a deep breath.

Keep going.

Keep going.

You have to get cover, she thought.

She forced her fear down and crawled even faster toward the car.

Bullets pinged all around her.

She didn't stop. She didn't stop crawling until she saw the wheel of the SUV.

When she reached the SUV, she pulled her gun out of its holster and crab-crawled to the open door.

Rob was already there. They watched as a gun moved the curtains over in the front window. Another round of shots rang out.

Harri heard the uniforms behind them calling for backup, but help would take time to get here. It had taken them half an hour and she didn't know if there was anyone closer. The way these men wanted privacy, probably not.

"I'm seeing only one shooter," she said.

"Same," he said.

Julian Vega joined them. "He's down, he's dead," he said.

Harri put her arm on his shoulder. "I'm so sorry," she said.

He nodded, his focus back on the window. "One shooter?"

Rob and Harri nodded. Gunshots rang out all around them.

"He has to run out of ammo eventually," Julian said.

"Or not. We don't know his firepower," Harri said.

"We need a plan," Rob said.

Julian returned gunfire.

"We're going to run out of ammo," Harri remarked.

"I have a plan," Rob said.

45

Lindsey

"I don't see how I can help you, Detective McDonald. I have to leave now for another appointment and I'm late already," I said, pushing the door closed.

Detective Peter McDonald put his hand against the door, stopping its momentum.

"What's wrong?"

Something in his expression shifted. His eyes became dead and flat, as his pupils dilated. I tried to shove the door closed, but he was too strong.

I stopped.

I had made a terrible mistake.

"You're not who you say you are, are you?" I asked.

46

Harri

R ob's idea was to ram the SUV through the shooter's front door. The construction appeared flimsy and they didn't have many other options.

"He could shoot out our front windshield and try to get us that way," Julian Vega said.

"True." Rob nodded. "I'll drive while you both keep away from the windows. Pop out at the last moment. We need to conserve the ammo until we get close enough to have a better shot."

Rob surveyed the layout of the compound. The shooter had taken a break. They hadn't seen or heard anything from him for the last five minutes. Each one of them knew without backup they were sitting ducks.

"There's that opening between the main house and that side building." He pointed to the right of the building. "If we drove there, then we could take cover against the house and try to take him from the front and the back. I go to the front door while you two go through the back to corner him."

"What if there's more than one of them?" Julian asked.

"All the shots are coming from that one window. If there

were more than one shooter, we'd have bullets coming from several directions," Harri said. "Should we go now?"

"Everyone have enough ammo?" Rob asked.

Harri and Julian checked their sidearms.

"I have four left," Harri said.

"I have two," Julian said.

"I have three," Rob said.

He crawled into the driver's seat, and Harri and Julian took up positions in back. Everyone's sidearms at the ready.

Rob started up the engine. He scooted down in the seat as far as he could while still seeing where he was going.

He gunned the engine. Harri peeked over the seats to see the small building getting closer.

Shots rang out and hit the car.

Pop.

Pop.

Pop.

Rob didn't stop driving.

The car slowed and shifted its direction slightly to the right. It was almost time. Harri peeked over and saw Rob grab the hand brake.

The sudden lurch of the car threw her into the seat. Adrenaline flooded her system again.

"Move, move, move," Rob yelled.

She threw open the door and fell to the ground.

Gun at the ready, she sprinted to the back of the building for cover.

47

Lindsey

Detective Peter McDonald slammed his full body weight against the door and forced his way into my sanctuary.

I backed into my dining room table and palmed the taser lying next to my keychain and hid it in my back pocket. Survive, I thought.

"I can't believe you didn't recognize your own brother," he said.

"You did something to your face."

"That's true, but my eyes are still the same," he said.

I stayed put, my heart thumping in my chest.

"I don't have any memories of you, Danny."

"At least, you know which brother I am," he drawled.

"You don't have Reece's or my eyes."

"True enough."

"How did you find me?"

What mistake had I made?

"Why Marjorie Wilson, of course." He laughed.

My heart sank. I'd been right. My need for human contact had left me open to being found.

"What do you mean Marjorie Wilson?" I needed to keep him talking.

"Me and Reece have been combing Hollywood and West Hollywood looking for you since Reece saw you at that Trader Joe's on La Brea. It was his idea to start asking around libraries. He remembered how much you loved the library in El Segundo," he said and cackled. "You haven't changed much, baby sister."

"What did you do to Marjorie Wilson?"

I thought of the pale pink-haired young woman. I'm so sorry, Marjorie. By her kindness, she'd become another casualty of my family.

"She's getting the deluxe treatment like all our special ladies," he said. "Don't worry, you'll get that same treatment, too. We've waited a long time for you."

"Like what you did to Natalie?"

Danny cocked his head at her.

"You don't know what happened to Natalie, do you?"

"She never spoke about you again," I said. "After we ran. She never said anything."

This news surprised Danny and not in a good way.

"We fucked her good and proper. Me and ole Dad. Well, Reece tried, but he was crying too hard. He was always too wimpy. We were all surprised when she had the balls to escape and take you with her. We didn't see that coming," he said.

I tried not to react to the revelation that my father had been part of this horror.

"What happened to our father?"

"He was the evilest motherfucker out of all of us until he couldn't remember who the hell he was. Dementia came on fast. We had to do something about him before he let something slip," he said.

His micro-movement caught my eye.

He was going for his gun.
This was it. What I had trained for all my life.
I only had a small second to do what I needed to do.
It had to be enough.

48

Harri

Harri and Julian, their backs to the wall, made sure they were not seen from the three windows on the side of the building as they ran toward the back door. Harri took the lead. She stopped at the end of the wall and peeked around the corner. The back was empty.

She counted 1,2,3 on her fingers and motioned for him to follow her. Harri, firearm at the ready, ran to the back door and slammed through it, gun out.

Harri went to the left and Julian went to the right. They were in an empty, filthy kitchen. The sound of a door slamming open came from the front of the house. A series of shots rang out. Harri headed toward the front and saw the back of a man about five feet away from her.

She raised her gun as he twisted toward her, his blazing blue eyes fixed on her. He pulled the trigger as she pulled hers. He dropped to the ground, dead. Her shot was true.

Rob stood in the doorway, blood blooming from his right shoulder.

"You got hit," Harri shouted.

"The bullet grazed my shoulder. I'm fine," he said.

Harri kicked the gun away from the man's hand.

Rob, Julian, and Harri look down at him. His brilliant blue eyes stared back at them empty.

"He's dead," Harri stated the obvious.

"Yep, and good riddance," Julian said.

"Are you seeing what I'm seeing?" Harri asked Rob.

"His eyes. Just like Lindsey Peters," Rob said.

"One of her brothers."

49

Lindsey

I let Danny talk about how he tortured each of the girls and then how Reece took over and mummified them. It was sickening to hear, but I needed him to keep talking so he didn't notice that I inched nearer to him.

My training told me that I should be relatively close to the gun when it was pointed at me to execute the move properly. I didn't think he knew what I was capable of yet and had the element of surprise.

"Why did you come back to El Segundo?" I asked.

The adrenaline was messing with my balance. I didn't want him to see me afraid or shaking. It would turn him on and make him more dangerous.

He laughed. "California girls are the best."

"Why did you fake your deaths?" I asked, one more step closer.

"We had to stage our deaths because one of our girls had escaped. She had been too terrified to say anything, but we knew that it was just a matter of time. Good old dad concocted a plan for our fake deaths in the Philippines," he said.

His hand dropped down to his sidearm.

"What happened the night Natalie ran?" I asked, another step closer.

"Reece didn't want to do what he was told, and he ran out of the garage, crying. Natalie was in the kitchen. She saw her friend on our table, naked of course."

Natalie knew exactly what they were capable of then.

He made his move.

In one swift motion, Danny Peters as Peter McDonald pulled his gun out and pointed it into my face.

"Sit," he commanded.

Instead, I threw my right hand against his wrist while shifting my head to the side. I hit the butt of the gun with my left hand.

The gun twisted out of his hand and clattered onto the ground.

I went after it.

He was right behind me.

50

Harri

As they waited for the rest of the Sheriff's Department to arrive on the scene, Rob and Harri did a preliminary search. They didn't touch anything, but it was the right house.

One of the bedrooms had been converted into a painting studio. Dozens of paintings leaned against the walls of the bedroom and hallway outside of it. Each one was of a different ghostly-pale woman with carved eyes on her chest, abdomen, and inner thighs. The women were beautiful and grotesque. Red paint was slopped over the floors.

"I bet you that red paint is going to match what was found in my bathroom," Harri said.

"I'm thinking you're right. And those eyes are the same shape as the ones on our girls," Rob said.

They went through to the bedroom next to it and found jars of what looked like organs in formaldehyde. They didn't stay there long. The techs could deal with that.

They moved on to the third door. Harri opened it with gloved hands and found an unmade bed, end table, and bureau. The place was spotless unlike the rest of the house.

A photograph on the end table caught Harri's attention. It was of two younger men and one older man in front of the building they stood in. Harri and Rob looked at each other.

The second brother.

They knew who he was, finally.

Lindsey had been right all along.

"Lindsey," Harri said.

51

Lindsey

I didn't get to the gun in time.

My brother's hands wrapped around my neck. The wig pulled off in his hands. This time I used that to my advantage.

I twisted around and ducked underneath his arms, getting him off balance, and enabling me to roll away.

"Clever girl," he whispered.

I hadn't managed to hurt him at all, but I got away.

"You have some moves, little sister," he said as he grabbed my ankles and dragged me toward him.

As I fought him off, I saw his gun under my couch. At least, it was out of the way. My kick caught him in the face.

He howled in anger.

I jumped to my feet as he lurched to his.

He grinned and came at me.

My right fist hit him in his ear over and over and over.

Danny grabbed for me as my right knee jerked up into his groin. He howled again, but still wouldn't let go.

We tumbled to the ground again. I kept hitting him in the head with the heel of my palm.

Smack.

Smack.

He managed to untangle one of his arms and punched me hard in the head. The pain rocked me back.

Stars filled my vision, and I fought against the blackness coming for me.

It was now or never.

I shook off the pain and kneed him hard in the groin again.

He fell off me, his guttural cries filling my small apartment.

52

Harri

arri phoned Tom Bards. His tired voice showed that he knew about the shootout already.

"We hit the jackpot and we have a massive problem," Harri said.

"Tell me." Tom's voice was unusually gruff.

"We have to find Detective Peter McDonald. He's Danny Peters, the older brother. We found a photo of him and the man we killed here along with an older man who looks like Franklin Peters. Lindsey is in danger. He had access to our database. We need to find him."

53

Lindsey

D anny didn't take too long to recover from the hard groin hit.

I scrambled up to my feet and pulled my taser out.

He grabbed my leg.

I shoved the taser into his neck and zapped him.

Danny convulsed and screamed as all 50,000 volts shot through his body.

I ran out of the living room and grabbed the cell phone from my bag.

I dialed 911.

"I need help, intruder. Assault," I yelled into the phone.

I dropped the phone and turned to find him stalking toward me. He'd recovered fast.

My instructor had only taught me one kill move. It was one he'd drilled into me over and over again. I'd only really gotten it right three times in practice.

I hoped I'd get it right this one time.

I needed to survive.

I had to survive. For all of us.

54

Harri

"Did we get them? Is there evidence of the mummified girls?" Tom Bards asked.

"We have to send the forensic team down here. But yes. This was the kill site. We found organs, Tom. And paintings. The techs will have a lot of cataloging to do," she said.

"Good. Thank you, Harri. I'm calling the FBI now," Tom said.

ROB AND HARRI had given their statements to the Imperial Valley Sheriff's Department and watched as James Garcia was taken away by ambulance. Uniforms and detectives were crawling everywhere.

Harri and Rob wouldn't leave until their forensic team showed up. This would be an interagency effort to catalog all the evidence. Tom Bards called back and told them to wait for the FBI team to get there.

So, they waited.

Harri's phone rang.

"A 911 call just came in. West Hollywood," Tom said. "A woman called about an assault in progress and left her phone on."

"God, I hope that's her," Harri said.

She hoped against hope it was. If it wasn't, then Lindsey was out there somewhere. With him. She prayed Lindsey could hold her own until the cops could find her. She paced back and forth in front of the SUV, frustrated the crime scene technicians were still hours away.

"Something happen?" Rob asked. He'd been talking to one of the deputies but noticed her movements.

"Danny Peters found Lindsey. I'm sure of it."

"How?"

"I don't know yet. But I know. I can feel it."

"They'll find her," Rob said.

Harri shook her head, panic welling inside of her. Would they find her in time?

55

Lindsey

Danny lurched at me, his gait loose and unbalanced. The taser had given me an advantage. Yet, he still came.

He shook his head, trying to clear his vision.

I breathed in and out.

My kill move required him to be almost on me. My heart pounded in my ears and blood warmed my face.

Danny lunged at me.

I sidestepped to the left, and as his body drew closer to mine, I slammed my arm under his chin, snapping his head back.

His neck cracked and he dropped to the ground.

Instead of checking on him, I grabbed my phone. The 911 operator was still on the line.

"Hello, he assaulted me. I fought back. He's on the ground. I'm at 900 Huntley Drive, between Melrose and Santa Monica. Upstairs."

"Help is on the way. Can you get to a door?" the 911 operator asked.

I pressed my foot into Danny's head and nudged it. He did not respond.

The kill move had worked as instructed.

I'd killed my brother.

I heard sirens on the street, growing closer.

The West Hollywood police station was only two blocks over and I wondered what took them so long.

56

PAB - Los Angeles, CA

Detective Harri Harper sat at her desk looking through all her open case files. She'd hoped being part of the task force would help her get into robbery-homicide. It hadn't quite worked out that way. Even though the task force had successfully solved the case of who had murdered the girls in the creek and had discovered another 10 bodies out on the compound in Salton Sea, the killers had been killed.

There had been a small amount of media attention in the aftermath, but the reporters moved on because there was no trial. The juicy details of the crimes never came out with all the suspects dead.

The task force was quietly dissolved. The deaths of Mason Reynolds and Christian LeGuerre kept the detectives from celebrating too much. They were a stain on their investigation. Detective Tom Bards took the heat for both, but all the detectives on the task force felt the guilt. They still hadn't collected evidence to connect the two of them to the Peters brothers outside of their friendship in high school. That fact didn't help the task force politically. The members had scattered back to their divisions and the FBI had taken over the case down near the Salton Sea.

The last Harri heard of the investigation was that Mitzi Jeffries had been put in charge of cataloging all the evidence that had been found there.

Reece Peters was the necrophiliac and mummified the bodies after death. He had become an expert at mummification and Mitzi Jeffries had some ideas as to why psychologically. However, Danny Peters turned out to be a garden-variety sociopath like Mitzi had profiled.

Reece had helpfully kept diaries of the Peters men's exploits over the years. Natalie Peters was their first victim. Maggie Johnson, Jennifer Lynch, and Lisa McNeill were abducted by the two teenagers for their father who was the alpha male that Mitzi described. He used his sons to procure his victims, then forced them to participate. Danny was a willing participant, but Reece was not. The two runaway girls came eight months later. Luca Giovanni and Rachel Morris. Detective Jackie Render had tracked them down and was helping the FBI with the ten other bodies.

Harri refocused on the file she hadn't opened since last August. Her annual investigation into her sister's disappearance and a trip to Oregon was a week away. Even though she had done it every September for the last twenty years, Harri's stomach flip-flopped with fear and anticipation. Jake Tepesky was coming with her and she hoped this time they could bring her sister home.

Detective Rob Lakin walked into the bullpen, his gait still awkward from the gunshot to his shoulder. He nodded to her and lowered himself down into his chair.

"How is your shoulder feeling?" she asked.

"Feels like it never happened," he said and grinned.

He opened up the case file on his desk. Harri noticed it was the Charlaine Lewis file.

"Still no evidence she was one of Danny Peters' victims?" Harri asked.

"No. She's open. I added the murder-book to the stack of files the FBI is looking into. I'm going to keep going on her, as well."

Harri nodded. The detectives in the Cold Case unit never gave up. Just like Detective Larrabee up in Seattle never gave up on Jennifer Stevens.

Lindsey Peters gave a long statement of everything her brother told her before she killed him. She explained how one of Danny Peters' buddies had seen Natalie Peters in San Francisco walking to one of her classes. It didn't take long for Danny to follow Natalie, figure out her alias, and run her over. He found Jennifer's address and came for Lindsey on the day of the funeral. Jennifer saved Lindsey's life that night.

Harri sent Danny Peters' fingerprints to match the fingerprints found at Jennifer's house. They were a match. Even though the prints were only circumstantial, Detective Larrabee finally knew what happened to Jennifer Stevens, even though Danny would never be brought to justice.

But that was sometimes how these cases ended, Harri thought. She opened up another case file. She would call Jake and see if he wanted to catch dinner tonight.

Just one week until she was back in the forest. Back on the hunt to find her long-lost sister.

57

Lindsey Peters
DAY 22

I stirred my coffee nervously and waited. Even though I was free, it didn't feel real. We'd been so wrong before. I knew that this wasn't the case this time, but old beliefs died hard. I still didn't know what to do with myself. I could have friends, lovers, a job that I wanted to do instead of one that kept me anonymous.

And now here I was, trying my hand at making a friend. Marjorie Wilson, her pale pink hair pulled back into a ponytail, smiled her crooked smile as she sat down across from me at Melrose Coffee.

"Hi," Marjorie said.

"Hi," I said.

Marjorie was as nervous as I felt. Her hands fidgeted with a straw. She'd been through a lot as well.

I plunged in. "Thank you for meeting me, I wanted to say I'm so sorry that I involved you in this horror."

"You didn't do anything. And you saved my life. If you hadn't done what you did, I don't know where I'd be. And really, I should be apologizing to you. He told me that you were hiding from the police. I told him where you lived."

"We should lay all of this guilt and frustration at my brother's feet and leave it behind," I proposed.

"I would really like that," Marjorie said.

"How is your neck feeling?" I asked, pointing to the thin red line on Marjorie's throat.

The El Segundo police had found her in a closet in Peter McDonald's house. He'd throttled her until she passed out. He didn't do anything else since he was hell-bent on getting to me first. Small miracles, I thought.

She smiled again.

"I won't be reading about serial killers anymore," I confessed. "I don't want to live in that darkness anymore."

"You're not a writer then," Marjorie asked.

"No, I was trying to figure out who my brothers were so I could somehow predict how they'd come after me," Lindsey said. "I'm actually a computer programmer."

"That's really cool," Marjorie said.

I flushed and stared out at the fancy shops across the street. This was my life now.

A life full of truth and friends.

I caught a flash of Natalie's face and pain spread through my body. I'm going to live this happy life for us, I promised Natalie. A life of joy and gratitude.

My sister gave up her life to protect me. I would make sure I'd live enough life for both of us.

I HOPE you enjoyed reading about Detective Harri Harper in The Creek Killer!

Click here to read Harri Harper's new case in The Hidden Grave or read on for Chapter One of The Hidden Grave.

58

The Hidden Grave - Chapter One

Detective Harriet Harper leaned back in the passenger seat of the rental car and closed her eyes. The strong sense of deja vu made her head spin. She was back again and hoped this time, the results would be different. Her sister Lauren Harper was still missing. Harri had come to Oregon every year to find Lauren's remains and she'd failed every time.

Harri and Jake Tepesky had picked up the rental car from the Portland Airport and were headed to their first destination. She'd programmed an address into her phone.

At least on this trip, Jake Tepesky, her sister's best friend in high school, was with Harri. He had been an FBI profiler for the last fifteen years, and she hoped his expertise might finally shake the truth loose. A tall order, she knew, because Lauren had been missing since 1994.

Harri was no slouch with cold cases. Her work with the Cold Case Unit in the Los Angeles Police Department regularly had her searching for killers who'd gotten away with murder years before.

This time would be different, she thought hopefully.

"You ready?" Jake asked.

Harri checked the back seat to make sure she'd grabbed all her luggage. "I'm all set. Thanks again for driving."

"I'm glad I can help. I know it's been quite the few weeks for you."

"Sorry we didn't get to meet over Lauren's case notes," she said.

Harri hadn't seen Jake Tepesky much in the last two weeks. The Creek Killer case she'd been on had overwhelmed her with its endless intra-agency meetings between the FBI, LAPD, and the Imperial Valley Sheriff's Department. She and Jake had become reacquainted through another FBI profiler on the Creek Killer case and had reconnected over Lauren's disappearance.

She'd done her best to keep pace with all the new developments on one of the biggest serial killer cases in Los Angeles in recent years, but the various agencies would be out there for months cataloging the evidence left behind and exhuming the numerous victims.

The count stood at ten last she heard. At least a number of missing person cases would be closed. The killer had left behind driver's licenses of some of his victims, which prompted the renewed search on the property.

Harri wished she could get that kind of closure for her sister Lauren. She had disappeared without a trace on a hike to the Tamolitch Falls over twenty-five years ago. This weekend was the anniversary of her disappearance.

She pressed her hand as sudden pain flared in her chest. She never felt well coming up here.

Harri stared out the window at the beautiful scenery of the changing colors of the fall season, a cacophony of oranges, yellows, and reds.

"I went through the case files three times." Jake interrupted her thoughts.

"And?" she asked.

"You're a very thorough investigator," Jake said. Harri gave him a small smile. For all her investigating skills, she had exhausted every single lead and had come up with nada.

Nothing.

"Did you find anything that I missed?" she asked.

"There wasn't much. Lauren had been at school for only three weeks and no one knew her very well. She hadn't had time to make any close friends. You thoroughly researched her roommate, Jacqueline Strauss, and the boyfriend, Charlie Burke. You tracked down the alibis. They were solid."

"I exhausted those leads. Charlie Burke played soccer the afternoon Lauren went missing. About twenty-five players swore he was on the field. Jackie pledged her sorority and thirty girls accounted for her movement."

"I don't think it was anyone she knew."

"You're thinking stranger abduction?"

"More like crime of opportunity."

"I came to a similar realization. That's why it's been so hard to track down," Harri said.

"They tend to be. The kidnappers always slip up somewhere, though. We have to find where."

"Do you think I'm wrong about the burial site?" Harri asked.

She'd asked a non-profit group of scientists trained to search for hidden graves to join them this time. It had taken Harri years to set up since she didn't have specific proof that her sister was buried in the same place as she disappeared.

"Where do we go first?" Jake asked.

"I always start with Tim Ledeyen. We've become friends over the years. He lets me know about similar cases that crop up in the city. And there's always the hope he'll remember something else from that day."

"How does he feel about being your first stop?" Jake asked.

Harri flushed.

The last few years she'd come up, Tim had been less than happy to see her. He'd barely known Lauren, but he'd joined Harri's search for her sister the first five years she'd come down. Recently, Harri had felt a certain coldness from Tim when they'd met. She believed Tim wanted to get on with his life. He'd moved on.

She could never do that. She needed to bring her sister's body home. Harri had no doubt that Lauren died all those years ago. It was a matter of finding her remains now and trying to piece together what happened back then.

"We're driving to Tim Ledeyen's now or to the bed and breakfast?" Jake asked.

"Tim's, unless you wanted to stop somewhere for a pee or coffee, or something."

"No, I'm good," Jake said and grinned. His handsome face lit up with a smile.

The morning sun created a halo around his face, and Harri's stomach suddenly did a couple of unwanted flip flops. Jake had been her sister's best friend in high school. They were here to find Lauren. There was no time for this nonsense, she thought. They'd enjoyed an intimate dinner together some weeks back, and Harri thought some spark was ignited for a second. Looking back at it now she was convinced it was in her imagination.

Harri hadn't slept in weeks and this trip always did strange things to her moods and her levelheadedness. Oregon was a fever dream every time she came up here.

"I booked us rooms at the Daniels Inn off the McKenzie Highway, Route 126. Tim Ledeyen's house is a few miles outside of Eugene. He's on our way to the Inn."

"Great, and the scientists? Where are we meeting them?"

"The pig team is staying at the Daniels Inn as well."

"I thought they were called NecroFind?" Jake asked.

"Although the pig team is more descriptive. Why are they called that?"

"They use pigs in their research. Bury them for long periods to see the changes to the surrounding site. I guess the nickname stuck."

"How big is the team?" Jake asked.

"I have a botanist, a geologist, and a dog handler with a bloodhound coming. Along with the head scientist, of course."

"Bloodhound?"

"Her name is Amy. Supposedly, she's been able to find graves this old before in Colorado," she said.

"Can't wait to meet them all," Jake said. "If you want to take a nap or something, I'll totally understand. I know you haven't gotten much sleep over the last few weeks."

"It's been crazy. That last case is far from over," she said.

"You mentioned you were coordinating between the various jurisdictions?" he asked.

Harri knew Jake wouldn't ask too many questions on an ongoing case. He'd been FBI. At the same time, the discovery of the new bodies by the field team had been all over the newspapers.

"As much as I could. I had to hand it over to another person on the team as I was coming up here. I tried to get everything done, but the case was moving too fast for me. They'll be there for months, just cataloging. To be honest, I was relieved to be coming up here."

That wasn't entirely true. At least, she'd be able to get some sleep here.

"Rest then. We should be there in an hour."

"I'll try to do that, Jake. Thank you," she said.

"Do you mind if I put on some music?"

"Better not be Green Day," she said.

That made Jake guffaw.

"Haven't listened to them in years. I'll put in something classical. I think that'll suit both of us."

Harri looked at him and saw his jaw clenched. This was hard for him, too. He had come up that first year to search and never joined in again. He never came back again. Lauren had been his best friend through most of high school. She knew they'd been close and talked to each other almost every day that first month of college.

"Thank you again for coming with me. This can't be easy for you either."

"I want to find her too," he said

He turned on the music. Something soft and romantic. The motion of the car made Harri's eyes droop, she let herself be dragged down into the darkness.

"HARRI, WE'RE HERE," Jake said.

Harri opened her eyes and squinted at the harsh afternoon light. He'd pulled into the driveway of a small Cape Cod home nestled between tall fir trees. Tim Ledeyen owned four acres behind his house.

"What else do I need to know about Tim Ledeyen?" he asked.

"He is an Oregon native who grew up outside of Eugene. He finished the University of Oregon and became an accountant. He has a wife named Molly and a teenage son named Dan. They're both teenagers. He's never been in trouble, not even a speeding ticket."

"That doesn't mean much," he said.

"True," Harri admitted.

"What kind of questions you typically ask him?"

"I take him through the timeline each time. He's remembered little things over the years."

"Like?"

"Cars he remembers passing him on the way to the park as he drove into the parking lot. Bits of a license plate. Bits and pieces like that. They haven't amounted to much honestly."

"Are you going to introduce me as an FBI agent?"

"No, if that's okay. I want to keep it personal. You were Lauren's best friend from high school. That's all he needs to know."

"All right then. I'll take your lead," he said.

They left the sanctuary of the car and walked up the paved path to the front door. Harri raised her hand to knock on the door but it opened before she made contact.

Molly's tear-stained face peered out from a darkened hallway.

"Molly, what's wrong?" Harri asked.

"Dan never came home last night. It hasn't been twenty-four hours and the police won't let us report him missing, but he would never do this to me. I know there's something wrong."

Jake and Harri glanced at each other.

"May we come in?" Harri asked.

Molly stepped aside and Harri and Jake entered. Molly motioned them to the left, toward the kitchen.

"Is Tim home?" Harri asked.

Molly shook her head no.

"Is he out looking for Dan?"

"Yes. He's been out since six this morning. He knew that you were coming today because, obviously, you come every year. He's sorry to have missed you, but we are just out of our minds with worry."

Harri put her hand on Molly's arm.

"Maybe I can help. I have a contact at the Eugene Police Department. He might be able to expedite the process some-what. Get your statement."

"Yes. God, please. We need more people searching. He's only sixteen."

"Are you sure that he's not with friends?" Jake asked.

Molly shook her head vigorously. "He's had some problems with drugs in the last few months. We sent him to rehab and he was doing really well. He was keeping with his curfew of ten o'clock every night. He wasn't hanging out with any of his old friends." Molly paused and took a breath. "Dan called us last night to tell us that he was coming straight home."

"Where was he coming from?" Harri asked.

Jake sat silently next to her.

"He'd been at a job interview in Eugene. He was hoping to become a barista at one of the local coffee shops near the University. It was a big step for him, and we were very excited, and he told us he was coming straight home and then he disappeared," she said in a rush.

Harri heard the hysteria rising in her voice.

"Did you call the coffee shop to see if he made it there?" Harri asked, taking a small notebook out of her pocket.

"Of course. The woman manager answered. He'd interviewed with her. She said he did great and was their top candidate."

"What time did he leave?"

"She said around five-thirty yesterday evening," Molly said, finally getting herself somewhat under control.

"How did he leave?" Harri asked, jotting the time down.

"I don't know," Molly shook her head. "We don't know. His car was still in the parking lot. The manager told us after she went to look. That's when Tim tore out of here like a bat out of hell to see for himself."

Harri nodded and bit her lip. His car still being there wasn't a good sign. But he could have run into one of his old friends from the drug days and fell off the wagon. A few months sober was not that long of a time. Harri assumed that's what the Eugene police would say. But Molly did not need to hear that right now.

"And Tim is still in Eugene right now looking for him?" she asked.

Molly nodded. Her tears started again. "Please help us. He's only sixteen and has had such a difficult time," Molly pleaded, tears running down her face.

Harri looked at Jake and took her phone out of her pocket. "Let me see what I can do." Molly burst into tears again and Jake sat there patting her on the hand.

He had a calming effect on Molly, who leaned back in her chair and breathed.

"We will help any way we can," Jake said.

———

CLICK HERE to read more of The Hidden Grave!

Also by Dominika Best

Harriet Harper Thriller Series

The Creek Killer

The Hidden Grave

The Broken Trail

The Night Blinder

Ghosts of Los Angeles Series

The Haunting of Sunshine House

The Haunting of Eva Murphy

The Haunting of Alexas Hotel

**Detective Harriet Harper returns in
The Hidden Grave**

About the Author

Dominika Best is the author of the Harriet Harper thriller series and the supernatural suspense series Ghosts of Los Angeles. She lives in Los Angeles with her family.

Never miss the next mystery!
Sign up at www.dominikabest.com

facebook.com/thedominikabest

instagram.com/thedominikabest

Made in the USA
Monee, IL
09 December 2022

20427735R00215